MISSING PICTURES

ANGELA HOKE

ETHAN FALCON PRESS

For the sisters that I wasn't born with but that God sent to me.

Also, for all you wonderful readers who have survived toxic relationships, traumatic divorces or other losses, being a single parent, and/or drowning in mental illness of any kind, and found the strength to find a new, different future, even if it required the assistance of (prescribed) medication, the occasional glass of sangria, unconventional exercise, enthusiastic sex, tearful prayer, well-meaning family and, of course, crazy, wonderful friends.

Contents

Praise for Missing Pictures

Five Stars! This novel was a raw, emotional foray into the harrowing and yet hilarious capriciousness of mental illness. – *Reedsy Editor*

Despite the flashes of darkness, the light shines through: a gut-bursting element of humour that thrusts up the rollercoaster to string us along for the ride before it plummets and then rises again — reminding us that even in our darkest moments, there may be something worthy of a smile. – *Reedsy Editor*

The prose is heartfelt from beginning to end, and reveals the character development of all three women with elegance, grace and beauty. – *Reedsy Editor*

Despite the gravity of the subject matter, the writing style underscores a humour that breaks through the surface to make it a story of triumph and uplifting inspiration. It teaches us that illnesses of all kinds can strike anyone, and rails against the stigma that far too often accompa-

nies a diagnosis of a mental health disorder. – *Reedsy Editor*

This is a novel that can meet you at your darkest moment and give you the power to decide to save your own life. – *Reedsy Editor*

Missing Pictures is a tender, evocative, broad emotional spectrum read. I was shaken by hilarity, descriptions of mental illness, betrayal, and the tender balance between reality and hope. – *Mackenzie Littledale, Women's Fiction Author, Editor and Mental Health Advocate*

The emotions are so honest and raw, but written in elegant, clear language. Claire is immediately relatable and a woman whose needs must be met with authentic friendship that is both feminine and powerful. – *Mackenzie Littledale, Women's Fiction Author, Editor and Mental Health Advocate*

Masterfully written. This is gorgeous writing. The words take on shape and contour and form, immersing readers in the scene with very real people and places. – *Mackenzie Littledale, Women's Fiction Author, Editor and Mental Health Advocate*

Mental illness is an area of medicine that still carries a stigma, which is why sadly, way too many people feel shame and try to hide their conditions. In her novel, *Missing Pictures*, Angela Hoke uses humor, drama and three lovable characters to put the spotlight on both the seriousness and hope that goes with depression and other mental illnesses. – *Jackie Pilossoph, Creator and Editor-in-chief, Divorced Girl Smiling*

Missing Pictures is a warmhearted, witty story about three girlfriends who without judgment, support each other unconditionally. The dating stories made me laugh out loud and the got-your-back friendships made me cry (in a good way.) – *Jackie Pilossoph, Creator and Editor-in-chief, Divorced Girl Smiling*

Hoke writes from the heart, and while entertaining and inspiring her readers, she also found a way to teach us many lessons of loyalty, self-acceptance and the courage it takes to never give up on happiness. – *Jackie Pilossoph, Blogger, Writer, Creator and Editor-in-chief, Divorced Girl Smiling*

Also by Angela Hoke:

4-time Award Winner,

A Whisper of Smoke

Award Finalist,

A Painted Lily

Date #1 - Roger Bigcock

I'M a few minutes early and also several years late, if I'm being honest. And I'm nervous. So I focus on deliberate movements, spread the edges of my dress out across the velvet cushion till it's smooth and symmetrical, like butterfly wings. And I trace the shape of my thighs through the silky material of my dress, because now that I've lost fifteen pounds using the highly underrated but inadvisable divorce diet, quadriceps have mysteriously emerged. And I breathe, in and out, long and measured and sequentially, until my pulse abandons its frightened fluttering and falls into rhythm with the slow beat of the jazz music piped from overhead.

I'm *centering myself. Being present.* My Group therapists would be pleased.

I check my hair in my compact mirror to make sure that my new extensions, dark red to match my actual shade, spill proportionately over my shoulders and down my back. I worry they look ridiculous, that *I* do, trying to be young, attractive. But Tasha and Gretchen insisted that my smart bob was more "business" and not enough *"bizness,"* and therefore counter to my mission.

To be fair, I'm unsure of my mission, exactly. I don't *need* a man

1

to validate me or make me whole or tell me my worth. But, and this is at odds with that firmly held belief, I am also seriously lonely.

I check my phone and see that he's now late, and that probably means something. But I have no idea what. Bad traffic? An attempt to build romantic suspense? Disinterest?

Hell if I know. Dating at thirty-eight is very different from dating at twenty. First of all, at twenty, I didn't have stretch marks and crow's feet, and a vagina that had spit out an eight-pound baby. But that's not the only difference.

Guys in college are still boys, barely past the stage of whoopee cushions and fart jokes. Men in their thirties and forties are matured, established. They know who they are. Plus, college guys are primarily looking for sex, like rutting dogs on the prowl, instinctual and led by their lesser appendages.

In contrast, these grown men I'm interested in via their on-line dating profiles are looking for meaningful encounters. Relationships.

So maybe his delay is fashionable rather than a portent. I'm going with that. Because in all honesty, I'm as excited as I'm capable of being these days as I await my first internet dating experience, sitting at this posh Nashville table for two, basking in the glow of charmingly mismatched punched metal light fixtures.

I've ordered a glass of wine to calm my nerves and have just taken my first sip when I see him walk in.

Roger.

He's attractive in an investment banker sort of way, dressed in a starched button-down under a stylish canvas jacket and pressed jeans, trendy, patterned socks and dockside shoes. A bit homogenous, but he's made an effort to be deliberately adult casual, and I approve.

His face lights up when he sees me, and I stand.

"Claire?" he says, and I nod. He gives me a quick, chaste hug and then we take our seats.

"You look beautiful," he says once we're facing each other across the table, and I actually blush. It's been a long time since a man has said that to me.

"Thank you," I say, and direct a smile toward my lap. Then I remember what I promised Tasha and Gretchen. He might think it weird, and I'm sure it's entirely unnecessary, but a promise is a promise.

"I need to ask you for something, and I hope you don't think it's too strange. But a single woman can't be too careful."

He pauses from looking at the menu and raises one eyebrow. "Okay…"

"I need to see your driver's license," I tell him.

"Pardon me?"

"To take a picture of it. And verify your information. It's standard protocol," I joke, and he almost smiles, but not quite.

He ponders this request, but after a moment he reaches into his pocket and retrieves his wallet, taking out his license handing it to me.

I grin at him again, widely, as though teeth and dimples will distract him from a situation that has become a bit strained. Still, I study his license, pleased to see that his information checks out, though his hair is a little grayer, his eyes a little less vibrant blue now in his present form. Then I take a picture of it and text it to Tasha and Gretchen, along with the name of the restaurant.

By the time I hand the license back to Roger, my phone is buzzing with responses. I glance at them quickly.

He's cute, sweetie! Have fun and be careful! Don't do anything I wouldn't do!' says Gretchen, followed by: *'Don't over-analyze it! You tend to do that.'*

'What she said,' says Tasha. Then a second, more "Tasha-esque" message pops up. *'Also, he's looks like a sexy accountant. Just your type! Hope you get laid!'*

I drop my phone into my purse, suppressing a real smile.

"Okay, now that we've dispensed with the formalities, shall we start the date?" I say, trying to sound cavalier, but coming off like the business executive that I normally am, convening a board meeting. I cringe inwardly, feeling awkward and wrong, but he smiles at me.

And then we start to talk. It goes well, for a while. I talk about my job, as if I'm currently working at it, gathering all the energy I can muster to sound enthusiastic and non-depressive. He talks about his. It's a little less professional than he made it sound on his profile – I'd thought he too was a business executive, and it turns out he's an "account executive" at a business.

After appetizers and two glasses of wine each, our conversation is growing more relaxed, less reserved. He looks at me over his glass, his eyes heavy-lidded, his lips curving upward. "So tell me something about you that not everyone knows."

Hmm. That's an unexpected question. I think about what I could reveal, and the prominent thoughts that come to mind are unspeakable, at least at this stage in a fledgling relationship: I recently got out of a fourteen-year marriage; I suffer from major depressive disorder; I'm unable to work right now because of both of those things.

I settle on telling him something harmless. "I like to sing. Actually, back in the day, I was kind of obsessed about it. I had my own stage name at the karaoke place, and I secretly dreamt that someday, I'd get discovered while belting out a Pink song," I say.

He doesn't comment on my use of the past tense. And I hope he doesn't probe much further, doesn't discover the truth. That was past me. Now I am an illusion. A dry, crackling husk.

He raises an eyebrow at me, and there's a spark in his eye. "That's adorable. I bet you're a wonderful singer."

I feel the blush again, and I take a sip and a bite to disguise it. "How about you? What's something that not everyone knows about you?" I ask, after I've swallowed and wiped my mouth with the cloth napkin. I lean back as far as I can in my seat, uncomfortable with the unexpected intimacy I feel at his words. And that makes me sad, both that a meaningless, throwaway compliment would approximate intimacy to me, and that it would trigger in me a withdrawal response.

"Well, not many people know this, it's true," he says, and looks away. "And those that do, well let's just say I don't think they've forgotten it."

He ventures a nervous glance toward me, I give him an encouraging, flirtatious look—or so I think. I'm very out of practice.

He tilts his head. "Are you in pain?"

"No," I say, and resume a neutral expression, but my cheeks are burning. I'm so bad at this.

He looks down, then back up at me through his lashes. "You promise not to judge me…"

"Oh, of course I won't!" I insist.

"Well," he says, hesitating, leaning towards me slightly. "I am very well endowed."

I spit out my wine. "I'm… I'm sorry?"

Now that he's said it, he puffs up, squaring his shoulders. "I have a very large penis. Abnormally large." He's looking at me expectantly. What he's expecting from me, I'm not quite sure… applause?

"I… I don't know what to say," I sputter, blinking at him.

He seems to take my fumbling words as an indication of my disbelief. "I can prove it," he says, pulling out his phone. "I've got pictures. Do you prefer flaccid or erect?" He begins to scroll through photo after photo, carefully considering the merits of each one.

At this, I cough on my spit, caught between eruptive laughter and incredulous anaphylaxis-like choking.

I take a sip of water and clear my throat. "Are you seriously going to show me a dick pic?" I say. I always thought such juvenile mating rituals were reserved for millennials with Instagram followers and cultivated fish-lip poses.

He sits back, retrieving his phone with him. His face registers indignation. "Please!" he says. And for a moment, I'm embarrassed that I've somehow misinterpreted this entire exchange. "I see a first date akin to a job interview, of sorts," he explains. "I'm simply demonstrating one of my most prominent qualifications, if you'll pardon the pun, so that you may make an informed decision about next steps."

He presents this reasoning so very sensibly, it nearly makes sense. I fight the absurd urge to say, *"Pish posh, quite right,"* in a British accent to match his disarming civility.

Then he's handing me the phone across the table, and unwittingly, I see a flash of fleshy, tubular penis – evidently he prefers the erect representation. I recoil, but I'm also intrigued. I've only ever seen two adult male penises in my life. I can't help but be a bit curious. Against my better judgment, I take the phone.

The image, including the penis in question, is quite the presentation. It is propped on furniture of some sort, maybe an ottoman, manscaped and exhibited for consideration like the offering that it apparently is.

I'm oddly fascinated at the artful staging if nothing else. "Why are these objects next to it?" I ask.

"The dollar bill is for scale," he explains, eager now that I'm showing interest. "A ruler would be too, I don't know, on the nose, don't you think?" I glance at him and he winks, eyes sparkling. "The watch is for authentication." He pulls back his sleeve to flash the distinctive and indeed identical watch.

Clever, I think.

But no, no. This is weird and inappropriate. I'm pretty sure this is not normal first date fodder. Or at least, not for the type of man I want to date, the type of man I assumed he would be.

His next sentence cements my resolve. "I'm also quite skilled in the bedroom arts, from a technique perspective. Would you like to check my references?"

References?

I quickly return the phone and turn away to fiddle with my purse.

"I think I hear my phone buzzing," I say. "It could be an emergency."

He tilts his head and studies me. "You know, most women appreciate a large penis," he says. "During sex," he adds, to make it clear.

"Yes, I'm sure," I say, as I pull out my phone.

He tries to hand me his phone again. "That's a real dollar bill."

I ignore him. "I was right!" I exclaim, scanning my own blank phone display. "There's been an emergency. My best friend has a... a hernia. It's pushing against her uterus as we speak. She's afraid it might fall out—her uterus, that is. That can happen, you know."

He blinks at me.

I put my napkin on the table and stand to go. "I'm so sorry, but this hernia uterus emergency can't be ignored."

I don't wait for him to respond. Instead, I pat him on the shoulder, grabbing my jacket and purse in one sweeping gesture, and hurry towards the exit.

As I slip out of the restaurant and walk quickly to my car, the Depression that is always lingering in the background is whispering to me that all men suck, and I'll never find a good one because they don't exist. But I'm a logical person, by profession and nature, and I realize something that could be important—this was not a representative sample! He was but one ridiculously inappropriate, genitally-blessed man.

Armed with that knowledge, notwithstanding the worrisome correlation of douchebag to impressive man-parts, I take heart that good men might still be out there as I head back to my empty house.

ONE

I'm Not the Only Crazy One

APRIL, THE FIRST TIME

IT'S NOT JUST ME. Those are the words I keep repeating to myself as I take a deep breath and walk into the room. It's a little sterile—stained, speckled tiles span the ceiling while dingy gray linoleum covers the floor, and white cinderblock walls complete the utilitarian feel. The only color in the room is on the whiteboard, which is full of phrases like "radical acceptance" and "positive self-talk" and "know your triggers" written in a variety of marker hues—reds, greens and blues.

I take my seat, the only empty seat in the space. The tables are formed in a u-shape, and the facilitator is sitting on a chair in the middle next to the whiteboard—she's sporting a butch, choppy hairstyle and cargo pants. The only thing feminine about her is the seashell necklace she wears around her neck.

"Welcome to Group, Claire," she says to me in a startling smoker's voice, scratchy and deep, as I turn my name tent facing outward and scan the room reading everyone else's name placards. As I do so, I try to take in a few details of my fellow patients. Or is it Group-members? I'm not sure what we are called.

It's hard to focus on anyone as I look around. I'm feeling really agitated and out-of-place, and that's when my newly-afflicted ADD kicks in the worst, which I've been told is a form of anxiety. So instead I turn my attention to the leader, whose name I learn is Veronica.

"Margo, what's an example of how we can be present?"

The woman on the end—Margo—appears bored as she shreds her handout into little bitty pieces. I suspect she didn't brush her hair today, because there are pieces of it sticking out at odd angles despite her efforts to smooth it down with her fingers every four or five seconds.

I wonder if Veronica's calling on her has more to do with trying to get her to be present in this current moment than it does with looking for input on the subject.

Margo yawns. "I guess you could not check your phone and stuff."

"Sure, sure," Veronica says in an encouraging way. "But I think what we are looking for are things we can tell ourselves or do when our thoughts start to go to unhealthy places."

Another girl, woman, raises her hand. She has the most beautiful, curly white-blond hair, pure and pale as an albino's. But her brown eyes are dark and striking, and I can tell she's tall, taller than me by at least a few inches if her long and lithe torso is any indication. She's making swirls in her journal based on the way the pen swivels in her hand.

"Yes, Gretchen?"

"You can focus on things around you to calm your racing thoughts. Like nature, or a song or sound. Something like that."

"Very good," says Veronica, writing down 'Focus on nature' on the whiteboard. "Does anyone have another idea?"

A few people speak up, and she writes a few more phrases on the board. They don't mean much to me—perhaps I'm struggling with being present, because my thoughts are definitely racing right now.

What have I gotten myself into? Do I belong here? Are these other people like me—depressed because of my situation—or are they seriously ill? I feel so out of place, but at the same time, oddly comforted that I'm not alone—lots of people have "issues."

Surprisingly, it's not overwhelmingly institutional in the room.

I'd not known what to expect, when my psychiatrist recommended an out-patient program at a psych hospital to address my worsening Depression. Or, rather, the psych wing at a regular hospital. But I'd envisioned shuffling patients in gowns, incoherent and blank-eyed, and indifferent orderlies in too-white scrubs dispensing medications from paper cups.

Instead, it feels like a classroom in a community college, and I try to think of it as such as I also make a concerted effort not to dwell on the locked double doors that lead to the in-patient ward.

I look at the handout that Veronica gives me, and I see a list of coping activities on one side and 'Being present' on the other. I'm supposed to pick the activities that will help me be present, but they all blend together. It seems like a simplistic exercise, and I wonder how or whether this could possibly help.

But I don't focus long, because I don't know what it says at all, even though logically I know it's not difficult. Even though I can *read*. Because that is one of the side effects of my Depression—I can't concentrate. On anything. And I can't figure out even the simplest tasks. These two cognitive breakdowns have stripped away my identity.

I am… was… a senior director of financial analysis at a Fortune 500 tech company. I constructed and deconstructed transactional agreements and provisions in my sleep, developing complex models, with a myriad of inputs and intricate assumptions, and whipping out spreadsheets and pretty presentations like nobody's business. I supervised a team of eight, and was a member of senior management, routinely interacting with transaction advisors and bankers and the board of directors. I was very good at my job.

But the deterioration was gradual, and then all at once, coincidentally (or not) just after my husband and I filed for separation, it became complete. And now, I can't seem to summarize my bills on a list for the lawyer. I know it's not difficult, but I can't figure it out. I can't even pay my bills, because looking at my bank account on-line gives me an anxiety attack so severe that I completely shut down. My dad has to do it for me. And as for reading comprehension, I can barely focus on the teenage vampire book I'm trying to read for the fourth time, a book I selected to read because of the simplicity of the themes and the easy language, because it now reads to me like an opus written in old English. Or like Greek, literally.

It's like I have pregnancy brain times a thousand, like I've lost fifty IQ points in a matter of months.

For the first time ever, I've discovered what it means to be less than, to not be exceedingly proficient, to be (temporarily) disabled. Not able to do my job. Not able to work. And while some people don't understand a disability resulting from mental illness, temporary or otherwise, because they can't see it, I can attest that it has had a very real, tangible impact on my mental faculties and abilities. It renders useless my years of study, my multitude of professional experience. It's left me, unbelievably, incompetent.

And without my mind, I don't know who I am, and that is scary as hell.

When is it time for break?

My leg bounces uncontrollably under the table, and I place a hand on it trying to calm it. It doesn't work. My anxiety, which is constant now, makes sitting still for long difficult. Makes listening and focusing impossible. From experience I know that, if I can't get it under control, I'll eventually escalate until I crash, that all of that extra adrenaline will overload me until my body just wants to sleep.

Aaron, the guy sitting two seats down from Margo, catches my attention as my gaze darts around the room. He's casually lounging in his chair, spinning a pen in his fingers, and he winks at me. He's attractive in a cock-sure kind of way, and I instantly am distrustful of him. I move my gaze quickly past him and settle on Cathy, the woman next to him. She is wearing a matching sweater set and a cross on a chain while she writes furiously in a notebook. She glances at me and then resumes writing, and I'm overwhelmed with the certainty that she's writing about me.

Veronica is still talking, but I don't hear her until she says the word "break"—that gets my attention, as she tells us to reconvene in fifteen minutes.

I let out a large breath in relief, and the man to my left—Jackson, according to his name tent—gives me a brief but pained smile in acknowledgement. Then he resumes lining up his handouts and folders so that they are perfectly square and precisely aligned in relation to the table. Under his breath, he is counting.

I slide my chair out and straighten my own pile of papers—my intake folder, the journal I'm supposed to write in, and the handout from the session.

I feel like I've just dodged a bullet, that I've survived something dangerous, and my heart is pounding. I want to leave, but I also am determined to stay. Because even more pervasive on my mind than my current infirmities is my intense desire to *get well.*

So I take a deep breath and close my eyes, and I try to focus on something peaceful—the sun shining through the trees in the morning, my sweet daughter's face sleeping. It helps, a bit.

I take comfort that we are all screwed up in one way or another. That's why both my therapist and my psychiatrist sent me to this place—because their help wasn't enough to fix my extreme screwed-upedness.

When I open my eyes, the girl to my right, two people down, is watching me. Her skin is smooth and caramel-colored and she has an immense head full of braids that are gathered back from her face and cascade down to the small of her back. She's small, probably five foot two in four-inch heels, and she looks too diminutive to carry around that substantial head of hair. She smiles and gives me a wave. Tasha is her name, and she seems friendly and, on the surface, normal. I wonder what's brought her here.

Gretchen, the woman who spoke up earlier, plops down next to her and they share a quick hug. I marvel at this—I doubt they knew each other before coming to Group, yet they clearly have formed a bond, one strong enough to warrant hugs. What does that say about what my experience will be like here? And what does it say about me that I want what they have?

Gretchen catches me watching, and waves to me too. Then, surprisingly, she beckons to me to join them. I look around to see if they mean me, and Tasha says, "Yeah, girl. we mean you. Get over here."

I pick up my things and bring them with me, even though I'm only moving eight feet. Gretchen pulls up another chair and pats it.

I sit and take a moment to set my things on the table, focusing on stacking them evenly, because I don't know what to say.

"New girl. Claire," says Tasha, forcing me to look at her. "What's wrong with you? You don't look crazy to me."

Gretchen gives her a shove. "Tasha! You're going to freak her out." She glances at me. I'm not sure what she sees on my face, but she reaches over and gives my hand a squeeze where it rests in my lap. I glance down at my hand and it captures me there, the fading warmth of her squeeze feeling remarkable and like a memory. It has been so long since I was last touched.

"I didn't mean nothing by it. She'll figure that out. Plus, I'm bat shit crazy. So I got nothing against crazy."

I risk a glance at Tasha, whose big eyes are twinkling. I can't fathom the positive energy it takes to twinkle.

How long has it been since my eyes twinkled? Since a smile even reached my eyes?

"But seriously. What's your deal?" says Tasha. "We don't judge."

"Depression, I guess…" I say. "Marriage stuff."

Tasha nods. "Oh, hell yeah. Marriage shit I get." There's a hint of aggression in Tasha's tone, but not toward me.

"And depression," says Gretchen, her voice as gentle as a soft breeze.

This time, Tasha reaches over and grasps my hand, stops it from obsessively pulling at a string on my shirt. I didn't even realize I was doing that.

"It will get better, girl. You are just at the beginning. Just starting all this," she sits back, gestures around. "You're new to it, I can tell. But we got you."

Gretchen is nodding.

"We're sort of experts," Gretchen says.

"Damn straight. We know what's what," says Tasha. "Hell, I got a great idea. We need to ditch and go to the strip club down the street. Get our freak on. Forget about all this depressing shit."

Gretchen looks at me as she elbows Tasha. "Tasha!" she says.

"You're scaring her again! And no, we're not going to a strip club. You're acting like a nut-head."

Tasha laughs. "Look where the fuck we are," she says, without irony.

Gretchen smiles at me. "You're going to figure out really quick that being friends with Tasha is mostly telling her there's no way we're doing that."

Tasha rolls her eyes. "And being friends with Gretchen is baking Snickerdoodles or pumpkin pie or some white girl shit, and watching one of those stiff-shirt reality shows like *90-Day Fiancé*."

Gretchen stares at her. "Chocolate chip... and how did you know?"

Tasha bursts out laughing and, most shocking of all, I feel my mouth turning up. It's foreign, this spontaneous twinge of facial muscles and hitching throat.

Friends.

Something I've not had beyond work in many years. And work friends... well, they are great. But sometimes they don't survive beyond the workplace. And that's as much my fault as theirs, because I've forgotten how to *be* a friend, somehow, in the last several years. I just haven't had the energy.

But in this moment, watching Tasha and Gretchen, and even realizing we probably have nothing in common at all except for the issues that brought us here, I experience an unexpected sliver of optimism. Maybe there's more to hope for than the strength to survive, or even escape, a miserable existence, and the insight to know whether I should make permanent my separation from my husband to do it. Maybe I can actually dare to wish for more than just the absence of misery—maybe there's good stuff yet to come.

TWO

We Can't All Be Crazy At the Same Time

JULY

THE KIDS ARE SPLASHING in the pool at my apartment complex, sprinkling us with the carefree, tinkling high-pitch giggling that only children can manage, even teenage ones. Brooklyn seems happy, and that makes my heart light and heavy at the same time—because while I'm glad she's enjoying playing with the other kids, it highlights to me how much she needed it. That little girl has been through a lot, and she deserves some unabashed joy.

Tasha's kids are bright lights. At fourteen, Hunter is laid-back and quick to self-deprecate to elicit a laugh in a tense situation, or tell a funny story in his enthusiastic manner. Conversely, Melanie is serious and responsible and diligent, the caretaker for everyone else. She's a little mother in tween's body.

I like watching Hunter engage my daughter in some good old fashion splashing games. He's used to having a little sister, and he treats my spunky almost-nine-year-old like she were his own. Brooklyn eats it right up with a spoon. She's always wanted siblings, while I've often wished I could give them to her. And as much as I work hard to be silly with her and watch teenage girl movies with her and cuddle her to the point of annoying her, she likes (actually probably prefers) being around other kids.

Meanwhile, Melanie happily pushes Gretchen's eight-month-old around in his swim ring, careful not to let him go for a second. Baby Carson is sucking on his fist, overly buoyant in both a baby life jacket contraption and the Sponge Bob swim ring, slathered in infant sunscreen and sporting an adorable little bucket hat. Melanie kisses his smooth round cheek as she's careful not to let him get too splashed by Brooklyn and Hunter's noodle fight.

The three of us, Tasha and Gretchen and I, are sitting under the pergola watching them and reveling in the shaded warmth on this beautiful summer day. We sip homemade sangria and Tasha and Gretchen flank the outdoor ash receptacle.

My apartment complex consists primarily of singles and some older couples. There aren't many kids that live here. So except for a group of twenty-somethings lounging and drinking beer on the far side of the pool, we virtually have the area to ourselves.

It would be perfect, were it not for my ever-present Depression. I'm still not able to work, and thank God I have good disability benefits through my job that allow me to pay my bills while I'm temporarily incapacitated. I know that's one advantage of devoting 60 to 80 hours a week to a profession and career path for fifteen years. And there are others, I know—a prestigious title, a good salary. But there were casualties too, and my marriage may have been one of them. But at least I'm out of bed, and I'm around people. I always try extra hard the weekends I have Brooklyn, and my friends' presence is helpful in this effort.

While we have spent the last few months forging our friendship over discussions of group therapy sessions, psych med cocktails and ex-husbands (or in my case, almost ex), this is the first time we've gotten together with our kids. Except, they are not all here. Gretchen has twin teenage girls who, while I've never met them, are conspicuously missing.

Melanie brings Carson over for a quick diaper change. "See, Mom. Told you I could be in childhood development before I'm an executive."

"I never doubted it, baby girl," Tasha tells her daughter as Gretchen deftly changes the swim diaper in a matter of seconds.

When she's finished, and after quick and slobbery kisses, Melanie struggles back to the pool packing Carson and his swim ring.

"What's she talking about?" I say once they are back in the water.

"We played 'I See My Future' yesterday," Tasha says, taking a drag from her cigarette. She must see our confusion because she explains. "We do it when they have days off from school sometimes. We pack a lunch and go sit somewhere in the city, and then we guess at people's lives and the kids imagine what their's might be. This time we went to the Farmer's Market at Bicentennial Mall downtown. There were all these people walking around in their smart, boring business clothes. You know, like slacks and stuff."

"Business casual," I suggest.

She waves her hand. "Whatever. Anyway, there were bunches of these business people, and Hunter said how he could be a finance executive and work on the fourteenth floor of the building that's shaped like R2-D2. Not the Batman building, because that's been *done*."

I smile because that sounds like him.

"And then Melanie said how she would be his boss, on the *fifteenth* floor, but that was only after she worked in childhood development in a third world country. She got that idea from some teachers that brought some little kids to the Market to have a picnic on the grass."

"That's cool," I say.

"Why do you do that?" asks Gretchen. "I mean, is it realistic? Like, do you have college funds set up? Because I have sucked at saving for my kids. Bills always seem to get in the way."

"No, but that doesn't really matter. It's about the dreaming. Maybe sometimes dreams don't come true, but if you can't imagine the dreams in the first place, you sure as hell can't reach them."

She reclines back, adjusts her braids, lifting them off her neck for a quick fanning.

We all think about that, because the truth in it rings clear as a tuning fork. And I like that my kid is having real fun with some serious dreamers.

ANGELA HOKE

"This is awesome," Tasha says after a minute. "I'm so glad we could get together with the kids." It's like she's reading my thoughts.

"Yeah," says Gretchen, but she's wistful.

"You okay?" I ask, as I top off her drink with the pitcher that's sitting on the table.

"This is nice, but I can't help thinking about the girls," she says, confirming my suspicion.

Tasha lights a cigarette, then leans over to light one for Gretchen. "When's the last time you talked to them?"

"Almost four months," she says, which I note corresponds to when she completed her most recent in-patient visit to the psych hospital, preceding our collective time in outpatient Group therapy.

She turns away, focuses on the kids for a moment. Carson is giggling as Melanie plays pop-up peekaboo with him in the water.

Tasha blows out a whoosh. "Damn. Why has it been so long?"

"Because of goddamn Jonathan," Gretchen says, and I'm taken aback.

Brooklyn executes a perfect cannonball from the diving board, making me smile, even as we jerk back at the enormous splash. I turn back to my friend, who has drawn her bare feet up under herself in the chair. "What do you mean?" I ask.

She sighs. "Ever since he got remarried, he's been trying to replace me. He wants his new wife, *Alicia*, to be mom to the girls."

"Well, that's bullshit!" says Tasha. "They already have a mom!"

"Yes, they do," I agree. "A good one," I add, reaching over to squeeze Gretchen's arm. She gives us a grateful smile. But then I think how the girls are fifteen, and they are old enough to call their mom if they want to. I'm not sure I understand how Jonathan could keep them from doing that.

"Sweetie," I begin, searching for the words to say. "I don't think he can keep them from talking to you, unless he has some kind of court order," I say delicately.

She shakes her head no, indicating there's no such order.

"Maybe you should give them a call?" I suggest. "Let them know you are thinking about them."

18

"Hell, yeah," agrees Tasha. "That bastard can't keep you from talking to them."

Gretchen's expression turns hopeful. "Do you think they would talk to me?" she asks, and my heart hurts a little at the desperation in her voice.

"Of course," I say, and I hope like hell it's true.

Her face lights up as she pulls out her phone. "Which one should I call, Macy or Raina?"

Tasha scratches her chin. "Who is the most talkative?"

Gretchen smiles. "Oh, Raina, for sure."

"Then by God, call Raina!" Tasha says, and I nod encouragingly.

Gretchen takes a deep breath. "Okay, here goes," she says, and dials, putting the call on speaker.

The phone rings four times, and I'm sure it's going to go to voicemail when there's a click and a beat of silence.

Gretchen looks at us questioningly. "Hello?" she says.

"Hi, Mother," is the response, the tone less than friendly.

"Oh, Raina! It's so good to hear your voice!" says Gretchen, as her eyes fill with tears. "How are you? How's Macy?"

"Wonderful," says Raina, followed by silence.

"Is your sister there? Can you put it on speaker, so I can talk to both of you?"

Raina sighs into the phone. "Macy doesn't want to talk to you," she says, after a beat.

Gretchen's face falls. "Why... why not?"

This time, Raina huffs into the phone. "Because of how you behave, Mother. Really? Like you don't know?"

Gretchen is momentarily speechless, her expression bewildered. Before she can formulate how to reply, Raina speaks again.

"What do you want, Mother? Why did you call?"

Gretchen seems to gather herself. "Well, I'm hanging out with my new friends, and the kids are all playing in the pool. You're little brother looks so cute. I couldn't help but wish you were here." Her voice wavers at the last bit, but I reach over and squeeze her hand and she maintains her composure.

"That kid is your kid, not my brother. Don't push him on me, because you got knocked up by the freaking plumber," says Raina, her words scorching as a sun flare.

"Electrician," Gretchen mumbles, but it's in reflex, because she has sucked in a breath at Raina's words as I gasp and Tasha whispers, "*Damn*," from her seat in the reclining lawn chair.

I want to say something so bad to that insolent child, I have to clamp my free hand over my mouth to physically restrain myself.

"Raina…" Gretchen says, when her breath returns.

"And another thing," Raina continues, her anger building. "I don't think we'll ever forgive you for what you said to Macy last time we talked. I mean, really, *Gretchen*. What kind of mother tells her own daughter that she's been a burden since she was born, because you only ever wanted one daughter? Who freaking says that to their kid?"

Gretchen's jaw goes slack, her face stunned.

"Raina… I would never…" she finally manages, but Raina cuts her off.

"I don't even know who you are. Don't call us again," she says, and disconnects the call.

We all sit there, utterly speechless, until Melanie breaks the spell.

"Gretchen, Mom, look at this!" she calls, and we look over. She spins Carson around, and he collapses in the biggest baby belly laugh I've ever seen, doubling over in slobbery giggling until his forehead rests against the front of the float ring. When he raises his head, his mouth is yawning open in absolute happiness.

We can't help but smile, even Gretchen, whose heart has to be breaking.

Since the kids are clearly having a good time, Tasha and I turn our attention back to our friend.

"Honey, are you okay?" asks Tasha.

"I… I don't know," says Gretchen, and she reaches over to lift her glass, taking a huge gulp of sangria.

"What was she talking about?" I ask. "That stuff she said, that doesn't sound like you."

She shakes her head vehemently. "I would never, ever say that," she insists. "I would never even *think* it. How could she think that I would say something like that?"

I don't know what to say, and neither does Tasha, it appears. We all sip our drinks in contemplation, until Gretchen suddenly sits up straight.

"Damn, I know what this is," she says.

Tasha flicks a fly away from her face. "What?"

Her eyes blaze. "It's fucking Jonathan. He's poisoning them against me!"

"Mom, was that you?" Melanie yells from the pool.

"No, it was Gretchen!" Tasha calls back, then explains. "Melanie is monitoring my 'fucks,'" she says, and tosses a glance toward the pool. "I mean 'f-words,'" she says with deliberation. "I'm trying to use 'alternative' words." She says "alternative" with air quotes.

I turn my attention back to Gretchen, reaching up and tightening my ponytail that has loosened. "You really think this is coming from Jonathan?"

"Of course! What else could it be? That bastard," she says. She takes a loose piece of tile from the ground and hurls it. It tings against the post of the pergola.

I've never met Jonathan, so I can't say if that's likely. But I'm almost sure that Raina referred to what Gretchen *said* to Macy.

"You sure he would do that?" Tasha asks, voicing my unspoken thoughts.

"You don't know what he's capable of," says Gretchen.

I flash to Noah, how wrong I'd been about him.

"Maybe she's right," I say, and Gretchen smiles gratefully at me. "I was so wrong about Noah, and I nearly lost Brooklyn because of it."

I look at my daughter now, slipping down the water slide on her stomach, a wide grin painted across her face, and my stomach twists at the memory of what it was like when he took her from me.

"Our marriage counselor told me five years ago to leave him," I say, almost to myself.

"No shit, what?" says Tasha. I'd actually spoken aloud.

"Yeah, tell us," says Gretchen, maybe thankful for the diversion.

I take a deep breath, hesitant to open up these wounds, but also feeling the need to share with the two people most likely to understand.

"Our marriage was bad for a long time. He quit talking to me years ago, had virtually stopped touching me. He never wanted to spend time with me." A mockingbird squawks at a squirrel, dive-bombing it until the furry creature scurries away. "But that wasn't all," I say. "He said things to me, hurtful things, snide passive aggressive comments that were hard to pinpoint or refute. And when I would try to tell him how he was making me feel, how he was making me shrink, he would tell me I was crazy, or that he never said whatever it was. Or that I couldn't take a joke—that was one of his favorite responses." I look back at my friends, who are rapt.

"It was hard to articulate why or how he was making me drown in this shitty despair, how it was causing me to disappear, but he was doing it brilliantly."

I pause, take a drink and a deep breath.

"Anyway, I was already seeing a therapist and a psychiatrist because my depression was growing, even though I fought it with everything I had. I begged him to go with me. Finally, though I'm not sure why now that I think about it, he agreed."

I pause, again unsure whether I want to resurrect these memories. They are painful.

Tasha takes the brief pause as an opportunity to weigh in. "Marriage counseling sucks ass," she says. "You go into the fucking, I mean 'flipping,' session for an hour and bring up all this bullshit in your marriage, not fixing anything, and then you have to leave together. It's the worst."

Gretchen nods in agreement. "I always had to take a Valium after we went," she says. "It made me a wreck."

I offer a wry smile to my friends. They really do get it.

Then I continue. "The therapist suggested we both write a letter to each other before one of our sessions, and that we exchange and read the letters prior to the session so we could talk about it. When we got to the session, we went over Noah's letter first. He said bull-shit in there like how I'd watched too many soap operas growing up and that I had an unrealistic idea of what a marriage should be."

Remembering this makes my blood pressure shoot up, my pulse pound a bass line against the wall of my chest.

Tasha looks at me. "What the hell?"

"Yeah," I say. "I was stunned. To claim that I thought soap opera relationships were real was ridiculous. It insulted my intelligence, and that's what I said in therapy."

I stop to take a drink, and my hands are shaking at the memory of the overwhelming frustration, and my growing sense of futility.

"It wasn't even a real complaint. It wasn't something I could realistically address, because it was total bullshit. A... deflection."

"Sounds like it to me," Gretchen agrees.

"And then it was time to go over my letter to him, which I spent hours writing, trying to express my feelings in a thoughtful, non-confrontational way. And you know what he said?"

Tasha leans forward. "What did that fizzler say?"

"He said that he didn't read it."

Gretchen's mouth drops. "Are you serious?"

I nod. "The therapist asked him why, and he said some crap about how he already knew how I felt, dismissing my letter like it was a waste of his time. It was the first time he let someone else glimpse the total disregard he had for my feelings. The contempt."

"Frack," says Tasha. "Then what happened?"

"Well, we left, and we didn't talk about it at all, but I was over-come, like I'd tripped and fallen into this sinkhole of despair. And the light couldn't get in there." I sigh, take a long drink. My girls wait patiently. "I mean, I had absolutely no idea what to do with that situation. And then the therapist left me a message asking for a private session with me."

"Mom, watch this!" calls out Hunter from the diving board. We all turn our attention to him.

"I'm watching, honey!" says Tasha. He grins at her, then runs and jumps and does a perfect flip in the air.

When he emerges from the water, we erupt in applause. "That

was flocking awesome, Hunt!" Tasha says, and he smiles from ear to ear, looking every bit the little boy I picture he once was.

"Teach me how to do that!" says Brooklyn, and I automatically call out to 'Be careful' in instinctive response.

Gretchen reaches for the pitcher of sangria, her hand visibly shaking. But she doesn't comment on it. "What happened when you went by yourself?" she asks me, instead.

I remove my sunglasses, rub my eyes, and take a deep breath as I put them back on. "He told me that he was concerned about me, that Noah was deliberately withholding love and affection, using psychological abuse to manipulate me. He said it was Noah's way of controlling me. Then he said he didn't normally say this to patients, but that I should seriously consider divorcing him."

"Holy shit," says Gretchen, and Tasha echoes the thought with a drawn out, "*Floook.*"

I sit there for a moment, remembering my shock, and also my stubborn disbelief.

"What on earth did you say to that?" asks Gretchen after a moment.

"Honestly, I didn't believe what he was saying about my husband. I couldn't. I couldn't reconcile what he was saying to the boy I met in college and fell in love with. I still thought that Noah was stressed or insecure because he'd recently gotten demoted at his computer programming job, and that he didn't realize how he was treating me. I just… wasn't ready to believe it."

Tasha shakes her head, though I'm not sure whether she's doing so in disbelief at the situation, or at my stupidity. "So, tell me you had some hot affair with a guy in chinos."

Gretchen cocks her head. "Do they still call them that?"

But Tasha is waving a hand in dismissal, waiting for me to continue.

"I stopped going to that therapist, and I stayed with Noah. And it turned out, that freaking therapist was right all along, and I wasted five more years of my life. Five of my…" I swallow back a sudden surge of sorrow before saying the rest, the words that don't want to come out. "Five of my child-bearing years."

Now Gretchen is reaching for my hand. "You wanted more kids?"

My eyes fill at this, as I try to maintain my composure. "Yes," I finally whisper.

Tasha leans over and gives me a hug. "There's still time," she says. But though I've not voiced it, even to myself, until now, I know my time is short. If it takes me a few years to find someone else, I'll be over forty. My eggs will be old, if they are even still alive. He stole more from me than my happiness and my mental health.

But as I fight the tears that are threatening to overtake me, I'm disgusted with myself. I'd never meant to make this conversation about me. I'd only hoped to commiserate with Gretchen on not knowing what your husband could be capable of, and hopefully distract her from the painful conversation with her daughter.

"I tell you what," says Gretchen, her voice brightening. "Whenever you have the baby blues, you can borrow Carson—you can change his shitty diapers and get up with him four times a night and clean up the baby food he slings across the floor and smears in his hair, and then when you are butt-assed tired, you can give him back to me. How does that sound?" she says.

But all I can think is, there's also the cuddles and the slobbery kisses and the soft wispy hair on his round little head. But I smile at her anyway and say, "Deal."

"This right here is why we're meant to be friends," Tasha says then.

"Why's that?" Gretchen asks.

"Because we flocking get each other, like no one else does."

"You know, you're right," says Gretchen, nodding. "We can be each other's therapists."

I can't help it—I smile at them, these two girls that in a short time have become unlikely friends, and I add, "We just have to make sure that we're not all crazy at the same time."

Tasha laughs loud enough that it feels like I'm laughing too.

"Here's to that," says Gretchen, raising her glass of sangria. "It's our one rule. We can't all be crazy at the same time."

Tasha and I also raise our glasses, and we all clink them, cementing the toast.

"Amen to that, sister," Tasha says, pulling her knees up to her chin, as Brooklyn and Hunter do tandem cannonballs designed for maximum splash effect.

We squeal under the spray, and it is a beautiful sound.

THREE

A Good Teething Toy is Funny AND Tasty

SEPTEMBER

I'M DREAMING about my husband. It's ten or twelve years ago, before our daughter, before the slow disintegration, and we are in bed in our old house—our first house, the one we built together as a monument to our forever love. I'm waking up and, seeing him there beside me, I snuggle up to him.

"I had the weirdest dream," I say into his chest, and even as I say this, I sense that something is not quite right, that I'm missing a critical observation.

I look around, trying to identify the source of my unease. But nothing stands out. The sun is streaming in the window from a low angle, baking my yellow walls up golden like piecrust. My sheets are twisty and soft, worn from the intimacy of marriage and many washes.

He kisses my head and runs a finger along my arm. "What was it about?"

I turn back into him, nuzzling into his neck. Still, my insides clench when I answer, bracing against a lingering ache. "That we were divorced. And it was really nasty and horrible."

He chuckles in my ear. "Well, that's silly! Like that would ever happen." He hugs me and kisses me again, and it does seem utterly ridiculous, in that moment, as I'm wrapped up in the certainty that we are happy—in love.

The buzzing of my phone invades my contentment, and I try to ignore it. But it won't stop, and it's pulling me away, dissolving my room and my bed and my husband, and then I'm waking for real—wet with sweat, and completely alone.

The dream lingers in my mind, and it's a vacuum in the pit of my stomach, a sucker punch to my gut. This dream that was a glimpse into my merciless subconscious, it could have been a memory, a cruel reminder that it hasn't always been this awful. That I was loved, once, by a man I trusted and adored.

But now the reality smacks me in the face—I'm divorced, officially, as of three weeks ago. I squeeze my eyes shut against the sudden sharpness of pain, forcing out tears that burn tracks into my hair. This surprises me, these burning tears. I'd thought they'd all dried up, spent like currency in the many months leading up to the end.

My phone buzzes again, and I grab it to silence it. It's Tasha. She's been calling me for days, and I haven't answered. I don't know what makes me answer it now.

"Hello?" I say, and it takes all my energy to expel that one word.

"She *is* alive!" she says. "I was beginning to worry about you."

Light is spilling through the slats in my blinds, bouncing off dust motes dancing in the air. It's too bright in here.

I close my eyes. "Yeah, I'm alive," I manage.

"Throw some pants on. You're coming over."

I shake my head, but of course she can't see it. I can't understand her words. I can't contemplate getting up, getting dressed, driving. All I can focus on is Loss, and his very close friend, Grief.

"Claire, don't make me come over there."

I sniff, wipe my hand across my running nose. "I don't think I feel up to it," I say, and I try not to sound like I've been weeping.

"Girl, pull it together and come over. You'll feel better if you do. Besides, we miss you."

I don't know why that makes me cry, but it does. Maybe because it's the "one more thing" on a pile of raw nerves and feelings that's already tipping over.

Or maybe it's because I miss me, too.

In any case, though I try to do it silently, she hears it anyway. "Stay right there," she says, as if I'm going anywhere. "We're coming to get you."

She hangs up, and I let the phone fall to the bed. And even though I haven't cried in months, I cry. I cry for that wife I used to be, the one who trusted her husband to never hurt her, and to always be there. The one that knew who she was, and what she could do, and it was no small thing. And when my tears dry up, I get up and pull on some flannel pants and slap some deodorant under my arms. My hair goes up in a messy ponytail and I wipe my eyes with a damp washcloth.

Minutes later, a determined knocking rattles my front door. I pick up my feet, first left then right then left again, and then I'm there, opening the door to the faces of my two girls. They hug me and then Gretchen's grabbing my purse and jacket to protect me against the sudden chill that has overtaken this mid-September day, and Tasha's yanking me out, locking the door behind us.

"Nice place," Tasha says as we walk towards the car. "Next time, maybe we can stay awhile." This is the first time they've been to my house, which I just got back in the divorce. Noah was allowed to live in it during the proceedings thanks to his legal maneuverings, but I was the one that ultimately could pay the mortgage, so now it was mine again.

Still, I was not yet keen to hang out in it, and I think Tasha sensed it. Too many bad memories and way too much negative energy.

In the car, I slap on my seatbelt as Gretchen squeezes my hand over the front seatback. Then they sing Lizzo with the windows cracked all the way to Tasha's place, while I sit next to Carson, secure in his car seat, shivering inside my windbreaker, not feeling really there.

Carson's asleep by the time we get to Tasha's, and Gretchen carefully takes him into Tasha's bedroom and lays him on the bed.

Meanwhile, Tasha sits me down at the messy kitchen table like I'm a small child, pulling my jacket off me as I collapse, limp and unhelpful. When Gretchen joins me, she starts flipping through a bridal magazine that seems to have been mailed to Tasha by mistake.

"Y'all didn't say anything about my hair," she says from the counter where she's making hot chocolate. Now that she mentions it, I notice it is quite different. Instead of tight braids down to her butt, she's got these snaking, twisty curls in a caramel color that go to the middle of her back.

"It looks cute," says Gretchen. "You cut a lot off."

"Nah, girl," says Tasha. "My braids weren't real. And these are crochet goddess locs. So they aren't real either. My real hair ain't that long."

If I could speak, I'd ask her more about that, and compliment her, but the words get stuck.

Tasha grabs a bottle of liquor from the freezer. "Do you want whipped cream vodka in your hot chocolate?"

I look at her. "It's 10AM." It's the first thing I've said to them since we got here, and my voice is dry.

She shrugs, flicking the snaking curls over her shoulder. "Your point?"

I shake my head no.

"Suit yourself," she says, and pours a healthy dollop in her own mug. "Gretchen?"

"Sure, why not?"

She adds a shot to Gretchen's and then hands us both our steaming mugs as she joins us at the table.

"So, that's a laugh, huh? I mean, like I'm thinking of getting married again. Ha!"

"Maybe it was delivered to the wrong address," I say, flipping the front of the magazine over. Gretchen takes a long drag on her cigarette. It's been smoldering in an ashtray, waiting for her to revive it.

"No! It's my name on it! Do you think someone subscribed me to it as a joke?"

I blow on my cocoa. My breath scatters stray ash across the table. "Who would do that?"

Tasha shrugs. "No idea. But it's pretty flaking funny."

"Save them for your idea charts, or whatever," says Gretchen, gesturing to two posters I've not noticed before, hanging on the wall.

"They are *dream boards*," says Tasha. "And good idea. Just because I'm done with the institution of marriage, doesn't mean my kids won't want to do it. Someday."

I look up at the posters and see now that each is labeled with the name of one of her two kids. Melanie's has multiple pictures of smiling black girls—one in a cap and gown, holding a diploma, another standing on the summit of a snow-capped mountain, planting a flag, and a third wearing a smart business suit and conducting a meeting in a boardroom. I can legitimately see her accomplishing all of those things.

Hunter's is more fanciful, or maybe not. He has a picture of an NBA player dunking a basketball and one of Mahershala Ali winning an Oscar. But my favorite is the one he's chosen of President Obama—he's not standing at the Presidential podium, delivering a speech as one might expect. Rather, Hunter has chosen a photo of the former President kneeling on the floor among young children, reading a book to them.

They truly are great kids. And I'm reminded again how good Tasha is at helping them dream of a beautiful future, when I'm doing my excruciating best just to remember to do laundry and cook meals for my own daughter.

"Can I put my feet on you?" Tasha plops her fuzzy-slippered feet into my lap. I look away from the dream boards and down at my lap. Three bunny eyes peer back at me from ratty pink fur. With a detached sort of amusement, I realize she must have driven in them.

"Uh, sure, I guess," I say, because she already has.

"I was on them all night last night," she explains. "Some kid or kids had diarrhea, and I spent my whole shift playing 'Where's the Shit?' in the locker rooms." Tasha is part of a nighttime cleaning crew on an irregular basis, often working in schools or health clubs.

She's flighty about work, at times, and impulsive in this as in all things, quitting and then starting again when her episode's over. I sometimes marvel at her ability not to worry about job security, but then I remember two important points: one, I have no room to judge since I can't function at work at the moment; and two, nobody likes cleaning up shitty, smelly locker rooms. Hence, she can always find another job.

Gretchen blows on her drink. "I thought you had a date last night? With that trucker dude?"

"Nah, had to work."

"What trucker dude?" I ask, as I shift my legs to get more comfortable. "Where'd you meet a trucker dude?"

"On *Flame*," she says, referring to a free on-line dating app she's obsessed with.

Gretchen crushes her cigarette in the ashtray. She has circles under her eyes that make me wonder if she's been sleeping. Not sleeping is the first sign with her, and I'm ever vigilant. "I want to see his picture! You never showed me."

"Kay," says Tasha, reaching for her phone. "But I don't know if I'm going to see him again."

Gretchen takes the phone from Tasha, and we squeeze in to look at it together. On it there's a photo of a muscular guy with tatts up and down both arms and around his neck. There's a glint in his eyes that I don't trust, possibly because he's tugging down the waist of his jeans with his thumbs in a suggestive way. He's very much not my type—he's wearing a muscle shirt, for Pete's sake.

"Why not?" Gretchen asks, studying him closely. "He's not bad looking."

"And very proud of his rig," I remark, noticing the way he's got his arm draped across the fender of a bright red tractor-trailer with orange flames painted down the side.

"That ain't all he's proud of," Tasha says with a wink, as she puts her feet down on the floor. I stretch my legs out in relief.

"So, why? What's up with this guy?" Gretchen says, lighting another smoke. I fan the ensuing cloud away from my face, but she doesn't notice.

Tash shrugs and looks away. "I wasn't going to tell you guys…"

Gretchen leans forward. She senses something juicy. "What?"

She sighs. "He flipping bit me."

I set my mug down and turn to face her squarely. "I'm sorry, he did what?"

She reaches to the neck of her shirt and pulls it down where we can see the top of her breast. There's an angry red bite mark marring her lovely cappuccino skin.

"Holy shit!" says Gretchen, and I gasp.

"It looks infected," I tell her, gently poking at its edges.

Gretchen agrees. "You should get some ointment. Hope you didn't catch something."

Tasha barks a laugh. "Like what, rabies?"

Gretchen raises one eyebrow and taps off her ash. But I'm staring hard at Tasha. She reaches for Gretchen's Camels and shakes one loose. "I know, I know. You don't have to say it."

I say it anyway. "Tell me you will never go out with that guy again."

She puts one hand in the air, as an oath. "I will never go out with that guy again," she says. But as I let out a sigh of relief, she adds: "Unless I'm really, really horny."

"Tasha!" Gretchen says, and I smack my forehead with my palm.

Tasha grins. "What can I say, he had a dick the size of a–"

Normally, I would be curious. But now that I've seen his photo, I don't want to picture any more of him than I have to. I cover her mouth with my hand.

At that moment, we hear Carson stir in the bedroom.

"You want me to get him?" I ask, but Gretchen shakes her head.

"He'll be okay for a minute more."

Tasha looks at me, then. "Glad you finally got out of the house," she says. "What's it been, three days?"

I shrug. "Four," I say, looking away. It's hard when Brooklyn's not with me. I'm used to being a mom all the time, and having her part-time is a huge adjustment. She leaves a hole in my home and in my heart when she's not there. And I don't even have work right now to distract me. Not that I could work right now. My brain chemistry remains hijacked by my Depression, and it continues to render the essential kind of job abilities—basic comprehension, some level of concentration, ability to form coherent sentences or be around... well, anyone—ineffectual.

The truth is, this has been one of the Dark weeks. I've barely eaten, and showering has been much too overwhelming to even consider. I'm skinny and smelly and my hair is a ratty mess. And I think I have fruit flies procreating in my kitchen sink because even running the disposal seems like an insurmountable task.

Tasha nods, pats my hand, like she knows it already. Which, of course, she does.

The three of us, we own our mental illnesses and hold them close. Like a rebellious sibling, we take care of them and tolerate them, even though they exhaust us. We take them out and discuss them, compare them, talk about strategies for disciplining them. Sometimes we even hate them, but not too much, because they are part of us—Tasha's Bipolar; Gretchen's Bipolar; Claire's Depression.

It's this connection that binds us, more than the Intensive Outpatient Therapy where we met, this bone-deep, mutual understanding that people living outside of mental illness don't seem to get.

Tasha looks at me expectantly, waiting for me to talk. But my Depression isn't interesting and, for that reason, it's hard to believe anyone wants to hear about it.

It's not angry and wet and hot, like Tasha's Bipolar. It doesn't give birth to tattoos and ill-advised shopping sprees, and it doesn't spin the "bad thoughts" that Tasha says spill over in her mind, suggesting too many codones and contins for a body to tolerate, or flashing pictures of cars driving into highway dividers and telephone poles.

It doesn't erupt in a series of words that are really messages, which at first could seem scary-funny in a did-Gretchen-really-say-that, hysterical way, but when you listen close they are a tightly-wound spiral down the rabbit hole. According to Tasha, Scary Gretchen says the messages all add up, and it's all one big MIND FUCK. But don't future fuck yourself, because then what's the point of anything?

No, my depression is a knob dialed down to its lowest decibel, a rumbling of Overwhelmed and I Can't Do This and a frantic but sluggish pursuit of Hope. It has no conversation, it only wants to: Shut. Everything. Down. It's a hermit, a brown recluse holed up in the corner of a dusty closet, content to wait in hiding for you, because you're going to need something out of that closet, like your confidence, your optimism. And that's when it gets you, with a small, corrosive bite. It's insidious that way, and it makes you scared to reach in there at all.

"You gotta get out of the house, girl," Tasha finally says. "Make yourself. Hell, go on a date. You can find someone on *Flame*, like I am." She pushes her phone my way. "See if anyone looks good to you."

I've already checked it out, and it's not my scene. They are mostly blue-collared, rough-looking guys with too much body art and too many motorcycles and trucks with naked women mud flaps. But I don't want to sound judgmental.

"I've actually been poking around on *Relations*," I admit. It's a paid site, but it has a fair representation of professional men on it. These are the kind of men I'm used to from work, the ones that wear matching ties and pocket squares and analyze spreadsheets in Excel. Men not like my ex-husband, with his rural roots and creeping insecurities.

"Oooh," Gretchen says. "*Relations,*" she says, like it is clandestine or naughty, and wiggles her eyebrows up and down. I have to admit, how she says it, it does sound rather sordid.

"You need some down and dirty relations," says Tasha. "I've never seen a woman that needs to get laid more than you."

I ignore that comment. Then we hear Carson babbling in the other room, and I try to take the opportunity to escape. "Let me go get him," I say.

"No, it's okay, sweetie. You stay here and tell Tasha about your *relations*. I'll go get him." Gretchen squeezes my shoulder as she walks to the other room.

Tasha grabs my purse from the floor and fishes out my phone. "So show me what you got," she says, as we hear Gretchen let out a strangled cry.

We both jump up and rush to see what's wrong. Even in my all-consuming lethargy, I find that I can still respond to the need of my friend. I discover a measure of comfort in that realization, a tiny redeeming thing that's a seed of hope in my belly.

We round the corner into the adjoining bedroom to find Gretchen standing at the foot of the bed, eyes wide and unblinking, mouth agape.

I grab her arm. "Gretchen, what's wrong?" I say, as Tasha lets out a hiccup-gasp. She's looking over my shoulder at the bed behind me.

Carson, I think, and whip around to see what has them both reacting so alarmingly.

And I almost choke on my own spit. Carson is sitting up in bed, blankets swirled around him, quite happily sucking on an impressively-sized purple vibrator.

My body seems to not know how to react. I stand there, blinking, a gurgling pushing past my lips that's not exactly laughter but rather a weak, synthetic echo of what laughter should be. To my right, Tasha's glee is a mouth yawning open as she coughs a dry, hissing sound, like she can't get air. All the while, Gretchen stands unmoving, horror painted across her face in a fierce, deliberate stroke.

But then Tasha stumbles back against the wall, and this breaks Gretchen free from her paralysis. She skitters across the bed and snatches the implement from Carson's hands.

He looks surprised and hurt that his new teething toy has been so rudely taken away, and I pull myself together in time to go around and reach for him before he starts an all-out tantrum.

By the time I grab him, Gretchen is sputtering and waving the vibrator around like a weapon.

"Oh my God! Who leaves this kind of thing laying around,

when there's a baby nearby?" she demands, pointing it in Tasha's face.

Tasha tries to compose herself. I can see the desire to be sympathetic war with the hilarity of having a giant purple penis looking you in the eye.

"I'm sorry," she squeaks, and then she's giggling again.

This only makes Gretchen more furious. "You're sorry??" she screeches, and her hands are shaking.

"Gretchen, put the dildo down," I say in my best stern cop voice, as Carson pulls on my hair and drools down the front of my shirt. "There's no need for anyone to get hurt."

Gretchen whirls to face me, brandishing her penis in my direction. I flinch, and snort, but Gretchen is serious so I try to be too. Still, there must be something in my expression that reaches through her indignation, because her mouth twitches. And then, all at once, she falls back on the bed and releases her unlikely weapon.

"Oh my Gooood," she says again, but now she's covering her face with her hands as laughter bubbles up from behind them.

And then, collapsing on the bed beside her, we're all three laughing—real belly laughing that's ugly to look at, with squinting eyes and scrunched noses and too much teeth, yet is also inextricably beautiful. We laugh, grasping hands, leaning into one another, Carson sitting in the middle of us slobbering, until my side hurts and I can't see through the tears.

When all but the last of the lingering sputters and snorts have subsided, we sit up, perching against each other in a three-pronged structure of support. Gretchen reaches over to pull Carson to her and plants dozens of kisses across his face, like she's sanitizing him with her affection, and he swats at her. For a moment, she rests her forehead against his wispy hair, and then she straightens suddenly and looks pointedly at Tasha.

"Please tell me it was at least clean?"

I suck in a breath. I hadn't thought of that, and now I look at Tasha too as we both await her answer.

A violent flush races up Tasha's neck and face, and she jumps up. "Who wants more cocoa?" she says, and streaks out of the room.

"Tasha!!" Gretchen screams, chasing after her, hurtling curse words and incredulity while she shields Carson's ears from the torrent.

I'm left alone for the moment, spent and dry, but not in the aching way that my Depression leaves me. This is a pleasantly hollow feeling, tingling around the edges, like I've had a laughter climax—an unexpected high from a drug that I'd forgotten how to take, but which I sorely needed.

A break in the clouds pours sunlight in through the window, and it lands on me. And it's bright, yes. But this time I don't turn away. Instead, I let it sink in a little, warming my skin, and my soul, as I listen to the voices of my friends bobbing and bouncing against the walls of the apartment in a sweet melody.

And, for that instant, I glimpse life again. It's distant, still, but it's shiny and beckoning, and I think I might want to go there. For the first time in a long while, it feels like maybe I can.

FOUR

Forever Your Girl, But Princesses are Fleeting

OCTOBER

HOW DO you know you're really sick? Because your life is reduced to a disjointed collection of days when you actually shower and see people, a scatter diagram of data points that punctuate the near-interminable pauses where you don't.

How will I know when I'm better? When all the days connect together again and life follows the line like a guide wire. Or a cliff's edge.

Right now, I'm still in the scatter graph period, intermittently mustering the courage to reach for moments that I can pin to my graph and cling to. Like dates with men that force me to put on mascara and a bra even if they are ultimately disappointing, or unexpected laughter with my friends on days when I didn't really want to see them. Mostly it's the moments with my daughter, when we sit snuggled under blankets on the couch drinking protein smoothies in lieu of lunches I'm too tired to prepare, watching movies in the Kids section of Netflix. But it's also my daughter that can bring me the most painful clarity.

So when you ask your kid on the phone, prior to her return to you, what she wants to do together when she gets back to your house, and her response is, "We don't have to do anything, Mom. *I know you need to rest,*" you know, with certainty, that you've devolved into a shitty parent.

It's funny, too, because I thought I was hiding it from her fairly well. When I'm by myself, I may not shower or eat or say words out loud for days. But I make a real effort when she's with me—all the effort, the only effort that matters. Except for the occasional smoothies, which she loves and seems to think is a treat, I make sure she has food to eat and clothes to wear, and that she gets dropped off and picked up from school on time. I watch kid's shows with her—Disney and Nick sitcoms with pre-teens in colorful, artfully assembled wardrobes and laugh tracks. I even make sure that we have periodic visits with my friends and their kids, which means we spend time outside, and that there is laughter involved, even if it isn't necessarily from me. I thought that was enough, that she would be insulated from my brokenness and think that all was okay and that the two of us were JUST FINE.

So by funny, I mean, I am a gigantic ass that's been fooling herself. Because, while I might not shed a tear in front of my smart, sassy, nine-year-old little girl with the dark red hair that matches mine, she gets it. She's no dummy. And she's not so little anymore.

It's not that I've tried to pretend nothing happened. In fact, in the beginning, when I was finally allowed to see her again without supervision, I was anxious to talk to her about it. Noah had robbed me of the chance to sit down with her and prepare her for what was to come. He'd stolen her and traumatized her by the shitstorm of despicability that he created, telling her God knows what when they'd disappeared. But I did NOT want to add to the mess, I wanted to diffuse it, to try, somehow, to undo some of it. So I waited until she was finally with me alone before I brought it up, because what real choice did I have?

I'd sat her down on the lawn chairs I was using as living room furniture before my lawyer finally was able to force Noah to relinquish one of the *three couches* in our house for my use during the separation, and I fixed us both Big Red floats, which are indescribably delicious, even when everything else tastes like white bread. She knew something was up, I could see it in her eyes. But she was quiet

—uncharacteristically so. And that made me worry more than anything.

I had thought long and hard about how to start this conversation, about what I could say without sounding like a raving lunatic consumed with rage. Because, whatever her dad had told her, she, inexplicably, *didn't hate him for it*. But now that the moment had arrived, my carefully chosen words were hiding in my depression-addled brain. I grew frustrated, as she patiently waited, and then finally she spoke first.

"It's okay, Mom," she says.

It startles me, this beginning. "What?"

"It's okay. I know that you and Dad are getting a divorce. I was sad at first, but now I'm fine. As long as I can see you both."

I'm stunned by her words, not that they're shocking, but that she sounds so grown up, like she's consoling *me*. And I'm sad, because of what her words imply—that she'd had to work through her feelings without me to help her. And that breaks my heart.

"Brooklyn…" I start to say. But I don't know what words should follow.

"I just don't want you or Dad to talk bad about each other. Because I love you both. Okay?"

I press my lips together, because after my initial overwhelming need to pour out all the supportiveness and mothering that I've stored up since it started, to empty my overflowing pitcher of maternal love, warm and thick and insulating, until it covers her up, everything else I want to say is how awful he is, how wrong he was to steal her away and lie and cheat to keep her, and how I'd meant for us to sit down together, the three of us, and have this conversation together.

"Okay, Mom?" she repeats, and her face is so earnest, her pale green eyes so round and tentative and yet insistent.

"Okay," is what I say back. Because above all, I don't want to make things worse for my baby girl by making her pick apart a wound she's moving past just to satisfy my maternal needs.

That was truly a harsh realization, that while my daughter had been hurting, going through the worst thing in her short life, I'd not been there to help her and protect her. I'd missed my window to be that person for her, locked out as effectively as a stranger standing outside a door, barricaded by her father. And so somehow she'd done it for herself.

Damn Noah for making it so. Damn him, and may he answer to God for what he's done.

But damn, my girl is strong.

The truth is, I will never forgive either of us for what Brooklyn has had to endure, unnecessarily. But this new evidence is unassailable—she sees through my ruse. And that is just as difficult to swallow. Because once again, despite all my efforts, I'm still failing to protect her.

After a generous glass of wine to fill the void in the pit of my stomach where the tiny kernel of psychic regrowth I'd sprouted had lived so briefly but now withers, exposed and deflated, I decide to come up with a plan. A plan to show my little girl that her mommy is here for her, and that I am more than a shell of a mother that just needs to *rest*, even if I don't believe it. I will *resolve* for it to be true, and thereby manifest it like a potter making art from clay, for her sake.

So I put on some real clothes, or at least a step up from pajamas —yoga pants and a t-shirt with no bra, my coat to protect against the brisk Fall air – brush my teeth and swipe on some deodorant, and I walk outside. In the middle of the day. When no one is making me. And then I get in my car and put it in gear and drive to the local party store, with one goal in mind—to find the best princess outfit a nine-year-old could hope for. Not the cliché dresses intended for Kindergartners, but a bad-ass princess outfit, like Princess Jasmine might wear, or what one might find on Diana Prince when she holds court on her island of Amazons. And maybe a tiara, but not the cheap plastic-looking ones with the gaudy stones that come unglued with rough handling, one that looks like it's made of real diamonds, maybe with crystals, the kind that sparkle like my baby's eyes.

It's a delicate balance, this shopping objective, because my daughter has not quite crossed the threshold into idolizing super heroes, and maybe she won't—she's a romantic more than a warrior by nature. Yet she's past the little girl versions of fairy tales—she doesn't need a prince to rescue her, though she still loves to be pretty like many girls do. No, if I know my daughter, what appeals to her about some of these more modern princess stories is, I suspect, the idea that she would be worth fighting for. Nothing wrong with that, as long as she doesn't define herself by it.

Because if there's one thing I've learned, it's that we ladies have to fight for ourselves.

This is a higher end party store, and I feel out of place at once when I enter, as the other customers are moms on serious party-planning trips, wearing cropped pants and cute sandals with rhine-stones and actual make-up. But as long as no one speaks to me, I'll survive. And it will be worth it, because the costumes are all well-made and designed to be worn again and again.

I peruse the aisles, looking for just the perfect outfit, when I see one that catches my eye—it's white and flowy, with a gold waistband and neckline. It's reminiscent of a Grecian princess, or Cleopatra. *That's the one*, I think. I head towards it and am delighted to find that they have it both in Brooklyn's and my size. Perfect! We can be Grecian/Egyptian princesses together. There are even decently made headpieces that go with it, and gold sandals.

When I get home, I still have over an hour before Brooklyn arrives. So I decide to transform myself in advance. I carefully apply makeup and am reminded, as I always am upon applying cosmetics, that I clean up pretty damn good, if I do say so myself. Then I begin the process of painstakingly curling my long auburn hair. It's a pain, sectioning off one piece at a time, using setting spray and a one and a half inch barrel curling iron. But then it's done, and once I add my headpiece, it is spectacular. Then it's time to put on the dress. It's not a great fit, but I'm thin enough that it drapes prettily. That's one thing I've noticed about clothes and being skinny—everything looks good on you.

When I hear the doorknob rattle, I jump up and rush out to the foyer in anticipation. I adjust my headpiece and straighten my princess gown, and my stomach flutters with something like nerves.

And then she's opening the door, flinging it wide the way she does and already shouting, "Mama, I'm here!"

Then she sees me and she stops dead in her tracks, letting her backpack slide down her arm, her coat fall to the floor. "Mama?"

"Queen Mama, at your service," I say, curtsying as best I can, considering I haven't curtsied since my third-grade dance recital.

She gives me the half-smile that I love, that makes my heart melt. "You look… good, Mama," she says, and I open my arms up to grab her in the obligatory hug. I squeeze her until she gasps and begs me to let go.

"Sorry, honey. I love you. I just missed my baby."

"Yeah, I know. Missed you too," she replies, pushing back from me. "So what's all this about?" She gestures to my get-up.

"Princess time! Here," I say, grabbing her hand and tugging her into the living room. "I have one for you, too!" I gesture grandly to the matching princess outfit laid out across the back of the couch.

"Oh," she says, pushing her red hair away from her face. She picks up the garment and holds it up critically, but doesn't say much. Certainly doesn't gush the excitement and words of appreciation I am expecting.

"I thought we could both dress up and then watch girly movies and make popcorn and chocolate chip cookies," I say, overly explaining in an attempt to increase her excitement.

She looks up at me then, her face a mass of freckles and flushed cheeks and big blinking green eyes—her dad's eyes. "Mom, can we talk?"

This catches me a bit off guard, but I nod. "Of course, honey." This time it's her leading me, taking me by the hand around the sofa so we can take a seat together. This is when I notice what she's wearing—distressed blue jeans with strategic rips and a form-fitting t-shirt with sparkly writing across the front. It's not revealing—she has nothing yet to reveal. But it's so grown-up. Like a teenager would wear, not a little girl.

Brooklyn takes a moment to gather herself, her ginger brows knitted in consternation. I hate seeing her distressed.

"Honey, what is it?" I say. She bows her head, and I put my

hand on it, feeling the silkiness of her hair, tracing the blonde streaks.

She looks up at me then, straightens her shoulders. "I think maybe you're trying too hard," she says, and I sit back, astonished.

"What do you mean?"

"The princess stuff. I mean, it's really nice, Mom. And I appreciate it. But… I'm not really into princess stuff anymore. I'm not the little girl you think I am." She squeezes my hand then, whether in reassurance or reinforcement, I'm not sure.

Despite my extreme desire to maintain my composure, my eyes fill with tears anyway. And then she immediately feels responsible, and that really makes me feel like shit.

"Mama, I'm sorry!" she says, reaching over to wipe my tear away with the tip of her finger. Her eyes fill up then, and it twists the heart in my chest.

"Brooklyn," I interrupt, straightening myself and grabbing her hand in mine. It's small and delicate, still a little girl's hand, but with nails painted neon blue, and not by me. "You don't ever have to apologize to me. I'm the mom, I'm the one that's supposed to take care of you. It's just, I don't feel like I've been doing such a great job. And I wanted to make it up to you."

She considers that for a moment before responding, looking away, over the landscape of the room, with its repainted walls and rearranged furniture, all designed to remake it into a home for just the two of us – to replace the look of the home that was once for three. I take the moment to compose myself, to reign in my fragile emotions with surreptitious deep breaths and calming thoughts.

She looks back at me then, her eyes wide and liquid but hopeful. "You don't have to make anything up to me. I just want you to be my Mom, like always."

Tears spill over then, and I grab her in a hug. "I'm your mom," I say into her hair, and it's true in every way except maybe the ones that matter, the ones where I'm the comforter, the protector, the strong one.

After a few minutes of tears and sniffles, she pulls back from me and roughly wipes at her cheeks—she doesn't like to cry. But she's beautiful, sitting there. This girl-child that's not so child-like anymore. And I smile.

"Okay," I say, sitting back to give her a little space. "I won't make you look like a princess. But you're not too old to be a goddess —no girl is ever too old to be a goddess!"

She smiles back. "A goddess? What does that mean exactly?"

"It means," I begin, with a great flourish of arms and hands, gesturing to her, to me, "that you are strong and tough and smart as hell, I mean heck." She purses her lips at me and laughs. "It means you don't need anyone to baby you, but you deserve… all the good stuff. To feel loved, and safe, and special."

"Okay, that sounds pretty good," she says, pulling the goddess gown from the back of the couch and running her fingers over it. "But can you straighten my hair maybe? And even… let me put on some of your make-up?"

"Of course, my sweet goddess Brooklyn," I say. "Not all the time, because I don't want to spoil you, and you're not old enough for make-up quite yet…"

She rolls her eyes at me and it's so normal and beautiful and I love it. I give her a playful tug on the hair. "But for today, since you are a goddess, you get whatever you want."

She jumps up then, suddenly full of the enthusiasm that she'd been missing before. She grabs the dress and heads toward the bathroom where all my beauty gear resides, but before she gets to the door, she turns and flashes me a grin. "You said whatever I want, right?"

"Yes, honey," I reply, then pause, suspecting a set-up. "Within reason."

And then my going-on-ten-year-old says something no mother is ready to hear: "Can we go shopping at Forever 21?"

But I laugh anyway, because these are the things little girls are supposed to dream of—make-up and pretty hair and provocative, trendy clothes. And it lightens my heart. My girl is still there after all, and I haven't yet missed all my chances with her.

FIVE

The Power of the Pu-tang

NOVEMBER

MY DEPRESSION IS SLIGHTLY IMPROVING, in that I am show-ering more frequently, and allowing myself to be dragged out of the house at least semi-regularly by my persuasive friends. I still save up most of my energy for my time with Brooklyn, so that I'm exhausted by our week's end and veritably collapse into the Dark-ness the moment she leaves. But I'm not complaining – I'm so grateful to have time with her again, more than the every other weekend I suffered during the divorce. Even if it did cost me thou-sands extra in alimony, I would have paid every penny I own to have her again.

Beyond that, and exacerbating it and/or because of it, I'm still struggling with concentration, cognition and extreme anxiety, but at least I'm not deep in the Hole anymore. Lately, sometimes, there are moments when I can even crawl up over the edge and stand there, wobbly, trying not to fall. The Hole still sucks at me, but there's a railing there, and I'm gripping it with all my might.

I've even been out on a few dates, courtesy of the questionably effective on-line dating app, *Relations*. And the last guy seemed to have real promise. His profile said 'retired lawyer', but he looked young so I figured he must be pretty well off. Also, he runs an arti-

47

sanal cheese shop in East Nashville where he makes his own aged cheddar—I Googled it. And I love cheese, and post-professional men. In theory.

But when he shit his undisclosed colostomy bag during dinner, which led to a confession that he'd been a drug mule for his shady clients and permanently destroyed his colon and got disbarred, I decided to give dating a break.

So my luck hasn't been great, but then, maybe my expectations are too high. And I still ask myself what I'm actually hoping for—Love? Affection? Companionship? Maybe a break from the loneliness… But for now, tonight anyway, I'm focusing on having fun with my friends, enjoying a few cocktails, and maybe hitting up the karaoke bar a little later if the mood strikes me, and if Carlie, my alter ego and not incredibly inventive stage name, decides to appear.

I haven't seen her for a while, but I sense that she's still in there… somewhere.

It's warm for a late November night, temperatures are in the high fifties, and the girls decide it's a good night to hit downtown. I've let my friends drag me to a new bar on Broadway called *Blue Oasis*, with à propos blue lights strung along the bottom of the bar top and all along the ceiling. I remember when this bar used to be a honkey-tonk called *Boot Scooters*, whose claim to fame was nightly line dancing lessons and ten-gallon hats you could borrow for the duration of your dance experience.

In any case, now it's a much swanker bar, in keeping with Nashville's recent hipster gentrification, but it still blares current country music, though interspersed with rap and Justin Bieber.

But I'm focused on none of that at the moment, though, because as unlikely as it seems, the cutest guy in the bar appears to be looking at me and smiling a very sexy half-smile. He can't be more than twenty-five, for goodness sake! Not that I'm complaining —he's within my newly determined, theoretical age range—my age plus or minus fifteen years. Sounds rather insane, and yet optimistic, when I really focus on it…

He's broad-shouldered and narrow-hipped, like a running back, or a college wrestler. His only flaw, if you can call it one, is that his brown hair is already thinning at the top, a precursor to a slow creep that will follow him for the next twenty years. But he's rakish and surrounded by the rowdy pubescent laughter of his friends, and I think, *Bachelor party.*

I flip my hair back as seductively as I know how, which is not saying much, and give him the tiniest return smile, because part of me still can't believe he's looking at *me.*

"How do you do that?" says Gretchen, eyeing me over her drink with a competing mixture of wonder and annoyance on her face.

"What?" I ask, turning my attention back to my friends.

"Get guys to look at you like that," she says, and her lips pucker in a pout.

"By not making that face," I say, laughing. She grins and gives me the biggest kissy-face pucker she can. She looks like a Kardashian taking a selfie. "Why are you asking, anyway? You've got Chris," I say.

"I know, and he's a good guy. But I didn't get to *date*, like you're getting to do. I met him when he came to fix the wiring in our laundry room, and that was that."

"That's how you met? He was your electrician? I didn't know that."

"It's not what you think," she says. "He found me crying because Jonathan and I had gotten into a huge fight about... hell, I don't even remember. But Chris was so sweet. He had my number already because I'm the one who called him to come work on the house, so he sent me a text after to check on me to make sure I was doing okay. And then we just started... talking. And it was nice, to have someone to talk to. Really nice, because it had been a long time since anybody really listened to me." She sighs, remembering, then takes a drink before continuing.

"I swear I didn't sleep with him until Jonathan was already talking to Alicia at work and we were separated. That asshole already wanted her before he even left me. He was freaking searching for my replacement."

"None of that bullshit tonight," Tasha says then, smacking Gretchen on the hand.

"None of what?"

"Divorce talk. It's off limits. Tonight is about having fun with our bad selves and, for me and Claire anyway, maybe getting laid."

"No, no, it's definitely not about getting laid," I insist, though I don't sound completely convincing.

"Okay, okay," says Gretchen, sufficiently chastised. "Well, then, back to my original question. How the hell does Claire do that?"

"It's her va-jay-jay power," says Tasha. She's drawing sugar skulls on a napkin with a red pen she found in my tiny going-out purse.

I sputter out a mouthful of Crowne and Seven. "My what?"

She scratches out her last drawing and looks at me. "Your va-jay-jay. Your pu-tang." She winks, adding, "Your love canal," as she gestures rather widely toward the groin area.

I do not appreciate the connotation.

I shake my head. "I don't have va-jay-jay power," I insist.

"Oh, yes you do, girl," Tasha says, and Gretchen's nodding too.

"She's right," Gretchen says. "The sex vibe is coming off of you in waves. Like poison gas."

"Gee, thanks."

"Hey, I say own it, work it, give that bitch a name," says Tasha, taking a sip from her Jack and Coke. "Plus, you went and got hot."

I reflexively fan myself and she gives me a playful shove. "Not that kind of hot."

"That is true," Gretchen says. "You're all skinny and your hair is all long and flowy. You were kind of... business-like when we met you. But now you scream 'sex' from your pores."

I decide to ignore the last observation and focus on that which is objective. "The good ole divorce diet," I say, swirling my drink in contemplation. In truth, I had recently marveled at my hollowed stomach. I didn't even notice it happening, just woke up one day to pants that hung on hipbones I forgot I had and a sudden absence of rolls when I leaned over to pick up the dog's squeak toy from the floor to resume a game of fetch. Who knew I'd ever be a size four again? I mean, seriously. At my age?

But I'm not perfect. My chin is too prominent and my nose is a smidge too long. And my flat stomach doesn't erase the vague line of stretch marks above my pelvic area, or the freckles and spots from years-old sun damage.

"I've got boob slideage," I add, not realizing I've said it out loud.

Tasha raises an eyebrow. "What the hell's that, and what the fuck are you talking about?"

"What happened to your 'fuck' moratorium?" asks Gretchen.

Tasha gives her a blank look.

"Not saying 'fuck'—what happened to that?"

"Too fucking hard," says Tasha with a wink, then eyes me, waiting for an explanation.

With anyone else, I'd be embarrassed. But these are my girls, so I explain. "Yours may be too... um... pert for you to relate, Tasha," I say delicately, trying not to call them small, or any of the other colorful descriptors that come to mind—mole hills, mosquito bites, itty-bitty titties. "But I have this... issue. When I lay down on my back, my boobs end up in my pits."

Gretchen snorts out a laugh, snotting out vodka and cranberry juice that we collectively rush to clean up with cocktail napkins. Tasha's masterpieces disintegrate in the effort.

Once she's gathered herself and cleaned her dripping nose, she says, "Mine do that too," and laughs again, though this time without the mess. "And..." she begins, taking a sip before continuing, suddenly serious. "My nipples have gone cock-eyed."

At this, combined with the earnest expression on her face, I burst into laughter.

"Gretchen, you're shitting me," Tasha says, as she reaches to lift up Gretchen's shirt. Gretchen swats her hand away.

"No I am not. One points straight and the other hangs like a googly-eye and points southwest." She puts her hands up to her chest and demonstrates with pointed fingers.

I'm stumped by the directionality. "Doesn't that depend on which way you're facing?" I ask.

But Tasha's fascinated. "Can we go to the bathroom so I can see?"

"No, you nut-head! I'm not pulling them out for display! I'm just remarking, that's all. Contributing to the conversation, as it were."

But Tasha's not giving up. "Maybe the next time we go skinny-dipping…"

"Uh, there will be no 'next time,'" Gretchen says, making air quotes with her fingers.

I'm smiling as I watch and listen to them. They're referring to the night we had one too many glasses of homemade sangria at my apartment complex, and then decided it would be a great idea to sneak over to the pool for a clandestine midnight swim. It was Tasha who decided it would be sans clothing, and it was a testament to Gretchen's high level of inebriation that we'd been able to convince her, for all of about sixty seconds, to strip and dip with us. Unfortunately, or not, it was too dark to see bits and parts.

Including cock-eyed nipples.

As it were.

I'm distracted by the titillating (pun intended) conversation, so I don't notice when a guy walks up behind me. He nudges me in the shoulder and I turn to face his crotch. It's compact, firm, uncomfortably eye-level, but pleasantly appealing the way a tightly wrapped package is, begging to be opened. My eyes reluctantly travel up his torso, across his retro Whitesnake t-shirt (*is that supposed to be ironic?*), to his face, and I see that it's the cute guy that I'd noticed from before.

He smiles at me as soon as my eyes reach his. "Hey, beautiful. I missed you."

"Excuse me?"

"I missed you before you came into my life," he adds, winking at me as he runs his hand lightly across my upper arm. It raises chill bumps in its wake in a most enjoyable way.

Still, the line was cheesy. I try not to roll my eyes, because… well, I'm not sure why. Because I don't want to scare him off, I guess. Yes, he's exhibiting interest, but I think of him like a gazelle— quick, sleek, muscular in a virile, animalistic way, but skittish.

However, I can virtually hear my friends rolling their eyes behind me.

Without waiting for an invitation, he pulls up a chair, turned backwards so he can straddle it, close enough that his leg is pressed to mine under the table when he sits.

"I'm Ryan," he says, reaching out a hand for me to shake. I take it, and he brings my fingers to his mouth and kisses them. Then he licks his lips. "You taste sweet," he says.

"Do I?"

"I think so. Can I re-verify?"

At this, Gretchen snorts behind me, but I don't turn around. Because I like his leg against mine, and my fingers in his hand. I suddenly want to be closer to him.

My girls are long forgotten. I know somewhere in the back of my mind that I'm probably being rude, but then I think that they'll understand. Or at least, they'll get over it.

After all, who can defy the power of the pu-tang?

Ryan is looking deeply into my eyes now, and his are unlined and long-lashed—like a baby cow. Damn, he's young. He says some stuff to me, I don't remember much of it, and then he's offering to buy me another drink at the bar, as mine has disappeared along with most of my inhibitions.

I suggest that he get drinks for my friends, too, and he pauses for a moment, considering it. Apparently I'm worth the supplemental investment though, and we girls are left on our own for a few minutes while his tight little ass wedges its way between two burly guys squatting on stools.

"You're not seriously considering this, are you?" Gretchen says, but she's smiling.

"Considering what?" I ask. "I'm just… enjoying. Am I allowed to do that?"

"Girl, you eat that little man-cake up!" says Tasha. "And save me a slice! Or better yet, get him to introduce us to his friends." She waves her fingers at the group of them, where they are alternating between playing flip cup and making lewd groin-chopping gestures at each other.

And then Ryan's back, and he's asking where I live and is surprised to learn I actually live in Nashville, as apparently most the girls he's met tonight have been visiting from other places. He tells me, when I ask, that he's from Austin.

"Austin's a cool city," he confirms upon further inquiry. "Kinda like here, but more hipster."

"Awesome," I say. *Awesome?* What's next—*Gag me with a spoon, because you're totally rad?*

"So what's cool to do in Nash Vegas?" he asks, and I look at my girls.

"Uh, we like to go to the karaoke bar sometimes. Except karaoke in Nashville kinda sucks, because everybody is good here. You know how in other cities, if you can sing 'Sweet Caroline' on key, you are the star of the bar? Well here, it seems like everybody that gets up there is a wannabe country music star. It makes it hard to stand out, if you know what I mean," I say, realizing I'm rambling, but thinking that ballroom dancing and painting/wine classes are probably *not* what he had in mind when asking about "cool" activities.

"Yeah, karaoke with bros is lit. David Allen Coe is my old school jam," he says, and I inwardly sigh in relief that I've answered something suitable, though I'm only partially confident that I understood his response.

I glance over my shoulder, and Gretchen is watching us raptly, her chin in her hand, elbow propped on the table. Tasha is tossing napkins at one of the other frat boys, and he's laughing and tossing bar nuts back at her.

Ryan says some more stuff, including his age, which has Gretchen kicking me under the table. I try to respond appropriately, though I feel inept, like I've never had a conversation before. And then he's leaning in toward my ear.

"It's really loud in here," he says. His breath tickles my neck and that chill is back again. It feels really good. "Want to walk outside for a minute? There's some tables out there."

He's referring to the back of the bar where there's a patio area with warming lamps which is open, I understand, on all but the coldest nights. I doubt we'll find a seat out there, because the place is packed, but I'm agreeable. He stands and takes my hand.

"I'll be back in a few," I tell the girls. Tasha waves me away and Gretchen shrugs, but she's eyeing us almost longingly.

He leads me back through the main bar area to the hallway that leads outside. As soon as we are out of sight from the rest of the bar, he's pushed me up against the wall and is kissing me. I am overcome with a waterfall of sensations. His kiss is eager and hungry and yet soft around the edges, tasting like beer and salt, and I worry briefly that I won't remember how to do it. But somehow my mouth remembers. And his body is pressed against mine, all six-feet, six-pack-abbed bit of it, even his tight little package. It's molded to me in the most perfect, intentional way. And his hands... they find their way under the hem of my long dress and trail along first the outside, then the inside of my thighs.

I literally gush—I mean, down there. I think for a second I might have peed, because that happens sometimes.

And I suddenly realize... no, remember—this is what it is to be really *touched*.

When his fingers dip inside me, I nearly collapse in his arms, and it brings to mind a vague recollection of this elusive concept, this thing that some women supposedly live with daily but which I barely remember—this magical fairytale known as *orgasm*.

But then his friends stumble out, dragging Gretchen and Tasha with them, slurring about going together as a group to another bar, and Ryan pulls away, releasing my parts, dropping my dress, freed by my va-jay-jay.

I get pulled along then—one indistinguishable component of this amorphous, rowdy collection of friends and strangers, migrating to another smoky, over-filled bar of live music that makes up in volume what it lacks in talent. As we walk long the dirty side-walk, dodging other people that have come downtown to party and enjoy the Nashville nightlife, I'm starting to feel tired and dizzy, but I don't stop. Because I'm drawn powerfully forward by the hope of another touch. *Lord, please, one more touch.*

And that's when I start to think, which has always been my problem.

Why do I want this so damn bad?

It's not so much that I've been hanging onto the tangible memory of not being touched. I haven't been consciously flashing back to my husband wincing when I accidentally brush his arm, his body recoiling because I lean in his direction. It's not that I've been focusing on the fact that, by the end, he hadn't kissed me in more than three years, not even a chaste kiss on the forehead or the cheek. Or that he had relegated sex to once a quarter, a supposed improvement, because a marriage counselor had warned him that I'd probably leave him if he didn't increase the frequency. Or how sex had come to feel like a violation, back-alley and sordid and wrong, the way no parts touched but the essential ones and the look of disgust that never left his face, even as he pushed away from me afterward and exited the room like it was on fire.

Because if I had ever focused on it all together, pieced cohesively in a collage of evidence in a case, I might have questioned aloud why I stayed in that. I might have seen that the evidence was there for a long time, years even, and I wasted them thinking it was going to change.

But I'm not there. For me, since things have been bad and then got even worse, this is all different levels of pain in the slush of pain soup within me, giving rise to a neediness that makes me now yearn for touch with every cell in my body. It's primal, this need. And though unspoken, and previously unacknowledged, it pulsates like a living thing, all on its own.

Does Ryan sense that in me? Is that why he's so drawn to me? Am I this wounded animal giving off a scent, a weakness, that predators sense? Or is it this lean body, born of sadness and the side effect of no appetite, and the long hair I've finally ignored long enough to grow out?

Surely it's not my conversation, which is uneven and broken by lulls where I momentarily realize I haven't done anything fun or interesting by myself that I can talk about. All my stories are old and involve a husband that left me years before the actual divorce. And of course he doesn't want to hear about my daughter—he's single, never been married, nine years my junior. Or so he says—he's still young enough to think that *inflating* your age makes you more attractive. He was looking for low-calorie pseudo-conversation, flirtations that lead to drinks, that lead to accidental touching of my newly tiny waist next to a pool table in a bar.

Or very intentional touching in a dingy backroom hallway.

We drift from bar to bar and the guys, too distracted or too drunk to keep up, eventually fall away. And eventually, as we call a ride to take us home, the physical imprint of Ryan's hands on my body fades. And I know it meant nothing, but I don't care. Because touch is my new drug. And I need it in a way I don't understand, but that overpowers everything else. Even my normally cautious instincts.

Date With Ripply Young Reston

I'M BEGINNING to think there's a reason why men in their late thirties and forties are available. Because no rational, sane woman wants them. They are the rejects, the defective, the unmarriageable. Either that or they are divorced because of something they've done—they are the liars, cheaters, disgusting specimens of manhood.

This realization, however, does not cause me to give up on men, exactly. Rather, it's redirected my efforts to a different demographic, as it were. The young ones. Now, I'm fully aware that I'm creeping up on thirty-nine, which by default means I'm pushing *forty*, and that number, taken out of context, might not be appealing to a younger man.

But I could pass for twenty-eight... or maybe thirty-two... in low light and beer fog. That's been proven lately in the test environment of the downtown karaoke bar, quite successfully, I might add.

So now I'm considering calling Reston.

I met Reston when I was still living in the apartment. He was hard to miss at the swimming pool—tan and muscular, with abs so ripped it looked like he had a series of speed bumps between his chest and his groin. Like a dual-purpose obstacle course, decorative and practical, to slow down the journey for the timid or the overly enthusiastic.

Anyway, Gretchen had approved immediately, her sexual fantasies being in high mode and dependent on exceptional physical specimens. There were no realistic love story dreams for her, maybe because, in all reality, she already has that. There are only steamy imaginings of elegantly contrived porn movie encounters.

And Tasha was fully on board with me dating the young ones because she firmly believes that the cure to what ails me is to get good and properly laid. Her only complaint was that his name sounds like a hotel chain.

My hesitation initially was, in fact, his age. And the secret belief that he was out of my league, physically speaking. But I've gained some amount of confidence in that area over these past months of failed dates and bar experiences. And his age, as I've mentioned, is becoming less of an issue. Less years theoretically equals less baggage. And, hopefully, more potential.

Anyway, he'd flirted with me, tossing the rubber football around with me in the shallow end of the pool, probably to watch my bikini-clad boobs bounce. I didn't mind. I liked watching him, too.

And we had ultimately exchanged numbers. He texted me a few times suggesting beer and chicken wings, or tail-gating before the college football game on the big screen. But I had been otherwise engaged with my daughter during those proposed times, and so was inclined to decline. He took it well, asking no questions about my daughter at her mention, as though she were part of the portion of my life he had no interest in. This assumption, of course, adding to the presumption that he was much too young for me.

But now I wonder if I was too harsh in my judgment of him. He very likely has no experience with children of prospective romantic interests. So maybe he didn't know what to say.

And here I am now, thoroughly disillusioned with men my own age, and willing to give young Reston a chance.

I pull out my phone, open a text to his number, and think. What do I say? How do I sound nonchalant and cool and slightly unattainable, but still desirable, all at the same time?

I settle with the following: *Hey Reston, It's Claire. Finding myself with no plans this weekend and thought I might take you up on those burgers.*

Not super smooth, but not terrible. Still, I hesitate before hitting 'send'. But then I sigh, because I really am lonely, and it might actually be fun. So I push the button that sends my text over cyberspace to his phone. And then I wait.

I try to busy myself with other things—checking Facebook, then reading a little teenage vampire romance till the eye rolls and ironic brooding gets to be too much. And that's when my phone vibrates—two buzzes, meaning it's a text I've received.

I open it, my hand shaking for some inexplicable reason, and it's from him.

'Good to hear from you, Claire! How's 7:00 Saturday night? I'll pick you up if you send me your address.'

I feel an unexpected giddiness, a pleasant nervous fluttering in my stomach, like the not-quite popular girl in tenth grade that inexplicably got asked out by the cutest boy at school. I'm excited to let my girls know, and they are excited for me, responding appropriate to their natures—Gretchen with her sweet encouragement, Tasha with her insistence that sex is the best thing since the invention of the smooth glide tampon.

I'll take her word for it, even if it's not been my personal experience. Maybe I've been doing it wrong.

THE REST of the week is filled with numb days that spill into dull nights, and lots of sleeping, always lots of sleeping. But then it's Saturday, and my impending date is giving me a reason to shower and shave my parts, even my naughty ones, though I don't consciously acknowledge any hope or expectation such grooming might imply. I spend the time to blow-dry out my hair, and then curl it in long lengths, fingering them apart so they appear natural and beach-y. Then I apply all the necessary layers of my make-up, even the ones I normally skip, and put on my pretty underwear—the matching ones, again denying that such coordination means anything beyond the need to feel coordinated. After spritzing my neck and the space between my breasts with sweet-smelling body spray, I put on my coral floor-length dress with the matching shrug and check myself in the mirror. It's like looking at a different person. Someone younger, prettier than I could ever be.

And then there's a knock at the door, and my stomach flips again.

Reston is standing behind it, smiling a cock-sure half-smile when I open it, looking fine in his ripped jeans and tight designer t-shirt.

"You look great," he says, and then looks down, as though bashful. It's endearing, but an unwelcome reminder that he's not far from being a boy.

But he's not a boy. He's a man, if a young one. He turns to lead me out the door toward his waiting car. He drives a late-model Honda Accord, practical and recently washed, and I climb into the passenger seat to find that it's clean on the inside as well. So far, I'm pleasantly surprised.

He suggests a local restaurant, sort of up-scale pub fare, and I agree. We listen to country music while we drive, and we both sing along quite companionably.

The restaurant is rather noisy, with several televisions playing sporting events and pop music blaring from the speakers. But he asks for a booth in the rear corner, and it's marginally better.

"So, what made you text me? Not that I'm complaining, but it was kind of out of the blue," he says after we've ordered drinks and appetizers.

I look down, feeling shy. "I was thinking about you," I say, and that's true enough. "I wanted to get to know you a little better."

"Well, I'm glad you did. And I'm an open book," he says. "As long as you don't ask me about my drug past or my time in the joint."

I look up at him then, shocked. And he laughs at my expression. He's teasing me.

I smile back and our drinks arrive. He offers a toast. "To hanging out, and maybe more," he says, with a *"wazzup"* nod and sexy half-smile that is so obvious I almost snort, and we clink glasses.

The rest of the dinner flows fairly easily. He's got three sisters, one older and two younger, and he's originally from Virginia Beach.

"What brought you to Nashville?" I ask.

"I went to Vanderbilt," he says, and when my eyes widen, he adds, "for a while."

I sit back, sipping my margarita and munching on a fried pickle. "You must explain."

"I got in for golf, and my test scores were good. But I flunked out. I guess I partied a little too much."

He looks chagrined at this. "Pretty lame, huh?"

"I'm not judging," I say. "So, did you ever finish college?"

He eats an entire fried pickle spear in one large bite. Thankfully, he waits till he's swallowed before he answers. "Yeah, I finished at Middle Tennessee. Got my business degree. But not much to do with it. General business degrees are not all that useful. For a while, I worked in a bank, but I freaking hated it. That's why I ended up managing the cell phone store—business degree is supposed to mean management training, I guess. I actually recently decided I want to be a paramedic, so I'm about to go back to school for that."

He asks me about my job then, and I answer in the way that I've practiced—in a way that makes me sound like I'm a professional while being very non-specific about my actual employment. He nods appreciatively, obviously concluding that I make decent money, but asks no further probing questions.

By this point, our food has arrived, and we talk about movies for a while. He's quite a movie lover, and enjoys expounding on the virtues of different directors, his favorite being Tarantino. And by the time the food is consumed, I'm full and more than a little tipsy.

He pays the check with no hesitation and we get up to leave. As we walk toward the door, I'm slightly unsteady on my feet, and he puts his hand on the small of my back to steady me. It sends a tingle that radiates up my back and makes me shiver.

"Cold?" he says into the back of my hair, his breath brushing my neck. I hadn't realized he was so close.

"No," I say.

Outside, he opens the car door for me, and doesn't ask me

where I want to go. I don't take offense to this. Because the answer would be, *wherever you are*. Instead, he drives me to the familiar apartment complex, parking in front of the units where his apartment resides. He opens the door for me again and takes my hand to help me out of the car, but doesn't let go as he leads me, wordlessly, to his apartment door.

He unlocks it with one hand, still grasping mine behind his back. And then the door's open and he's pulling me inside. I notice random things during the few seconds it takes him to shut and lock the door—the huge television on one wall, the black sectional sofa with red and orange pillows, the stack of laundry on the floor.

And then he's kissing me. My back bumps up against the wall, but not hard and it doesn't hurt, and his body is pressed against mine. I can sense his desire as strongly as I can feel my own, but he doesn't rush it. He kisses me slowly and thoroughly, his hands in my hair massaging my scalp, cupping my face. The room spins a bit, even with my eyes closed, but I relish in the kiss. It's good, wet but not sloppy. After a few minutes, he takes a breath, breaking away with a pull of soft lips from soft lips, and he looks at me.

"Can I touch you?"

The anal retentive voice in my head corrects him—"*May I,*" I think, but I don't say it. Instead, I nod. He steps back, so that there's a few inches space between us, and he looks at my body, slow and appreciatively. I involuntarily arch my back, merely from the power of his gaze, this look that I barely recognize, this expression that says he wants me.

Me.

He reaches forward then and runs the backs of his fingers down my bare shoulder, slow and delicately, raising goosebumps in their wake. Then he trails his fingers across my collarbone to my chest— the high part, which is ribs and breast-tops—and he hovers there, making my skin tingle with anticipation. His fingertips brush across the front of my breasts, first one and then the other, and my nipples stand up and ting when his fingers brush past them, even through the fabric. He runs his palm down my stomach then, but stops where the tops of my panties rest, which he would clearly see if my dress weren't in the way.

Without my conscious decision, or even permission, my body reacts, arching and meeting his touch, and it ignites him.

He crushes his mouth to mine in a kiss that is the king of all kisses, and his fingers are roaming, pulling up my skirt, undoing buttons and zippers, vaguely fumbling with pockets and wrapper. And then he's inside me. I gasp from the surprise, my eyes popping open, my mouth forming an "*Oh*," and he pauses there, letting me experience the fullness of him fully before he moves, just a little, and I gasp again, closing my eyes in surrender, gripping his shoulders with my hands. And then he's withdrawing, and my body doesn't like it one bit. It latches onto him, willing him to fill it again, and he does and I nearly explode. And then he's pushing into me, filling me, releasing me and filling me again, and I'm riding and grasping and pulsing and I know nothing except his cock and my need, my incredible, physical need.

He pumps inside of me harder and harder until he cries out and shudders and then I'm shuddering too, contracting three, four, five times, until my bones melt and I slither partway down the wall.

He holds me close though, not letting me hit the floor, and laughs into my neck and hair.

"Damn," he says, and I thoroughly agree.

Damn, indeed.

I stay over, and he wakes me at some point for sex again, and it is quick but fun. And though he doesn't quite hold me, his back against mine is comforting and foreign and nice.

And I'm no longer a divorce virgin, twice over.

Boom!

SIX

The Appeal of a Good Bologna

APRIL, AGAIN

FIRST, it was Ryan. Then it was Matt, at another bar, another back room. Then it was Kevin, audacious and deft with his hand under the table, surrounded by people. A series of interludes, touches that left me on fire and ravenous and physically awake in a way I've never known.

That's what led me to Reston, because let's face it, my other dating forays had been a complete disaster. He is young, and cute as hell, and so freaking *firm*.

And it was hella fun… for a while.

Our first date, it turns out, had been rather perfunctory. A lead-up to the main event, so to speak. And since that first night, the pull between us was overpowering. As soon as we would see each other, the energy we created ignited the room with protons and electrons swirling in increasing frisson, creating friction that made my hair stand on end and creating this atomic frenzy that is beyond human control, but that required immediate, kinetic, *action*. It was tempera-ture-raising and uncomfortable and immediate, and we, or at least I, was left with the distinct impression that there was quite literally nothing else to do but to tear each other's clothes off.

And then the sex was just as frenzied and animal and damn hot, with me mounting him on chairs and couch cushions or any other convenient surface, and him spinning me around to ruck up my skirt and take me, hard, from behind against that very same couch.

The sexual pull between us was truly and scientifically electric, but it was also a tiny bit surreal. When we came together, I could almost separate from it, not that I wanted to. But something drew me away from fully being present, so that a part of me watched our interaction like it was a movie scene. Still, if I couldn't completely engage on every level, being with Reston consumed my thoughts enough that it squeezed out all the rest. All the bad, all the worrisome, all the fears. And that was a good thing.

It turned out, sex could really be fun, in a way sex has never been for me.

And suddenly I am thinking about sex all the time. I fantasize about it, wishing tangentially that there was love associated with it, but that wish doesn't diminish the physical need. I want to be touched, in every way, shown love, or some form of it, with tangible skin-to-skin contact if not quite affection and intimacy.

Unfortunately, Reston is only twenty-seven years old, and his idea of hanging out after sex is watching male-oriented HBO shows that are drowning in too many sports references and fart jokes and that spray more gratuitous profanity around a scene than a 1980s Porky's movie. And he's got a decent job, but his idea of a nice date is the local Mexican restaurant on taco night.

The truth is, I can't talk to him about anything real, because it might make his head explode with two much adultness and grownup shit. Consequently, I don't really say much at all.

So we parted ways, quite amicably, with the generous offer on the table to remain "fuck buddies," though I'm not quite ready for that level of self-reflection, the conscious decision to meet up with someone for the sole purpose of having sex, knowing there is not even the pretense of a possible relationship.

But even after my very mature decision to end the relationship, it doesn't stop my intense desire. I know that it's screwed up, that I am probably seriously damaged and that these are undoubtedly not the healthiest feelings in the world, but it felt so damn good to be wanted, to be loved, in whatever form I can get it.

And I could get it—easily. Even if I chose not to take Reston up on his offer, there are plenty of men that I could meet up with and drink wine and eat duck confit with that would service me, and I could even pretend it could mean something, though it wouldn't.

But that's not what I want to do. Or not really. I don't want to be a slut-puppy, as Tasha would say, and not in a derogatory way, chasing sexual encounters like an 18-year-old boy. Not that I'm judging—because, believe me, I *really* get the appeal.

And so all this self-restraint is leading to even more self-reflection. Why am I so consumed? Is it my age that has given birth to this need? I always heard women hit their sexual peak in their late thirties… Is it a mid-life crisis, or me experiencing the single life I never got to enjoy?

Or is this overwhelming desire born of the complete and deliberate deprivation I endured?

I don't know, and maybe it doesn't matter. All that matters, at this moment, is that it's 10 am, I'm alone in my house, and horny as hell. And all I can think of is, *who can I call? Ryan, Matt, Kevin…*

Reston.

And it's tempting. Very, very tempting.

So I do what any rational, non-slut mom would do—I call one of my best friends for support.

"Tasha, I need sex. But I don't want to do something stupid," I say, when she answers the phone.

"What's stupid about needing sex?" she asks. "Sex is like food. You need it to stay alive. I say, get laid! What happened to Reston? Can't you call him?"

Shit, she's not helping. And I really want to… get laid, that is. But I hesitate. First, because I would rather there be feelings involved. But second, and maybe more importantly, I'm afraid I'll sink into the abyss—that if I feed the need, I'll never get enough of the drug.

Yes, I'm screwed up.

But I don't try to explain all that. Instead, I say, "It's... not enough."

She sighs. "Okay, fine, if you say so. In that case, I know what we've got to do. Throw some clothes on," Tasha says, so I do.

When she arrives to pick me up, I'm curious. She's wearing such a sly grin as she drives and sings along with the radio, for a moment, I wonder if she's taking me to a male whorehouse despite my reticence. But she laughs when I ask her and keeps her mouth shut.

And then we're pulling into a parking lot for a store I've never been to before—its windows are blacked out, and the neon sign says 'Intimate Exchange'.

"Uh, what is this?" I ask.

"It's a sex store!" Tasha says, rather gleefully.

I can feel the blush cover my face. "I can't go in there!"

"Of course you can. This is exactly what you need. Trust me!"

She practically drags me in the door, and my embarrassment is complete. But I'm also a bit curious.

Whatever my preconceived notions, the establishment does not disappoint.

The first thing I notice when we walk through the door is a display of flavored lubes, accompanied by a full-size cardboard cutout of a woman leaning forward to display an impressive collision of breasts, and licking her glistening fingers. Headless mannequins flank the display, sporting erotic lingerie and holding whips and handcuffs, and all I can think is, *why does a person need flavored lube?* I wonder at it, but it's a secondary, passing thought, because my attention has been diverted to something even more shocking—an expansive wall of vagina.

There are pocket-sized ones and ones shaped like penis-length tunnels. Ones attached to legs and torsos behind glass, to protect the merchandise from over-eager customers, as it were, and ones attached to full-body mannequins, with disturbing, orgasmic faces. There are varying vaginas representing every conceivable shape and feature—with vulvas that range from delicate petals to harsh, demanding lips, sporting corresponding labias that span from diminutive and virginal to skillfully undulating. And they come in all colors—fleshy Caucasian and varying shades of coffee to ebony, and some kind of in-between ethnicity that could be Latina, Native American or Middle Eastern—very multi-cultural. There are pulsating ones and twisting (?) ones, and ones that appear to swallow a man's appendage like a meat grinder. *(Why?)* It's a virtual wonderland of vagina.

I see a pocket version sitting out on display, and I pick it up, curious. I turn it on and go to stick my finger inside when Tasha snatches it away.

"Focus, Claire," she says.

"But, but, the chomping pussy…" I say, as she pulls me away.

And then I see it, what she meant for me to see, what we came for—the *Wall of Dildos*.

They are everywhere—red ones and white ones, purple and pink ones, clear ones and black ones. I wonder briefly why the dildos are so vibrantly colored, and except for a few exceptions, not made to look as realistic as the vaginas.

"Because women don't want realistic penises," Tasha explains. "And besides, you're not going to see it once it's in use anyway."

Good point.

There are curved ones and straight ones, even pulsing ones. There are big ones and small ones and every size in between. There's even uncircumcised ones. It's quite overwhelming and yet fascinating. And I come away with one prevailing thought—if these are supposed to be representative of the variety of real shapes and sizes, I have been very, very sheltered indeed!

But there's one displayed prominently on its own shelf that grabs my attention and has me faltering in astonishment and wonder—it's a gargantuan Caucasian flesh-colored phallus, thick and long as a log of bologna at a meat counter, artfully veined in a realistic roadmap of synthetic blood vessels.

I approach it slowly, as though it might come to life suddenly, my hand reaching out tentatively. I want to feel its girth, which, honestly, might require both hands…, to prove that it's as robust and unlikely as it appears.

"I don't think you want that one," Tasha says, though she's eying me speculatively.

I look down at my narrow loins and back at the cock. "What... how..." I sputter, as she gently redirects me.

"Look away, my child," Tasha says. "Look away." She slowly guides me back to the main wall, but I am still drawn to it, peering after it over my shoulder.

"I can't unsee..." I say, and she nods in agreement, patting my arm. "It'd be like screwing someone's arm..." I mutter as she directs me to more realistically proportioned varieties.

"Here's what you need to focus on," she says, as she gestures grandly toward the wall of penises, still varied in size, but none quite so large as the bologna cock. "What are you most interested in," she continues, selecting a few from their pegs on the wall to examine more closely. "Clitoris stimulation? Penetration? Rotation?"

Rotation?

"I'm not sure," I admit, but I'm insanely intrigued. I take one and study it—it's an odd-looking contraption, with dozens of little squares built into its flank that apparently go in and out when turned on. Hmm.

Tasha delicately plucks it from my fingers as she appraises me, one brow raised, her finger resting contemplatively against her lips. "I think I know the one," she says, laying the gathered examples aside. She pulls one from the top row, stretching up on her tall heels to reach it, and hands it to me. It's called the Bootie Bunny, presumably for the tiny bunny at its base, its ears long and reaching. It has giant beads inside which rotate, and then I see the added feature that the entire shaft also rotates.

"I don't know," I say, handing it back to her. But she stops me.

"No, this is the one. Trust me. I've used this one, and it holds up. Lots of them have tricks and whatnot," she says, nodding to the array. "But what you need is function *and* durability."

Still, the size was troubling. Larger than the few penises I've seen in my time, though not by much, I'll admit.

I study it again, and my pu-tang slobbers at the sight of it—*traitorous bitch..*

Anyway, I decide to trust her expertise. Bootie Bunny is going home with me.

I weather the extreme embarrassment of handing over my cash to the salesperson and listening to his well-practiced and informative cleaning instructions, and I take my new purchase home and carefully hide it in its new resting place in the bottom of my tampon drawer, chosen for its current irrelevance to my pre-teen girl-child, and quite safe from teething babies.

Date With Banjo the Booty Bunny

CANDLES, *check*. Wine, *check*. Soft, sexy music, *check*. Easily accessible underwear, *check* and *check*.

Now all that's left is my date. I open the package carefully, using scissors to cut around the outline. It falls out onto my lap after a minute and it's surprisingly heavy, solid. I go to the drawer in my second dresser, which I've stocked with forty-eight double-A batteries, courtesy of same-day delivery. It cost me an extra twenty bucks, but I didn't have to leave the house. I retrieve two, carry them to my bed.

I consider making this ceremonial, but that seems silly. Still, I hold my breath once they're inside until the motor reassuringly starts humming with the click of the button, vibrating the entire device, including the strategically placed rabbit ears. Another click, the beads rotate around, morphing the malleable plastic form in contortionistic fashion. One more click, and the entire shaft starts to rotate.

My date, *check*.

No more words necessary. Except this – it's the best date I've had in months.

SEVEN

Tattoos and Bull Rides Go Together

MAY

I'VE BARELY HUNG up the phone when Gretchen calls me. Without preamble, she launches into the conversation. "Did Tasha call you?"

"Yes," I say. I'm already trading pajama pants for yoga pants and contemplating a bra, but quickly discarding the notion.

"She sounds kind of off, don't you think?"

I run a brush through my hair and a handful of red strands come out in my hand. Normal shedding, though. Nothing to be alarmed about.

"She does," I confirm.

"I'll pick her up and bring her to your house. Chris said he'd keep Carson."

"I was going to go there. She asked me to come over."

"I think it would be better if she got out of her house. Trust me on this. We'll be there in thirty."

We hang up, and I look around my house helplessly. It's a mess, and I try to conjure the energy to straighten it up. I pick some clothes up off the floor and throw them in a hamper, wipe off the counter, and then I'm spent. I pass the next few minutes playing a game on my phone with candy and swiping that does nothing to ease my increasing anxiety.

Anxiety, my other constant companion, walking hand-in-hand with the Depression, feeding it, feeding off of it. It's hard to know whether I'm anxious at the thought of them coming over—because, as much as I love them, sometimes the thought of being around people is overwhelming—or if it's because I'm worried about Tasha.

She had sounded "off" on the phone. Agitated.

The knock on the door startles me, flipping my stomach and churning it in an unpleasant way. But I take a deep breath and let my friends in.

Tasha gives me a quick hug and quickly heads to the kitchen. "I need a drink," she says.

Gretchen gives me a look, but I'm not Tasha's mother, so I don't object. She fixes a Crowne and Diet Coke and immediately heads outside to the patio where she can smoke. We follow behind her and take seats on the patio lounge chairs.

I've always loved it out here. Especially when I first moved back into the house, and it was full of awful, negative memories. I cleansed the house with holy water and burning sage, and redecorated it as best I could within my budget, but even now it's still hard. But out here, this has always been my sanctuary. In the spring, it's surrounded by floating blossoms from the cherry trees that flank it, as the aging sugar maples farther in the yard stand sentinel as they bud and spread. And in the summer, the landscape is lush and colorful with knock-out roses and pink and purple crepe myrtle trees.

Tasha drinks half the glass and smokes two cigarettes, lighting one from the other, before she finally settles back.

"So you going to tell us what's going on?" I ask.

"Same shit, different day. Why do ex-husbands have to be such assholes?"

Gretchen raises her eyebrows. "What did Malcolm do?"

"He's so damn rigid. I always watch the meteor shower with the kids. *Always*. But he won't let me have them because they have 'plans'."

Gretchen braids her long blonde hair over one shoulder. "Is it your scheduled time?"

Tasha opens her mouth slightly, a look of confusion crossing over her face. "No. What does that have to do with it?"

"You do know that you are supposed to go by the parenting plan, right?" I say.

"You don't really have to," she says, taking a deep drag.

"Uh, yeah, you kind of do," says Gretchen. "It's a court order."

"But we switch and stuff all the time," says Tasha, and Gretchen and I give each other a look. *Exactly.*

The truth is, Malcolm is very accommodating with Tasha. He is flexible all the time, unlike our exes, and she obviously takes it for granted.

"This is just like when we were married," Tasha says. "He was always trying to control me. Life should be spur-of-the-moment and fun, not freaking boring and rules and whatnot."

Interesting. This is the first time that she's ever mentioned what happened between them.

"Is that why you split?" I ask.

She shrugs. "He always wanted me to be so responsible. But that's not me! I'm spontaneous! That's what makes me so fucking awesome!"

Gretchen runs her fingers through her braid and starts again. "I think spontaneous is okay. And you are fun," she says, flashing Tasha a smile. "But that doesn't mean you can't be responsible."

Tasha shoots Gretchen a look of annoyance. "You sound like Malcolm."

I swat at a mosquito, and it's interfering with the zen of the outdoor space. It's not quite summer yet, by the calendar, but it's already very humid, the trees dense and alive with crickets as the sun sinks, splashing the sky in color. "What exactly did he think you were irresponsible about?"

She shrugs. "Like when I forgot to pay bills. Or I guess I spent too much money occasionally. But that didn't mean he had to call me crazy."

That seemed like a non sequitur, and I glance at Gretchen. She shrugs. "Why did he call you crazy?" I ask.

"I used to scream sometimes," she says, looking away. She stares out at the trees in the distance, budding with spring blooms and baby leaves.

I think of what to say. I'm surprised, because I've never seen that side of Tasha.

"For real?" Gretchen says.

"Well, yeah!" Tasha says, whipping around, glaring at us in challenge, as though we were questioning her right to scream.

"He used to piss me off, always asking if I was taking my meds, acting like I was a lunatic."

"Were you? Taking your meds?" I ask.

She looks down, picks at some beads on her top. "I screwed them up now and then," she says. "They kind of sucked, like the side effects and whatnot. Made me feel like shit, or tired all the time, or freaking gain weight. There were those days, you know, when it seemed better without them."

I understand that sentiment. I know the side effects can be awful, though for me, it's hard to distinguish possible side effects— lethargy, numbness, fatigue—from the effects of my Depression. However, it rarely ever is truly better without the meds. Being less than is better than being completely sick. But sometimes not by much.

When you're mentally ill, you may always be ill. I mean, the illness never goes away. But you're not always *sick*. And here's the sucky part—your mind forgets how bad the sick really is. Because you still feel like shit, oftentimes, even on medication, and so you think that's the extent of it. Take me, for example. I still struggle every single day, even diligently taking all the medication I take. I feel my Depression, like an albatross hanging on my back, covering my eyes and squeezing my lungs and heart, muddling up my brain —I feel this all the time. But without the medication, at least right now, I would be a writhing, drooling mess in a puddle on the floor, unable to face anyone or think about anything or live life at all. I know this because if I accidentally fall asleep before taking my night meds, within a couple of days, the darkness that always lurks in the shadows, flicking out now and then to capture me, but ever-present nonetheless, becomes a superstorm cloud blocking out the sun, and I am left whimpering and praying for relief. It's terrifying. So I remind myself that as shitty as the meds sometimes make me feel, it is staving off the full extent of my illness.

But when you haven't felt that in a while, haven't recently stood on the edge of the cliff staring into the abyss, or even worse, fallen into it, you forget how bad it can really be. And that's when you fool yourself into thinking that the side effects suck worse than the sickness.

Gretchen gets it, too. I can see it on her face, her own battle with illness, or past decisions to not take her meds correctly, or maybe even to attempt to self-medicate in other ways, and the impact they had on her life, her marriage.

"It pisses me off," Tasha says. "Him always trying to change me, even after we're divorced! It's bullshit."

She sits up straight, abruptly, and looks at me. "Let's talk about something else! How's the young'un?"

I assume she's referring to Reston. "He's not," I say.

"Oh? Why not, honey? What happened?" says Gretchen.

"It wasn't enough," I say. "I didn't feel anything."

"Damn Noah screwed you up, girl," says Tasha. "Doesn't that piss you off? That he's fucked you up for other guys?"

"Well, I haven't had the best luck in men," I say, not directly answering the question.

"Maybe you should try *Couples*," says Gretchen. "I saw a commercial for it. It's supposed to be for people that seriously want relationships, not just hook-ups."

But Tasha won't be deterred. "But aren't you mad? How do you *feel*?" she asks, looking at me intently.

I suddenly *feel* uncomfortable, but I sense that she's not going to let me off the hook.

"I... I don't know how I feel," I finally say. "I feel nothing."

Tasha studies me. "I don't believe that," she says. "You just forgot the fuck how."

Gretchen seems intrigued, also interested to know why I'm so unfeeling. She taps her chin. "Think about the last time you felt something besides sadness and hurt."

I think back, and surprisingly, my mind goes to Reston, to how the sex with him was hard and athletic. We met each other with equal aggression and fervor, and there was nothing domineering or controlling about it. And I think about how it was a release for me, and not just a physical one.

"There was something..."

Gretchen pats my hand. "What?"

I hesitate to say this. I'm not even sure what I mean by it. "When I had sex with Reston, I felt... better."

Tasha waggles her eyebrows, and with the cigarette in her fingers, poised at her lips, she looks like Groucho Marx. "I'm sure you did."

I smile. "Well, yes, but that's not what I mean." I hesitate, trying to formulate my thoughts. "I thought I'd want to be made love to. Because I miss that. So much."

Gretchen nods in understanding. She knows me. "I would have thought so, too."

But Tasha is getting more interested. "What are you saying, that you like it rough now?"

"Not rough, exactly. Just hard. Almost... unfeeling."

I feel a rush of guilt at that. I'd been raised a Christian, with a pretty strict moral code. And while my husband wasn't my first, up until now, I'd only ever made love with someone that I actually loved. And I don't think God is condemning me now—after all, I can't re-virginify myself, no matter what some churches might say. I'm not seventeen and dating boys anymore. I've been having sex for years. It's a natural part of being a woman, for me. Plus, rather than the ultra-strict interpretation of God's intent regarding sex, I've come to believe that God just would prefer us, as humans, to try to keep it special, because that's when we realize the true gift He meant for it to be.

And it can be incredible, when it's done in love.

So what I'm feeling now goes against a deeply ingrained belief.

My thorough enjoyment of it, sans the emotion, is triggering guilt, and an accompanying sense of discomfort.

Tasha appraises me, then nods knowingly. "Oh, I get it. You want to be properly fucked."

I wince at that. It sounds so harsh and raw. That one statement seems to expose something about me.

But is that it? I think about the release that he gave me, like something in me that was wound tight as a spool of wire was sprung, let loose, to unravel and take me with it. Like I don't have to hold on quite so tightly.

Gretchen sits up straight in her chair. "I have a thought. It might even be an epiphany. Maybe that kind of sex helps you release your anger," she says.

"I'm not angry," I immediately say. It's an automatic response, programmed, rote.

Tasha shakes her head in disbelief and her locs swing around, slapping her face. She swats them away. "Why the hell not? Why wouldn't you be? Your piece-of-shit ex-douchebag ruined your life."

But I don't know how to answer, exactly. Because anger seems so foreign and distant to me. "Because... I don't get angry. I don't know how to be angry."

Tasha readjusts her boobs in her bra where it's crept up. Gretchen and I don't have that problem – our boobs create a shelf that keeps our underwire in place. "What do you mean you don't get angry? What does that even mean?" she stares at me, eyes wide.

I shrug.

"Well, hell, girl. There's your problem. Getting pissed is good for the freaking soul. It's one of my all-time favorite emotions!"

I think about this, how I've been conditioned by my Christian upbringing and a manipulative husband to empathize, not get angry.

But she's right. He hurt me and destroyed my life and he did so many things to intentionally wound me, but that's not even the worst of it. Because I probably did stuff too—not to the extent that he's done, not even close, actually. Still, I'm sure I failed in lots of ways over the years – being too driven, too consumed by work, even if it was borne from a desire to escape the poverty of my childhood rather than ambition. It's that my ex-husband left me feeling not just abandoned, abused, or disgusting, but he also left me feeling completely impotent. Not the sexual kind of impotence, though that was real enough, but the kind of impotence where you can't hurt the person back that so thoroughly hurt you.

And so now, apparently, I'm drawn to mindless hard sex, the kind where I feel nothing but the physical sensations, till all thoughts and feelings are driven to the far recesses of my mind. Because, apparently, this hard, unfeeling sex is quelling some deeply buried anger, the very anger I've never allowed myself to feel.

Tasha sees the emotions, the thought process, travel across my face. "See?" she says. "You have every right to be hella pissed. And you damn well should be!"

This time I nod. "You're right. I should be. But I'm not sure I know how. I've spent basically my whole life learning how not to be angry."

She rolls her eyes. "Geesh, you're such a WASP sometimes," she says, but it's said in love. "We need to do something crazy so you can tap into your anger. Because I guarantee you, it's in there somewhere."

Gretchen gives up on the braid and pulls her long hair into a high ponytail, using the holder she stores on her wrist for that purpose. "Yeah, something besides screwing a dude sideways till Sunday," she says and grins. "Though I still want to hear more about that…"

Tasha nods emphatically. "Me too. And there's nothing wrong with that. But now that you know that you're pissed, or at least that you *should* be, we gotta think of a way to get rid of that shit."

I'm intrigued. "What do you have in mind?"

Tasha's face lights up. "We should get matching tattoos!"

"Uh, no," I say. Because, no. I'm not opposed to tattoos, but her idea of a matching tattoo would involve a half-sleeve of skulls and nymphs. Not exactly conducive to capped-sleeve frocks in the professional workplace.

Her bottom lip pokes out in a pout. "Why not?"

"Just… no," I say.

She doesn't stay discouraged long. "Okay, well then, how about we go bull riding?" she says, her eyes alight once more.

But this confuses me. "Like at the rodeo?" I ask, thinking about Professional Bull Riding and the proverbial eight-second rule, which I learned from watching a very sad movie on precisely that topic.

"No, dumbass. Like at the bar!"

Gretchen and I look at each other.

But Tasha is not deterred. "Hell yeah! Let's ride that bull until it freaking throws us off! And then we'll go dancing till we fall down."

Gretchen looks at me. "Well, what do you think, Claire? It's your call."

And here's yet another example where these unlikely friends get me out of my comfort zone. "Aww, hell. Why not?"

Tasha does a fist pump. "Yes! And wear something short—we're riding a fucking bull!"

BULL-RIDING turns out to be fun, but perhaps not as therapeutic as Tasha might have predicted. Rather than the athletic exercise that would have required intense concentration and leg-gripping to master Toro the mechanical bull for eight seconds, the bull controller (a man, of course) moved it rather slowly and sensually, so that the ride was more of a dance than a conquest. So the better for the entertainment of the crowd, predominantly beer-chugging frat boys.

But Tasha is dissatisfied, still antsy and searching for release, so we go to a club with a good cover band, and we drink cocktails and dance until the point of collapse.

It is after midnight by the time we find an unoccupied table and sink into the chairs.

"So how do you feel?" Tasha asks, holding her hair off her neck with one hand while fanning herself with the other.

"Decent," I say. "Pretty good, actually."

Gretchen rubs an ice cube across her chest. "Any better with the anger that you're not acknowledging?"

I think on it a moment. "It's still there," I say.

Tasha smacks her hand on the table, shaking it. "I know what to do—let's go key his damn car!"

Gretchen and I speak in unison. "Tasha, no."

"Why the hell not? Fucker deserves it. And I guarantee, it will make Claire feel a hell of a lot better."

I capture her hand, which is waving in the air to emphasize her points, and squeeze it. "I'm sure it would," I acknowledge and let go. "But I also would like to be employed again, eventually. An arrest record would not be a great add to my resumé."

Tasha gives me a look. "Only you would be talking about freaking resumés in a bar." Then she smiles and shakes her head at my pervasive practicality.

"Fine. Then we need to break some shit."

WITHIN THE HOUR, we're back at my house, standing in the garage in my pajamas, a stack of my wedding china sitting on the shelf beside me. Tasha has been talking to me for a few minutes, trying to get me in the right state of mind. She's already wound up, bouncing on the balls of her feet, full of kinetic energy.

"Are you mad yet?"

I sigh. "I'm not really mad. Mostly I'm hurt."

"Why aren't you mad, honey?" says Gretchen, who's leaning against a low cabinet studying the pattern on one of my saucers.

"I don't know."

Tasha gets in my face. "Didn't he treat you like you were disgusting?" She's emitting a pungent aggression, and I step back involuntarily.

I blink. "Yes, for years," I say.

She steps back and throws a hand in the air as if to say, *"See there?"* "Didn't he say hurtful things to you?"

"Yes, all the time."

Gretchen sets the saucer atop the stack. "And didn't he make you feel like the crazy one?"

This is making me feel worse, not better. But I nod.

Tasha's back in my face. "Didn't he take Brooklyn away in the most skeevy way possible?"

I swallow. "Yes."

"Just because you had the nerve to say you wanted out of that bullshit dysfunctional situation?"

I feel a jolt shoot through me, a surge of searing heat that travels from the base of my neck down to my private parts. "And because of the money."

"And for the goddamn money! He stole your fucking life!"

The jolt comes again, spidering out in fingers, like a lightning strike that forks and splits before striking home. "Yes, damn that bastard, he did," I say. My words are quiet, but I am shaking. With anger.

She knows she has the advantage now, but she doesn't back down. "He shit on your whole life together, just to hurt you, to use you one last freaking time."

I'm breathless, and my heart is pounding. "He did!"

Tasha's cappuccino face is flushed and I notice, as an aside, how pretty she looks. "Doesn't that make you mad? Doesn't that make you want to scream or yell or break something?"

I'm nodding now, but she doesn't stop. "Doesn't it make you want to kill that piece of shit mother fucker, or at least see his balls cut off and stuck down his throat?"

I laugh at this, and I realize that I'm also crying.

I wipe my nose on my sleeve. "Maybe not that, but I do wish that I could hurt him. I wish he felt a little of the hurt he's caused me."

Gretchen reaches out, squeezes my hand hard. "Of course you do, sweetie," she says.

"Now break a mother fucking plate!" says Tasha, and she hands me one.

I look at it and run my hand over the pattern we picked out together, back when young couples still did that. We thought we'd have them forever, and so we fussed over whether to get six or eight place settings, thinking we'd feed our children on them at Thanksgiving and pass them down to our great-grandchildren when we died.

It was all an illusion. A big, terrible lie.

I notice my reflection in the glossy surface of the plate – opaque and blurred, but solid. Real.

And I throw that plate hard against the cold, hard concrete floor of the garage.

It shatters with a great crash, scattering porcelain shrapnel about and startling my friends, but only momentarily.

"Fuck yeah, girl! Now do it again!" Tasha hands me another plate.

"He hurt me," I say simply, and I bring it down hard. It breaks into pieces, and Gretchen hands me another.

"He didn't have to. Once he stopped loving me, he could have left. He didn't have to act like I was crazy when I sensed it. He didn't have to torture me."

"No, he damn well didn't!" Another plate.

"He didn't have to destroy me so thoroughly, when all I wanted was for him to be happy, for us to be happy."

Smash.

"He could have just let me go." This time, the piece placed in my hand is a teacup, and I throw it against the wall so hard, the delicate handle ricochets and hits me in the chest.

"He didn't have to take everything from me."

Someone hands me the platter then, and I hold it high over my head. They take a few extra steps back, but Gretchen is nodding to me in solidarity and support, while Tasha's eyes are bright with shared outrage.

I bring it crashing down, but it only cracks, bouncing once and then gyrating until it settles to a stop. I stare at it, this representation of our broken marriage, of my cracked but not shattered self.

Not shattered.

Gretchen comes to my side and takes my hand again. "You will heal," she says, and it's preternaturally quiet in the wake of the preceding destruction.

Tasha takes my other hand. "Don't you feel better?"

Looking at the mess and then at my friends, I let loose the walnut of bitterness I've been holding deep in my chest, let its hardened outer coating dissolve a bit.

"Yes, a little."

And it's true. The anger helps, quite a lot. Though it still doesn't help me understand what happened to us, to him. But that's a question, a quest, for another day.

Gretchen, ever the encourager, says, "Well, that's something."

Tasha's more pragmatic. "I need a fucking drink."

We laugh.

Me too.

Date With Probably-Too-Good-to-be-True Brandt

ON GRETCHEN'S ADVICE, I decided to try the on-line dating app *Couples*. As fun as my Bootie Bunny has been, he lacks for conversation and post-coital cuddling. And he never picks up the check.

At first glance, the men on here do seem a little different. They tend to talk about their careers, teenage children and adult hobbies like golf and marathon-running on their profiles. I take this to mean that they are established, financially secure, good dads. This is in subtle (or not-so-subtle) contrast to the often vague job description and marital status of men on *Relations* or the college alumni standing and backpacking pictures outside hostels advertised by the men-children on *Flame*. And as much fun as it is to be pressed up against a firm, young, ripped body of a twenty-something, and as much entertainment value/post-date girlfriend fodder as I've experienced with my dates from *Relations*, what I really need is a man who knows what he wants and knows how to be in a relationship. Not to mention, the whole concept behind the *Couples* app is that it's for people legitimately looking for long-term relationships.

And, just maybe, I might be ready for that, at last.

So I flag several guys as possibles, and get more than a few hits back. But it's Brandt that ultimately grabs my attention. After initial contact, we agree to converse over email for the particulars, and I like that. I learn that he's divorced with one small son, that he's in his early forties, and that he's a vice president of operations at a large manufacturing company in Franklin. He's articulate and courteous, at least in his written correspondence.

On paper, he's great… so far. But I'm still reminded of the colostomy guy and what a disappointment that was.

So based on my experiences thus far, I try to keep a reign on my excitement.

Nonetheless, I find myself feeling hopeful as I get ready. I decide to mix it up, and do things differently tonight, even if it does border on superstitious neurosis. I don't even wear one of my flowy dresses, which I've found are easily accessible and perhaps not the most prudent choice for a first date. Instead, I wear a royal blue cold-shoulder top, dark jeans with embroidered pockets and black wedges. I add to it dangly gold earrings and a gold dangle-chain necklace. I look chic and rather pretty, if I do say so myself.

Dinner is at a gourmet southern style restaurant with fancy hot chicken that is fancy because it has extra secret seasonings and pickled onion garnish. I figure I should try it, since Nashville Hot Chicken has become the hot thing, no pun intended, and I've never had it before. The restaurant also serves spiced Old Fashioneds and Mint Juleps with blackberry compote.

I try the Mint Julep. It's delicious. And probably 2,000 calories.

Brandt is handsome and distinguished, with a cleft chin and light brown hair on the top of his head that is not combed over. I appreciate this, because I know him to be forty-five years old from studying and photographing his drivers' license. His smile is disarming and his crows' feet are endearing, making him seem jovial and trustworthy at the same time. But it's his body that is remarkable. He's wearing a "slim fit" button down like the younger men wear and jeans that hug his parts exactly right, and I can make out his impressive musculature just fine—which was probably the point.

"I like this place," he says, looking around, after all the preliminaries and compulsory driver's license inspection are dispensed. There are aged wagon wheels on the wall and Ball glass canning jars hanging as light fixtures from the ceiling. The floor is wide-planked, like an old barn floor, but polished. "It's charming and yet hip."

"Agree," I say, sipping my delectable libation.

We sit and chat as the courses come—first, an appetizer of fried green tomatoes with pimento and mustard sweet potato puree, then hot chicken with garlic smashed potatoes for entrees. I learn that he is successful and seems entirely competent at his job, as he talks about optimization and P&Ls and quality measures. But then he asks about mine.

"I am senior director of financial analysis at Originate Global Technologies," I say, because technically I still hold that position. But then I hesitate and decide to go for the truth—at least some of it. "I'm actually taking a leave right now to spend a little more time with my daughter. The divorce has been... hard on her," I tell him, and he nods.

"It was tough on my little guy, too," he says, then looks away, lost in thought.

"How old did you say he is?" I ask, and he turns back to me, smiles.

"He's three-and-a-half," he tells me, and I can see his pride. "He's a monster, talkative and high energy and exhausting to this old man! Oh, and playing soccer, which I'm 'coaching.'" He says this with air quotes. "They don't even let us keep score. It's hard on me, being quite a competitive person when it comes to sports. But the kids don't care. And we get to make a human tunnel for the kids to run through at the end. I think the kids play the game just so they can run through that tunnel."

He laughs. "Yeah, I'm utterly exhausted, all the time. But I love him to pieces. Wouldn't trade it for the world."

My heart warms. "I know what you mean." Nothing sexier than a dad who loves his kid.

"What about Brooklyn?" he says. "Tell me about her." And it's not lost on me that he's the first of my dates to really ask.

"Oh, well, she's almost ten but going on eighteen, of course." I begin, then blush. "But that's cliché."

I should explain her better than that.

"She's smart and so strong. She's handled the divorce way better than I have," I pause then, afraid I've revealed too much. He raises one eyebrow but says nothing, so I continue. "I think she's beautiful. Breathtakingly. She's got long red hair, like me, and gorgeous curls. But she has her dad's striking green eyes. When she starts wearing make-up, she's going to be a red-headed bombshell, and look out boys!" I laugh again, but it's nervous. I'm still not describing the essence of my daughter. I'm not sure if it's safe to share her with him that way.

But then I see that he's still waiting patiently, that he seems to genuinely want to know, and that makes the difference. "She loves swimming and crossword puzzles and some boy band called Run and Fly that started on the Disney channel. She says hilarious things and wants to wear grown-up clothes and still lets me snuggle her at night and read books together. She's fierce, and she's going to become the most incredible woman," I say, and I turn away to hide the tears that spring to my eyes—whether it's at the thought of her growing up, or of how wonderful she is... well, I think it's both.

"She sounds really special," he says, and raises his glass. "To our amazing kids," he says, and I toast to that.

We talk about our careers for a while after that, how we got to where we were, what we like and dislike about our jobs. Anyone else would probably think it an extremely boring conversation, but I like it—it reminds me what it was like to be treated like a professional, to be respected for my mind and accomplishments.

It reminds me of who I used to be, and I miss her.

And then we talk about family. I tell him that I'm extremely close to mine, though my parents live and work in Cincinnati. I don't think my dad will ever retire—he's an electrical engineer at a chemical company, and he loves it. My mom is semi-retired, teaching reading to remedial students in an after-school program, and knitting me stuff in her spare time. She sends them to me about once a month—scarves and beanies, afghans and sometimes even toilet paper covers, which I didn't know was still a thing.

He laughs. "Was it ever a thing?"

I smile in response. She also sends me devotionals and prayer cards when she thinks I'm down. I have quite a collection of them, but I don't tell him that. Instead, I tell him about my older brother, who is an officer in the navy, stationed in Hawaii. "He met a Japanese girl there, and they got married but 'are not in a hurry for kids.' She's only twenty-eight, so she still has time left on her biological clock."

"Noted," he says.

Then he asks me what I like to do for fun. Fun is an elusive concept, especially the last several years of my marriage, though I'm finding it again in bite-size pieces, mainly with my two crazy friends. But through it all, and though Carlie doesn't make frequent appearances, I still love karaoke. It is the one time that I can act completely silly, performing for an imagined crowd of fans, and be free of the weight of life.

He laughs when I tell him this. "Okay, that was unexpected," he says, still chuckling. "I thought you were going to say running half marathons or hot yoga—something either very driven or hipster cool. And with that body, one can only assume you're a fitness freak." He winks at me then, and I realize he's flirting with me and probably a little tipsy.

"Why thank you, charming man," I say and blush. "But no, I hate fitness. Unless it's in the guise of something else entirely, like salsa dancing. Or roller skating…"

Or sex, I think, but don't say.

He laughs. "Got it," he says. He asks me what songs I like to sing, and I give him some of my signature ones—modern-day classics with range and sufficient challenge by Pink and Jewel and Faith Hill.

"An eclectic mix," he says.

"Acknowledged," I say and smile.

"Where is your favorite place you've ever performed?" he asks.

I don't even really have to think. "Oh, Japan, for sure," I say, and he looks surprised.

"Really? I thought you were going to say some bar here in Nashville. I mean, this is 'Music City.'"

So I explain the issues with singing karaoke in Nashville, how it isn't all that fun because so many people are too serious, trying to make it, and pretty much everybody is really good. "It's hard to stand out. And what's the point, if you can't pretend you're a star?" I explain.

"Aren't you trying to make it, too?" His eyes are twinkling. He's teasing me.

"Well," I say, "I wouldn't turn down the proverbial record deal, if that's what you're asking. But I'm not holding my breath."

He laughs. "So why Japan?"

"Well, for one, it's the birth place of '*karaoke*,'" I explain, using the correct Japanese pronunciation of the word. "But they are so supportive there. They sing along with you and are enthusiastic applauders when you're done." I tap my lip as I remember. "Then again, you're really only singing to your friends, because they have these clubs full of small rooms called 'karaoke boxes' that are private, so maybe the enthusiasm is not that remarkable after all…"

He laughs at this, and I warm up inside. I'm making a man laugh. That's pretty cool.

He asks me why I was there, and I explain it was for work, and that launches another conversation about where all we have traveled.

Before long, all our plates have been cleared away, and we are finishing our second bottle of wine. I think I've had more than him. Is that why the conversation has come so easily? I'm not sure. I think it might be something like chemistry between us, and not only the sexual kind, for once.

In any case, I probably shouldn't be driving, and I'm just now focusing on that. It's like he reads my mind.

"I hope this doesn't sound too forward, but I live about three blocks from here. In fact, I walked here tonight. I'm not sure you should be driving yet. Would you want to come back to my place for a little while before you drive home? Or, if you want to spend the night in my guest room, we can have a night cap and I'll bring you back to your car in the morning. I want you to be safe."

I wonder vaguely if he's playing me, but I am slightly swaying in my seat, and my depth perception has become variable, as the near-empty wine glass alternately looks close and far away as I stare at it.

Then again, that could be because of the swaying.

In any case, I do think he's right, that I should not be driving. I could take a cab, but that would be super expensive because I live on the outskirts of Hendersonville, and I'd have to take another one in the morning to come back and get my car. I look at my phone—almost 11:00 pm. Gretchen is asleep by now, and Tasha's working an overnight shift.

Shit.

"Okay, sure. I'll come back with you to your place. I'm not sure about staying over in your guest room, though. Let's play that by ear."

He smiles, and it's not smarmy at all, I'm relieved to see. "Good!" He pays and helps me up, then puts my hand in the crook of my arm as he leads me out of the restaurant and the couple of blocks to his house.

We're in East Nashville, and his home is an adorable refurbished shotgun house with bright red shutters and a dark gray door, trimmed by huge white moldings. It has a pretty front porch, with hanging petunias and a white rocking chair. It is inviting and homey and awesome.

"No funny business," I say to him as he unlocks the door, while to myself, I'm repeating: *I'm not going to sleep with him, I'm not going to sleep with him.*

I end up sleeping with him, but without sex. Instead we share some really soft, deep kisses and a little hands stuff, but he is a gentleman, despite the fact that I stripped down to my panties and one of his t-shirts and pressed close against him all night.

Yes, I could have worn more clothes. But I was quite tipsy after another glass of wine at his house, and I really wanted to feel that tight body against mine. In all honesty, I wouldn't have protested if he'd touched me more, but with the dawn of the next morning, I'm giving him total props.

Breakfast is quiet but companionable, with coffee and blueberry muffins from a bowl on his counter, and then he's kissing me goodbye next to my car and promising to call.

And, surprisingly, I really, really hope he does.

EIGHT

Smokers Are Slow Runners

JUNE

IT IS Gretchen's idea to have a Bible study followed by an unconventional workout session—she says that we need to work on ourselves, take care of our mind, body and soul with more deliberation.

It's a little out of the blue. She's never really said much to us about God or church. But she seems insistent, and we're agreeable.

So first they come to my house. Carson is excited because he remembers that I still have a roomful of Brooklyn's toys that I can't bear to part with—a shrine to my continued hope to have more children, though, with my aging eggs and thus far less than promising prospects, is seeming less and less likely.

He yells "Toys!" as soon as Gretchen releases him, squirming, onto the floor, and takes off to the toy room that adjoins the den. We can see him rummaging through the toy box and tossing aside undesirable dishes and dolls in a series of thunks. And then he finds the one he wants—a train engine—because he squeals in delight, as we all settle on the couch to talk.

I've put coffee on, and its aroma fills the room as we wait for it to finish brewing, and Gretchen takes her position perched at the edge of the couch, ready to lead our session.

"Do you have your Bibles?" Gretchen asks, pulling hers out of her purse. It is a thinner version than the more modern interpretive ones, her maiden name engraved on the front corner, hopeful and semi-permanent, its gold lettering mostly intact.

"Yes, ma'am," I say, dutifully reaching for mine on the side table. I had to dig mine out of the study, beneath a pile of recently purchased vampire romances and previously acquired literary works. But now that I've resurrected it, I remember that I like the feel of it in my hand, that it's familiar to me. I brush my hand across the smooth leather of its cover, liking the malleable, flexible feel of its collection of thin pages in my grip.

"Me too," says Tasha, pulling out a pocket-size version, fluttering with tape flags that apparently mark her favorite passages from the gigantic tote she always carries. Aside from the prick of surprise at the sight of the well-used look of the Bible, inspiring a momentary flash of inadequacy at my own pristine volume, I experience a flash of nostalgia at the site of the tote, which is cloth and stained and enormous, reminding me of the giant Esprit purses we had in middle school.

Seeing us thus prepared, Gretchen takes a deep, fortifying breath. "Are you ready?" she asks, and I wonder at her obvious trepidation.

"Sure, honey," I say. "This is your show."

She pulls out some folded papers from her bag. "I printed these at the library," she says. "But I only had enough money for one copy, so we'll have to share."

"No problem," says Tasha, as the coffee maker stops dripping. Tasha jumps up to pour us cups, adding milk and sugar to her own, and without being told, leaving Gretchen's black, but adding artificial sweetener to mine.

She brings them to us and then retrieves her own, and settles back on the couch. Gretchen's hands are steady as she takes a sip, and then holds the papers close to her face to read them—she's getting near-sighted, but refuses to buy reading glasses.

She begins to read then, a discussion of loss and dealing with it. After a brief introduction to the topic, consisting of the most of one page of text, she directs us to the first scripture.

"Jeremiah 29, verse 11: *For I know the plans I have for you, declares the Lord, plans for welfare and not for evil, to give you a future and a hope.*"

We dutifully refer to our own Bibles, following along, mine worded in the translation of the New International Version, Tasha's the American Standard Version.

"Also this one," she continues. "Philippians 4, verses 6 through 7: *Do not be anxious about anything, but in everything by prayer and supplication with thanksgiving let your request be made known to God. And the peace of God, which surpasses all understanding, will guard your hearts and your minds in Christ Jesus.*"

When Gretchen finishes, she refers once again to her sheaf of pages.

"Okay, now for the discussion questions," she begins. She turns to us. "When is a time that you have felt the most despair in your life?"

Tasha leans back a bit, and her face goes a bit ashen. "That's kind of depressing, don't you think?" she says.

But Gretchen is insistent. "It's supposed to help us work through stuff. Trust me, there's a point."

Tasha regards her briefly, but then nods slightly. She takes a breath, a slow one, deep and long, with a steady outflow at its end. "I'd have to say the first time I tried to kill myself," she says, and absently rubs at the scar that runs three inches up the length of her wrist. I've noticed it before, but never asked about it. We are like that, the three of us. We don't generally force each other to remember the wounds of the past—at least, not unless there's a damn good reason. Like needing to find your inner anger.

I hope there's a good reason now.

But now that she's opened the door to that particular event, I want to know more. To maybe understand it a little, and in doing so, firmly avoid such a compulsion for myself. "What happened to make you do that?"

She sighs and looks at it now in earnest, tracing it with her fingertip, its shape long and ragged, like a ripped seam. "Malcolm said he was leaving and taking the kids. He said I was crazy, and I screamed and screamed at him for hours, it seemed like. That usually worked, you know," she adds, looking at us. "I usually got my way, first because he didn't want me to lose my shit, and eventually, when I would wear out and then cry, because he didn't want to hurt me. But this time…" she pauses, takes a sip of her coffee, the cup trembling in her grasp. "This time, he seemed to want to leave *because* of all that, because of my temper and my crying and… all of it. And then I thought… damn, he's right. They don't deserve a wife and a mother like me. I should just let them all go."

Gretchen reaches out and rubs Tasha's shoulder, which has shrunken with her tale. Tasha leans into Gretchen's touch, like a cat will when you scratch behind its ears.

Gretchen withdraws slowly, and Tasha reaches up to clasp her hand before letting go.

"I waited till they were asleep to do it," she says. "I didn't want them to find me. I thought they'd be better off, and that they wanted to be rid of me. I was doing us all a big fucking favor. But he did find me—Malcolm, that is. And he called his sister to watch the kids and took me to the hospital."

A bird lands on the window sill then and squawks loudly, making us all jump. It's the male mockingbird that has been flying around lately, courting a female that has built a nest in the eaves outside.

Tasha stares at it, but doesn't seem to see it. She's in another place, lost in her memory. "I didn't lose that much blood, but I had drunk almost a fifth of whisky before, so I passed out for a while at the hospital. I woke up to find Malcolm crying, hunched over in his chair, his head buried in the bed beside me. He was holding my fingers so tight, and he didn't know I was awake until I squeezed them."

"Then what happened?" I ask, as lost as she is in this scene, watching it as though I'm standing in that hospital room, with its blinking monitor and dripping IV, standing on the scuffed linoleum and feeling the soft whoosh of the wall heater kicking on.

"I went to the Twinkie House for the first time. Oh, you mean with Malcolm? He stayed with me," she says, shrugging. "I think because he didn't want the guilt—he thought I'd do it again if he tried to leave."

Except, I think, *he ultimately did leave, and you're still here. So maybe not just guilt.* "Or maybe he really loved you," I say, feeling a pang of jealousy, and then instantly a flush of remorse.

Gretchen has been quiet, but now she speaks. "How did you get past that?" she asks.

"I tried harder," Tasha says, and then she takes a beat, thinking. "I didn't like to see him hurt either, it turns out."

Gretchen looks back at her papers now. She runs her finger along the page until she finds the passage she's seeking. "Moments of loss or times of great pain are often when we seek out God, because we can think of nothing else to do. Perhaps we even feel that we've exhausted all other alternatives, and there is nothing left but to seek God. But I say to you, your pain might never have been so great had you turned to God first! It should be the first thing you do, not the last.

"First Corinthians 10, verse 13: *No temptation has overtaken you that is not common to man. God is faithful, and he will not let you be tempted beyond your ability, but with the temptation he will also provide a way of escape, that you may be able to endure it.*"

Gretchen turns to me then, as I knew she would. I've tensed up and I'm gripping my coffee cup so hard my knuckles have gone white.

"Claire, what about you? Can you share a moment from your past where you felt overwhelmed by despair?"

But I don't want to. There are moments when the hurt bubbles up and washes over me unexpectedly, flooding me with memories, both the hurtful ones and the good ones, both of which are equally distressing. Such moments are unbidden and mostly startling, leaving me feeling assaulted, limping along afterwards as I try my best to recover. And there are moments when I purposely examine the past, take it out and turn it over, trying to find the cracks in it, the hidden crevices that concealed the germs that ate away at my marriage. I know I must do so, when I feel strong enough to weather it, because that is how I will learn. That is how I will avoid repeating the path that brought me here. But even those explorations have their cost, leaving me hollowed out and empty, requiring the slow and deliberate refilling of my spirit.

Plus, I'm feeling decent today. I've had three really good dates with Brandt, and while the Depression is not gone, I'm cautiously… hopeful. Things might be changing for me, finally, and I don't want to jinx it. I'm afraid that it is fleeting, that this brief glimpse of a happier future will evaporate like the dew on the morning grass.

But Tasha saves me from speaking. "Do you really believe all this, Gretchen?"

I look at her in surprise, at her well-used Bible with its rainbow of tape flags. "Don't you?"

Tasha fiddles with one of her dangly earrings. "I don't know. Sometimes it feels like when I need God the most, there's just… silence."

Gretchen pauses, thinking about this. "Maybe it's not silence, maybe it's that you don't like the answer you're getting."

She shrugs, but considers it. "You could be right. But, still, it's hard not to doubt. It probably has something to do with my Grandma on my mama's side. She used to tell me, 'Don't be soft, Tasha, and especially don't go letting people see it,' if I was having an episode, back before I knew what it was. And then she'd tell me to just pray on it, pray hard to Jesus, and my thoughts would get clean. But it didn't really work like that. So I guess that was when I first starting having my doubts, God rest Grandma's soul. It wasn't until I went to the Twinkie House that I found out I needed, you know, like medications."

She runs her finger absently over the scar along her wrist.

"So Gretchen, no offense or whatever, but I mean, do you really believe it that much?" Tasha asks again. "Always?"

"I have to," Gretchen says, standing up suddenly, startling us. She moves to the kitchen where she starts to clean the counter on the island, even though it's already clean.

"Gretchen?" I say, seeing her agitation and wondering what it means.

She stops cleaning but doesn't look at us. She stares at the counter, the rag in one hand and the kitchen cleaner spray bottle in the other. "I have to believe that He's listening, that things will get better," she finally says, but it's quiet, almost to herself.

Tasha goes over to her and carefully removes the cleaning supplies from her hands, then takes both of her hands in her own.

"Gretchen?" she says, softly, till Gretchen finally meets her gaze.

"It's my girls' birthday," Gretchen says, and Tasha draws her into a hug. I immediately join them, wrapping my arms around the two of them, hoping that we can draw away some of what Gretchen must be feeling by the sheer power of our surrounding love.

After a minute or two, she stirs in our embrace, and we pull back. Then, collectively, we walk to the couch and surround her once more, I sitting close on one side, Tasha on the other.

Gretchen takes a few deep breaths. "I have to believe that I'll see them again," she says, with only the faintest hitch. "I have to believe that God will help bring them back to me again, somehow."

Of course you do, I think, but what I say is, "Of course He will."

Because, of course, she must believe this—how else can she survive it? How could any mother?

We sit close beside her for a while in silence, because no words are needed. Tasha and I have both have had brushes enough with losing our children that we can imagine the fear. But after a while, she reaches for her coffee, which by now has gone cold, and she takes a long sip. Then she begins to speak.

"Raina was always a spitfire, basically from birth," she begins, smiling to herself. "She was bossing everybody around by the time Macy learned to walk. But she always looked after her sister. I always loved that about her...

"And Macy, oh my sweet Macy. She's the sensitive one. She was the one that could tell I was getting sick before I even knew it myself. She sensed it somehow. But she wouldn't ask me about it, she would just suddenly be next to me. Always next to me," she adds, and smiles sadly at us through tears. "Kind of like you guys are for me right now."

We squeeze her in tandem and she leans into Tasha first, and then me, in acknowledgement.

I look for something to say that might distract her from her pain.

"It's hard for me to even believe you can get really sick," I say. "You seem so much more normal than I feel."

"Girl, you should have seen her when she first got to Group! She's a wackadoo when her meds aren't working," says Tasha.

Gretchen's mouth turns up a little at that observation, but her eyes retain their faraway look. "Anyway, I don't mean to make it sound like Macy is weak or helpless, because she's not."

"Sensitive does not mean weak," I say.

And she gives me a small smile, but she's remembering now. "There was one time that Raina got sideways with her volleyball friends. She was a shark at volleyball. I think she focused her frustrations into it." She smooths back her wispy white-blonde hair from her face where it has fallen in front of one eye.

"Anyway, those girls were always her other sisters. But she could be bossy, as I said, and she did or said something to piss them off—I think it was when things had been shitty at home and she was probably stressed about it... But whatever she did, they didn't speak to her for a while."

She smiles then, fully, though it's at odds with the teary look of reminiscence in her eyes. "She would never admit that it bothered her, that she was really hurt by their rejection. And she had a hard time ever saying she was sorry, for anything. Got that from asshole Jonathan, of course. But Macy couldn't stand to see her hurt. So Macy called all of Raina's friends and arranged to meet them at the coffee place by school. She talked to them and said... I don't even know what. She explained Raina, somehow, and then those girls were all calling Raina again and coming to the house, and it was like nothing ever happened."

She reached over and swirled her coffee cup, eyeing its diminished contents contemplatively.

"But it took a toll on Macy. I don't know if it was the emotional energy it took to have those talks that drained her, or if she secretly felt hurt when Raina suddenly disappeared, spending all her time with her friends again. See, Macy made a sacrifice when she did that for her sister. Because, for that little bit that Raina was at odds with her friends, Macy had her best friend back. They hadn't been that close, spent that much time alone together, in years. But Macy cared more about Raina's happiness than her own, and she did that for her, and then she holed up in her room listening to John Legend for the next several days."

She sighs heavily. "I tried to talk to her about it, but she insisted nothing was wrong. It made my heart ache for her. Mostly because I get it. More than anybody else, probably."

She looks at us then, her expression raw.

"It's Macy I worry about most," she says, and we both squeeze her hands. "If either of them are going to have... *it*, have inherited this *crap* from me, it's my sweet Macy. Raina is a fighter—a strong one. And she'll fight off any demons that come on her, and protect Macy till her dying day, of that I'm sure. But she can't fix everything. She can't fix...," she pauses, gestures to her head. "This."

She shudders in between us, and I sense her losing her composure. I want to do something to ease her mind and her fears. I reach for the papers to search for scripture, the words that God is speaking to us, right this minute. And it doesn't feel natural to me—as much as I've had faith, on and off, over the years, I'd never researched it. And maybe that's why I've never truly been able to rely on it.

But now I'm looking, my immature faith reaching out in hope, and I fail. All the words are foreign, their meaning escaping me. So, instead, I speak from my heart.

"I think faith is beautiful," I say, with a twinge of envy, but also sincerity. "And hope is never crazy, even if we may be." My mouth turns up at this small joke, and it brings a small smile from Gretchen through fresh tears.

Even Tasha's uncharacteristically subdued, but not for long. "Enough of this soul crap. Didn't you also say we needed to work on our bodies, too?"

Gretchen really does laugh at this. "Yes. I thought we could go to the park and work out on the playground equipment."

"Really?" I say. "That's an interesting idea."

"No more freaking tears," Tasha declares. "Let's go to the playground!"

She gathers us up and herds us to Gretchen's car, strapping

Carson in his seat still clutching the train engine, and we all ride together, blaring music of Tasha's choice—Rhianna, I think—until we arrive at the nearest city park.

It's an older park, mostly painted metal—swings and basic straight slides and old fashioned monkey bars and merry-go-rounds. It has lost favor to the more modern wooden and plastic structures, and so it's nearly deserted when we arrive. But that's okay. I'm kind of glad we almost have it to ourselves.

Once we spill out of the car and unbuckle Carson, we all look to Gretchen for direction.

"Well, first I thought we could do some pull-ups on the monkey bars," she says, and so we do, and even Carson gets into the action on the lowest bar. My biceps are screaming by the time I've done ten reps. I am disgustingly out of shape.

Tasha's either already bored or also feeling the burn, because she asks, "What next?"

"We swing."

"Really?" I say. "That's it?"

"Yeah, it's supposed to work several muscles," she insists, as she places Carson in the toddler swing.

We all take our places on the swings, three of us and Carson lined up in a row, and we pull on the chains and swing our legs in opposition, the old muscle memory from childhood returning. Though, I don't remember it being so taxing!

We swing until we're swinging high, except for Carson, who is yelling at his mommy, "My turn!"

And then I'm soaring, and I lean back and stare at the sky as the momentum I've built continues my back-and-forth motion. And, for a moment, I have the urge to jump off when I'm at its highest point, like I did when I was a kid. To feel what it's like to fly, to be free. But I resist, because as tempting as it feels, that could only end in broken bones at this point in my life.

And then, one by one, the pendulums of our motion slow and then stop with the dragging of our feet in the gravel, and my friends look as I feel—physically spent. It's not an altogether unpleasant feeling.

But now I'm into this and liking the color in Gretchen's cheeks even more. Her eyes had dimmed briefly back at my house. They are bright once again.

She smiles. "Now we jog."

Tasha laughs. "That's not very inventive."

Gretchen shrugs. "Maybe not, but effective."

So we put Carson in the stroller, and we head to the paved jogging trail. We prepare, stretching and taking deep breaths to recover from what we've already done, when I have a thought. "Actually, I read once that you burn more calories if you do a 30-second sprint and then walk, and then sprint again."

"Okay, sure," Gretchen says. "I'll try that."

We line up on the track, Gretchen standing behind Carson's stroller with her hands on the handle.

"I don't think that's made for running," I say, dubious.

"It'll be fine," she insists.

Then Tasha yells, "Go!" and we do.

Here's one thing I learn, unequivocally, from our work-out session at the park—smokers do not make for good runners.

Within twenty feet, Tasha is wheezing and bent over her legs on the track, so Gretchen leaves the stroller with her, mid-stride, and presses on, at my heels. Our feet are pounding on the pavement, and then I hear her footsteps trail off.

"Run, Claire, run!" she cries at my back, as I, alone, continue sprinting for all of about five more seconds, before my lungs are on fire and bursting, and my legs give out quite suddenly. I collapse on the pavement, spread eagle-style, gasping like an asthmatic, as my friends come hurrying up. And then there are two adult faces and a stroller with a quizzical toddler surrounding me.

"Are you okay?" Gretchen asks.

"You were flying!" says Tasha.

But I can barely speak, so they help me sit up. And that's when I feel the wetness in my crotch, and I start laughing.

"I think I peed myself," I say, and Tasha's eyes widen for the split second before her face dissolves into laughter.

Gretchen pats my hand. "Maybe you need vaginal rejuvenation," she says, quite seriously, but her eyes are alight.

"Does that help with bladder control?" I ask, genuinely curious.

But Tasha's more pragmatic. "Girl, don't we all!" she says.

They help me up, and Gretchen pats my back. "That was awesome, Claire. I didn't know you could run like that," she says, and all I can think of is Macy, and how she inherited her sweet sensitivity from her mother.

"I didn't either," I tell her, squeezing her shoulders in a one-armed hug. "Thank you for reminding us of what we can do. Thank you for reminding us to have faith."

Her face splits into a wide, joyful grin that thrills my heart to see. "I did that?" she asks.

"Yes, Gretchen. You did that," I say, and together we work to haul up Tasha, who is now sprawled on the track, smoking a cigarette.

I refrain from pointing out what would be the most obvious improvement to their overall health, as Gretchen lights up, too.

"God is good," Gretchen says, smiling, as we walk back towards the car.

"All the time," Tasha says right after, as though automatic. She smacks her forehead with her hand and then shakes her finger toward the sky. "I hear you, Grandma! You don't gotta make a big point about it."

One step at a time. But I have found a little faith.

NINE

When You Need COBRA, but It's Not from the Sex Store

JULY

IT'S BEEN OVER A YEAR. Fourteen months since our separation, since my time at Group, almost a year since the divorce. Fourteen months since the worst of it, and I'm still struggling from Depression. Fourteen months, and despite taking seven pills a day representing a cocktail of antidepressants and anti-anxiety medication intended to make me New! Well! Happy!, I'm still overwhelmed by the simplest of tasks. I'm still struggling to pay my bills, or review my finances, to read a book or watch an entire movie. I still struggle to be present for Brooklyn when she's with me, only to crash the subsequent week, exhausted from the energy it takes to act like I'm okay, even if only for a little while. I'm still overcome by the insurmountable prospect of facing each day, knowing it will be less than it should be.

It's been long enough that I've transitioned from short-term disability to long-term, and as a result, I was forced to resign from my position at my company—the position I had worked so many long hours for, exceeding all milestones and expectations, achieving promotions and earning bonuses, for the better part of the last decade. This happened on a Tuesday, as my short-term disability period came to an end and my boss gently informed me that they could no longer hold my job for me. I signed papers, enrolled in COBRA benefits with my dad's help because it feels too complicated and overwhelming for my addled brain, sent in my company credit card and security badge. And then I sat outside and listened to my friends talk about their boyfriends and/or sexual escapades and children and lives, while the loss of my career was barely a sidenote.

My career has tumbled off the cliff, and I don't know who that makes me, but I haven't truly mourned that loss yet—I think I'm still denying it, choosing to believe that this is all still temporary, that my career, like my life, is not over but only awaiting my return.

After, I tried, briefly, to do some contract work as an analyst, but I was distracted, flitting from one thought to the next with no correlation, no logical progression or emerging thought patterns or plans. Numbers and information on the screen scrambled into a morass of circling digits and data points, seemingly random and intentionally incomprehensible, an incredibly complex code for which I had no key. I was ineffectual, and without intervention, it would quickly be apparent to my employers that I could not produce what my resume promised. This realization sent me into a mini-breakdown, a frenzied panic and resultant descent into nothingness, which was just as well—it allowed me to withdraw from the engagement before my secret was revealed, truthfully claiming my recurrent illness as the cause. It allowed me to retreat back into the well of Depression, believing, insistently, that if no one on the outside of my small circle knows about my illness, it will not be as real.

But, as my girls and even my parents will say, at least I tried. And I will try again, and maybe next time it will be more successful. Because I want to resume my life—with everything in me, I want to be myself again, whole and competent and accomplished, not wounded and broken.

I suppose I've improved a little, enough to rally for my dates with Brandt, so that he's not yet really glimpsed my downs. I'm fairly adept at this deception, in short bursts. And for those brief moments, it's actually pretty good, a reprieve from the darkness, a string of moments wrapped in contentment where even joy, while still out of reach, seems to be skimming my fingertips, almost within my grasp. And the love-making is so intense and beautiful, it makes me think I didn't know the meaning of that term before now.

I am beginning to feel something… I'm not ready to name it, but it's surrounding, and seems true and inevitable and dare I say, right.

Still, even with all the good these encounters bring into my life, afterward I'm often relegated to days of sleeping and no showers, completely depleted. But it doesn't deter me from taking a fortifying breath, putting on my best face, because I'm determined, during those encounters, to be the version of me that I insist is the real one.

But here's what I don't understand—why isn't it the real me *right now*? Hasn't it been long enough? Haven't I processed enough of the trauma, forged my way through the memories and realizations to find a path, albeit indirect and intermittent, of healing? Or if my Depression is a punishment rather than a consequence, haven't I suffered enough, paid enough of a price for my shortcomings, for my successes?

If not, when the hell will it be?

There's a secret, hidden fear in the darkest part of me, a fear that I don't want to acknowledge because I don't want to give it power—the fear that my Depression is not just because of my marriage, my wounds, but because I am really and truly ill.

And beyond that, I'm very afraid, terrified even, that I will never be well again.

That is terrifying enough on its own. But what would Noah do with that, if it turned out to be true? Would he come after Brooklyn?

So now I'm waiting for my doctor, hoping that he will have some new answers for me.

The door opens to the waiting area. A nurse in pink scrubs reads my name from a clipboard. "Claire Colson?"

"That's me," I say. I follow her through the door and to my doctor's office. I know the way, of course. For the last couple of years, I've frequented these sage green halls often enough.

Inside Dr. Warren's office, I take a seat on his comfy red-patterned sofa, and try to calm my nerves to the backdrop of instrumental relaxation music, try to clear my mind of the stress that I've managed to work up over the last 20 minutes in the waiting room. Thankfully, I don't have to wait long.

He walks in, his balding head adding ten years to his appearance, making him seem fiftyish instead of the early forties I know him to be. He's wearing his typical pressed khakis and white button-down shirt, though his tie is always a surprise—this time it's a collection of artistically rendered frogs that look like an impressionist painting of a vague landscape until you study it closely.

"Nice tie," I say, as he takes a seat in his brown leather chair.

"Thanks! My oldest daughter picked this one out." He pulls up my chart on his iPad. "So, how are you feeling since I last saw you?"

People who've never been treated for mental illness may not realize this, but psychiatrists are not really there to talk to you. They only want to know how you're doing from a clinical perspective—still depressed? Check; anxiety attacks? Check; diminished cognitive function and concentration? Check and check. They aren't really interested in whether you're having PTSD flashbacks, or still obsessing over your ex-husband's abuses.

If you want to talk about your troubled childhood and self-destructive tendencies, your eating disorders or obsessive compulsions, you're looking for a therapist, not a psychiatrist.

So I know how to answer this. "I'm still having trouble with depression, concentration, and anxiety." I give him a few pertinent details, then I tell him about my brief attempt to return to work, as he makes notes with an Apple pen. "Is there anything else we can try? I feel like I should be... better by now."

He refers again to my chart for a minute, but then he lays it in his lap and gives me a look no one wants to get from her psychiatrist. "We've tried several different medications since you've been coming to see me, and I'm also concerned that we aren't getting better results. I believe you have treatment-resistant depression."

While it seems rather self-explanatory, I ask the obvious question anyway. "What does that mean?"

He gives me a wry smile. "It means that your depression doesn't respond well enough to medications to manage your symptoms."

I let out a huge breath. "Well, that freaking sucks," I say.

He unconsciously straightens his tie, smoothing it between his forefinger and thumb along its length. "Surprisingly, a huge percentage of depressive patients are treatment-resistant. It's not the end of the world, it simply means we should consider other alternatives."

"Like what?" I ask, but I'm already drowning in defeat.

"Well, like ECT, for instance."

Shit. I know what that is—electroconvulsive therapy. Shock therapy, as it was called in previous decades. My grandmother had it years ago when she went through a particularly difficult depression, and it robbed her of several memories.

Still, I'm shocked at the suggestion. "They still do that?"

He nods. "Yes, it's still fairly prevalent because it is very effective. Much more so than medication."

I picture old movies of mental hospitals and deviant psychiatrists with flickering electrodes. "But isn't it kind of barbaric?"

"It's much safer than it once was. And we know more about how to do it effectively, including the appropriate duration, than we once did. So the side effects are significantly less." He uncrosses his legs and leans forward slightly. "Claire," he says. "You might have a chance at actual remission."

Remission. I didn't even know there was such a thing. This is appealing and is the one thing I've heard in months that almost assuages my deep-seated, unmentionable fear that I'll always be sick.

"Let me do some research about it," I say after a few minutes of consideration.

"Sure, sure. I'll give you an information packet about it, too. In the meantime, we'll up your antidepressant a bit," he says, as he writes out an electronic prescription on his tablet.

And then my session is over, and I'm leaving, reeling at the thought of undergoing ECT. I'd have to be desperate to do such a thing. But in all truth, I feel the desperation creeping in.

. . .

WHEN I GET HOME, I take a nap because I'm exhausted from the emotional cost of my psychiatrist visit, and I want to have some energy for my date with Brandt later. When I awake, I start the long process of getting ready, feeling as much excitement as I'm capable of feeling at the prospect of seeing him again.

For once he's not picking me up or meeting me at a restaurant—he's asked me to come to his house at 8:00. As I drive there, I'm a bit nervous. I've been there a few times since our first date, but usually late at night after substantial amounts of wine and good food, stumbling to the bedroom as we kiss and touch and tear at each other's clothes. This is the first time I've ever gone over early. So either he wants to start the sex phase of our night early, or this is a new step in our relationship.

As I'm pulling into his drive, I do a quick check of my face and hair in the rearview mirror. Then I'm walking up the sidewalk to the front door.

I hear the rapid little footsteps before the door opens, so my brain acknowledges on a subconscious level what it takes my conscious brain a moment to figure out. *His son is here.*

The door opens, and there is an adorable little boy in a striped shirt and elastic-waisted jeans standing there, his father towering over him.

"It's a wady!" says the little boy.

"Yes," agrees Brandt. "It's my friend, Ms. Claire."

"It's Ms. Claire!" says the boy.

They step aside to let me in, then pause in the entryway. "Claire, this is my son Elijah."

I crouch down and reach out my hand. "Hi, Elijah. It's nice to meet you."

He gives my hand a smack, like he's giving me "five," and runs off, yelling, "You wanna see my trains?"

"Sure," I call out after him. I look over at Brandt, raising one eyebrow in question.

He shrugs, kisses me on the lips. "I thought it was time."

Before our kiss can progress, a little voice calls from down the hall, "Ms. Claire, come on already!"

"I'm coming!" I say, flashing Brandt a grin.

He follows me down the hall, placing his hands briefly on my waist, which sends a shiver up my spine. His touch is electrifying. We get to the kitchen/family room—Elijah has small, colorful train cars spread all over the family room floor, tracks included. I turn to join him there, while Brandt heads to the kitchen area where something that smells divine is steaming on the stove.

"I'm cooking pasta," he explains, as he lifts a lid off a pot and stirs.

"Sounds great," I say, as I kneel down on the floor, arranging my dress around me.

Elijah then proceeds to name all his trains for me—they have magnets on the front and back so they can join together on the track, and the front one is mechanized.

"You wike my trains?" says Elijah.

"Oh, yes," I tell him. "They are awesome."

"Yeah, they are very awesome!" he agrees. He picks up the red one, holds it up to my face. "But this one is the best."

Before long, it's time to eat, and Elijah takes his place in a booster seat on one of the dining chairs, while Brandt sits next to him at the head, and I sit across. Brandt fills two glasses of wine for he and I, and he raises his glass to me.

"To good company and a good dinner," he says.

I clink his glass and mumble, "Cheers," thinking all the while that, except for Brooklyn missing, I can envision what our family would look like, what it would feel like.

We talk with Elijah, mostly, at first. He tells me about his "school" which is actually pre-school daycare, and he mentions his room at Mommy's house only once, but it makes Brandt flinch a little. But then Elijah is done before we've finished half our meal, and he wants down. Brandt jumps up to grab a wet rag to wipe the sauce off Elijah's face, then barely sets him down before he's running back to his trains. Brandt joins me back at the table, flashing me a smile.

"I hope this was okay….," he says, nodding to his son playing on the floor in the next room. "I thought it was time that you met each other." He reaches for my hand. "You are becoming important to me."

I don't quite know what to say, but I'm incredibly touched and something stirs in me, a swirling in my belly that is one-half fluttery nerves and one-half longing.

He sits back then, wipes his mouth on his napkin. "So, enough about us. Tell me about what's been going on with you."

So I tell him about Tasha and Gretchen, the impromptu Bible study, the funny work-out in the park. I've mentioned my friends before, in passing. But now he's interested in the story, and he begins to ask probing questions.

"Why doesn't your friend, Gretchen, get to see her girls?" he asks.

I pause then, thinking how much to share. Thinking how this conversation could easily lead into discussions I'm not sure I'm ready to have about myself. But then again, maybe it's time for that, too. If we really are developing feelings for each other, he should know.

I take a deep breath and a sip of wine. My hand is trembling slightly. "She suffers from mental illness," I say slowly, studying his reaction. "She's estranged from her girls—they live with her ex-husband."

His face betrays nothing. Instead, he takes a slow sip of his own wine before responding. "What kind of mental illness?"

"Bi-polar disorder," I say. "I've not ever seen her really sick, but I think it can get pretty bad."

"How did you meet her? You said that she's a stay-at-home mom, so it wasn't at work…"

"No," I say. I hesitate again. This is the proverbial and literal moment of truth.

"I met her, both of them actually, at group counseling. I… went through a deep depression because of my divorce." I wait then, not sure if I should say more. Not sure if it's safe.

"And you became friends with them? They don't seem like your type."

"Well, I'm not sure what that means," I say. "I hadn't really maintained friendships while I was married. I needed someone to be there for me. They never judged me—they just loved me."

"What about your family? Couldn't you have turned to them?" he asks.

"Yes, but they don't live here. My brother is stationed in Hawaii. My parents live in Cincinnati, and they both still work. They tried to be there for me as best they could, but I needed more than that."

He looks at me for a long moment, and I'm not sure I like where this is going. I feel like he's judging them.

"Is that why you're not working now? You said you were taking a leave to get used to being a single mom, but is it more?"

Shit. He's figured me out. I'm not going to tell an outright lie, no matter what he might think of me.

"Yes," I finally say. "I'm still suffering from depression."

He sits back and is quiet. I don't like it. After a few long moments, he speaks. "How do you pay your bills?"

"With my disability insurance," I say. "I worked my ass off for that benefit. And now I literally can't do my job. I'm not taking social security disability, only my insurance benefits. That's what they're for."

He lifts his hands. "Don't get defensive. I'm trying to understand."

We both pick up our glasses, look away from each other, and take simultaneous sips.

Then I feel his eyes on me, and he reaches out and touches my arm. "Claire, look at me."

I do. His eyes are kind. "I'm not judging you. I just want you to be honest with me."

Tears spring to my eyes. "I'm trying," I say. "It's hard."

"I know. I get it." He squeezes my hand, leans in for a kiss. Our lips meet slowly, soft and sweet with wine. He lingers there, and it reassures me.

He breaks apart. "Want to help me put Elijah to bed?"

I smile through the tears that still sit but don't fall. "Sure."

AFTER A QUICK BATH, animal pajamas and two picture books, Elijah is finally asleep, and Brandt leads me quietly out of his room, his finger to his lips as he silently shuts the door. Without a word, he takes my hand and leads me to the bedroom.

"Are you sure?" I whisper. "I thought I'd be going home, with Elijah here."

"You can't stay all night," he says as we enter his room. "But I want you to stay for a while, if you will." He turns to me, takes my face in his hands.

I nod, and we kiss. We slowly take off each other's clothes as we stand there, our lips connected in a slow, sensual kiss. And I feel emotionally connected to him as well, like I never have before. My fear is slipping away.

Once naked, he lowers me to the bed and climbs over me. He looks into my eyes, holding my gaze without blinking as he enters me. And it's slow and sweet and completely intimate. When he comes, he laces his fingers with mine and hugs me tight as he shudders into me. Then he kisses my cheeks, wet with the tears I hadn't realized had slipped out, and pulls me into his arms to sleep. At least, for a few hours. And I succumb, happy for the first time in a very long time.

TEN

Bad Thoughts Are No Laughing Matter

AUGUST

I'M ALREADY CONCERNED because Tasha hasn't answered her phone in three days. And when she finally does, it's with a text response to my posed question, *'Are you okay?'* which was a short, but alarming, *'Not so much...'* I immediately throw on some moderately clean clothes and jump in the car.

I have been riding high, as high as possible for me, since my last night with Brandt. But as I drive to Tasha's, all my thoughts are on my friend. When I get to Tasha's apartment, the door is ajar and I can smell the cigarette smoke. I push it open, knocking as I do, and find her sitting on the floor next to the coffee table, eyes heavy-lidded and leaking tears through her mascara.

I close the door behind me and fan away the smoke from the smoldering ashtray before kissing her on the head and sitting down across the table from her, also on the floor. She's not supposed to be smoking in the apartment when the kids are here – it's one of the many rules Malcolm imposed as a condition for her getting to see Hunter and Melanie.

Speaking of the young'uns... "Where are the kids?"

"Playing some video game in their room," she says, swiping at her nose.

116

"Even Melanie?" I ask, surprised. Mel has never been much on video games. She's an interesting dichotomy of pre-teen and girl-child, alternating between texting or Instagramming with her friends while listening to sufficiently fringe pop music through her earbuds, and deconstructing dog-eared copies of Harry Potter with a highlighter.

"Yeah, I think they are avoiding me."

I give her a sympathetic look and reach out to squeeze her shaking hand.

"So, talk to me."

At this, she starts to cry. And I can tell it's not the first time tonight. "The thoughts are bad," she says, looking away.

"Tell me about them."

"They are racing around in my head—thoughts about cutting myself with the paring knife in the kitchen that is so fucking sharp; and thoughts of taking Tylenol PM till I don't wake up." She looks up at me now, and she has the saddest, most desperate expression on her face.

"I even thought of jumping off Percy Priest dam," she whispers, and I try not to gasp at the thought of the giant turbines and the long, long fall to rocks and foamy water below.

I want to ask the obvious question, but I know how it will sound. How much we all hate it when someone asks it. But it has to be asked.

"Sweetie, have you been taking your meds?"

"Yes!" she wails, as someone knocks at the door. We both turn at the sound, and I'm surprised to see it open, an unwelcome face poking through.

It's Diego, her sketchy neighbor with the bad teeth and pock-marked cheeks I've occasionally seen skulking around the neighborhood. He has the look of too many hard drugs, or so I imagine from my limited exposure to mug shots of meth-heads on TV.

He looks surprised to find me there, despite my car parked in the driveway, and quickly looks to Tasha for instruction.

She laughs loudly, like she hasn't just been crying. "Diego! You remember Claire?" She gestures toward me and he nods politely, his fake smile brandishing the teeth I'd rather not see.

"I was… checking on you," he says, having finally found his voice. "But I can come by later."

Later?

"Sure, sure," Tasha says, smiling too big and waving him out. "Another time, for sure."

That's when I notice the pill bottles on the table. The first is Klonopin—Tasha's go-to for dealing with anxiety. But it's the second bottle I focus on now. There aren't many pills in it, maybe five or six, and I don't know why it raises my suspicion, but I grab it.

Diego Mendez, it says, clear as day on the label. It's a prescription, if the label can be trusted, for hydrocodone, 40 mg.

I look at Tasha and she looks away. "What the hell is this, Tash?" I ask. She busies herself with lighting a new cigarette.

"Nothing," she replies, her eyes big and round and full of shit.

"You've been freaking using, haven't you?" I'm pissed now. She full well knows that using other shit will mess up her good meds. The ones that keep her well.

"They're not mine!" she insists, but she won't look at me. "He must have left them here by mistake!"

I'm quite familiar with her opioid addiction. She told me about it not long after we met. It started when she had the car accident ten or twelve years ago, and continued as she saw pain management doctors who fed her growing dependence. But she had gotten clean before I met her in group—part of her stay in the hospital—and I thought, until now, that she'd stayed clean.

My frustration is overflowing, and I shove them toward her face. "This is why you are sick," I say, willing her to look at me. "This right here. Is it worth it, this high you get when you take these? Is it worth the price of wanting to kill yourself?"

I have her for a moment, and then her eyes fill again and she looks down. "I don't know," she says, and at least that one thing is honest.

Then a horrible thought occurs to me, and my eyes widen as I pocket the pills. "Shit, Tasha. What did you give him for them? What did he make you give him?"

At that moment, her kids spill out of the back bedroom, first Melanie and then Hunter. Hunter seems oblivious, playing on his phone, but Melanie's eyes are bright and focused on us.

"What's going on?" she says, as she kneels by her mom. I expect her to put an arm around her, comfort her in some way. But instead, she jerks Tasha's chin so that they are facing each other, inches apart. She's searching her pupils.

"Gosh-damn Diego," Melanie says, and I'm surprised to hear the curse come out of her young mouth, but I understand it all the same.

It's a testament to the depth of her mother's despair that she doesn't react to Melanie's curse, only looks forlorn.

But I jump on Melanie's apparent knowledge. "What do you know about Diego? Has he been around?"

At this, her face dissolves into a look of revulsion. "I found them," she says. "In the bedroom."

"It's not what you think! Not that, I swear!" Tasha says, but I can feel the disgust overtake my face as well, and Melanie and I both look away, neither wanting to think about what she saw.

Mel stands suddenly. "I'm going for a ride on my bike," she declares, storming out. Hunter follows her, yelling for her to wait up.

"Tasha…" I say once they're gone, and even I can hear the judgment in my voice.

She can hear it, too.

"You don't understand, Claire! You've never been addicted to anything in your life. You don't know the pull it has!"

She's right, I don't. Honestly, it must be awful, to have a need so strong that it would make you want it, knowing it can… *will* make you sick. To make you want it so bad that you would degrade yourself with the likes of Diego.

"I've been feeling so, so bad," she says. "The pain is everywhere. It's this scorching acid in my blood and in my head, black and…" She struggles for the word. "Suffocating," she finally says. "It's crawling under my skin."

And then I wonder the same old question that I always wonder when this happens—did she mess up her meds first, which makes her feel like shit and want to use, or did she succumb to the temptation of using, which then caused her to mess up her meds?

Either way, it sucks. Because using might make her feel better in the moment, but it also paves the way for the deep dark hole that holds the Bad Thoughts. After the highs of wanting tattoos and new hairstyles and to spend money she doesn't have, this is what follows. They are all a precursor. I should have seen it. I didn't want to see it.

And the Bad Thoughts. I know my own version of pain, but even that, I can't totally relate to. I've only ever felt them once, and they were fleeting and so scary and foreign that I instantly sought help—help in the form of my friends, Tasha and Gretchen.

I look at the pills again and put them in my pocket. Tasha watches me but doesn't say a word. But her hands are shaking, and the tears are brimming once again.

"I think we should take you to the hospital," I say as kindly as I can. Because, more than being angry, I feel scared for her. And a deep, co-dependent empathy that she is in so much pain.

But she shakes her head. "No, no," she says. "I'm not going to do anything stupid. I promise. I can keep the Thoughts under control."

"Tasha, come on. They can help you feel better. You need help."

"I can't go to the hospital," she says. "Malcolm will take the kids away."

For a minute, I see the irony in this. Treating her illness, like any rational person would want to do, can get her in more trouble than not seeking help. It doesn't make sense. But then, I know this fear all too well. The fear that an ex-husband has the power to take your children away with a word. And just hearing this chills my veins and brings me firmly onto her side.

And the truth is, when she's well, she is a great mom. Funny and present, loving, if a bit inappropriate at times, and fiercely protective. Her kids would kill for her, they love her so much. And they're *good* kids—kind and hopeful, excited about all the possibilities of life the way Tasha is. *She* did that, even with all her self-proclaimed (to

Gretchen and me, at least) fucked-up-ness. She raised good kids, and they raised a good mom.

They need each other. Children need their mothers.

And despite what I said, about the hydro making Tasha sick (and maybe it did contribute—again, I'll never know which came first), Tasha can't help her bipolar. She suffers from an illness that is caused by her body, no different from people that suffer from Crohn's disease, or diabetes, or epilepsy. No different from me.

And I only know my pain. You can never truly know someone else's, or what it can drive them to.

"When's the last time you ate?" I ask her, noticing the dark circles under her eyes. *Or slept, or smiled.*

She shrugs. "I fixed the kids ham and macaroni for dinner last night. They had cereal for breakfast, leftovers for lunch, I think."

"What about you, did you eat?"

She looks at the black screen of the TV. "I'm not hungry."

"You have to eat," I say. "It's almost dinner time. Why don't I run and pick up some food for you and the kids?"

This time, she raises her eyes to mine—her beautiful brown eyes that are now dull and sickly.

"Will you stay and eat too?"

"Of course I will!" I tell her, rising from the floor. I walk around to her and pull her up and into my arms. She feels tiny there, where normally her small 5'1" frame is outshone by her large personality, now she feels small and frail.

On the way to retrieve a complex order of Mexican takeout, I think again about Tasha's Bad Thoughts. This is her sickness, just like Gretchen and I each have our own characteristics when we're sick. This is Tasha's. It must be pure hell. I think again that she should get help, that I should get her help. But her words about Malcolm and the kids stop me. Because while I may not get it completely, *that* I get.

The night that I had my own "Bad Thought," I had just left my 30-minute supervised visit with Brooklyn. The one imposed by a court that believed, because of my ex-husband's disturbing ability and even more chilling willingness to deceive, that I was a danger to my daughter.

When people hear that, they automatically assume there must be some validity to the charge. Perhaps it's human nature to believe that someone, a trusted spouse, would not raise such a claim without some underlying truth. But I was never dangerous. Up until the very end, when I had to take a leave from work so I wouldn't be fired because of my diminished performance, I worked through my depression, paid my bills, read my daughter stories and took her to the zoo. I made homemade chocolate chip cookies so she and I could split the leftover dough, and spent sixteen hours piecing and sewing a very ill-fitting Native American costume for a two-hour Thanksgiving party at Brooklyn's school. I pushed and pushed until I couldn't push anymore, and pushed my depression down at the same time. And the only one that saw my despair was Noah, and he reveled in it. All of which is probably why the depression ultimately overtook me, why God stepped in to force me to take care of myself before I disintegrated completely.

But in all this, I was awake and vigilant and maternal for Brooklyn. I spent all my excess energy on her, what little remained. I never abused alcohol or drugs, just took my increasing prescription of anti-depressants with a vigor that was almost religious. And I was absolutely never, ever dangerous. So for Noah to say I was, to use this most vile deception to take Brooklyn from me, and me from her, was beyond devastating.

On the night of this visit, I was in the depths of a despair that I'd never known—because I missed my daughter to the point of physical pain, but also because Noah had been able to take my child away so very easily. Without evidence, without my version of the story being heard. And it was well before the judge dropped the restraining order at Noah's attorney's well-timed request, and also before my ex-husband admitted to me that he had done it all, not because he really believed I was dangerous, but because *I had not offered him enough money.*

So I snuggled my daughter and ignored the evil, satisfied smirk on my husband's face not four feet away, until the brief minutes ticked by and I had to hug my child goodbye. And then I drove away from my daughter, who at 8 years old was confused but not weepy, and I wept for us both. And when I started across the low bridge, the sudden urge that pierced my sadness, the very strong and visual desire to drive off the bridge and into the water, almost... *almost* seemed like the right thing to do. For everyone.

Thank God I resisted. Because once I crossed the bridge and the dangerously strong compulsion waned, it scared the shit out of me. And that was the first time, since Group, that I called Tasha.

Without hesitation, she let me come to her house. And she and Gretchen, who was there too, almost as though they were waiting for me, fed me leftover spaghetti and let me cry and then, inexplicably, made me laugh—not enough to ease my pain exactly, but enough to remind me that it was still possible. And that was the true birth of our friendship.

I have to do the same for her—be her friend, provide what she needs the most, even if she doesn't know what that is.

By the time I arrive at the Mexican restaurant, I resolve to assess how she's doing when I return, and then make a decision—whether to encourage her, or force her if I have to, to go to the hospital or not.

TASHA SEEMS MARGINALLY BETTER over dinner, even cracking a smile here and there as Hunter tells us funny stories. He has a way of doing that, making her smile, despite herself. Where Melanie is worry, Hunter is joy.

"Mom, you shoulda seen it. See, me and my boys were lifting at the gym, you know trying to get all swole."

I raise my eyebrows at Tasha and she shrugs.

Hunter sees our confusion. "You know, ripped. Cut. Whatever, you guys are so old. Anyway, we were doing squats, and Brandon did 250 which is nothing, and I did 325, which is not my best, but there it is. But then Mario, he was trying to beat all of us. He put 400 on the bar, trying to look all cool, and he goes to do his squat and he... Mom, can I say shits?"

She smiles, and it does my heart good to see it. "This once, honey."

"Good," says Hunter. "Because I don't know no other way to describe it. He shits all over the freaking floor. I mean, not just a little, I'm talking a full-blown ass explosion. Sorry for saying 'ass', Mom. It runs down his legs and everything. And then he starts laughing, which makes him shit more. So then we're laughing, like, our guts out, and we have to take the bar from him because he's about to drop it, and then he runs to the bathroom, shitting, farting —you know, sharting—the whole way."

I'm laughing hysterically at this point, the way only Hunter can seem to inspire, and Melanie is slapping him for cursing and for making her stomach hurt. And I look over, and even Tasha is laughing. For a minute, it is real, but then it turns hollow, and I'm not the only that notices. Melanie does too—I can see it when she looks at her mama with sorrow and fear in her eyes, when she takes her mother's hand and squeezes.

But then dinner's over, and the kids retire to the bedroom they share on Wednesday nights and every other weekend. Tasha worries about this, when she's well, having her teenagers share a bedroom. If she had the money, and the room, she'd give them separate bedrooms. But it's a good-sized room, actually the master in the apartment, and she's hung a curtain between the two sides. And she makes them sleep with the door open—not that anything weird would happen, because as I said, the kids are good kids. But with the door open, there's no questions.

I help Tasha clean up the dishes, and then we sit together on the couch. She's quiet, but I can sense that she wants to talk.

I'm patient, so I wait until she's ready. It takes about three-quarters of a cigarette before she begins.

"I didn't sleep with him," she says.

"What?" I say, because I'm startled that she's bringing it up—it's not what I expected, but I know what she's talking about.

"With Diego. Melanie didn't catch us having sex."

"Okay…" I say, suddenly wishing I smoked. I need something to do with my hands.

"She caught us kissing and he... he had his hand under my shirt."

I try not to cringe, because even the thought of first base with that man is repugnant.

So I ask the question that I must ask. "Why, Tasha?"

There are so many ways she could answer that, so many questions I could be asking. She settles on answering the most important one.

"It's been bad lately. The thoughts have been creeping up for a while now. A couple of weeks at least... maybe a month."

A month?

"I tried to ignore them, at first. I thought I could keep them away. But it's like drowning, Claire. After a while, they fill up my head and then I can't breathe. I can't escape them, and it would be so easy, so damn easy to give in."

I grab her hand, grip it tight.

"I think I only missed my meds three or four times," she adds, because she knows that's my next question. "And not all in a row," she's quick to add. "But I guess that was enough."

"I understand, honey. I know it can happen, and I know how bad it sucks. But why Diego?"

"Because, Claire, the pills help drown the voices. I wasn't trying to get high. I was trying not to go crazy. I was trying not to do something crazy."

I know when she says 'voices', she doesn't mean in the schizophrenic sense. She means the overwhelming compulsive thoughts —we've had this discussion before. Still, I want to understand. "The voices — what do they say?"

"That all the pain will be over, if I just do it. That I won't hurt anymore. That everybody will be better off if I'm gone."

The scary thing is, there's probably some truth to the first two arguments. But the last one is so very *not* true.

"You know that is bullshit, right? We would all be devastated without you. Your kids would be shattered."

She looks at me, considering. "Most of the time," she says. *Most of the time she knows it. But not ALL the time. And it only takes one moment, one quick but permanent decision.*

We both sit with that thought for a while, listening to the kids thump music in the bedroom with the door cracked. After a few minutes, I look at her. She gives me a weak, exhausted smile.

"How long have you been taking your meds now, without missing?"

She shrugs again. "Eight days," she says. "The thoughts, they should be getting better by now. Any time now."

That's another shitty thing about mental illness. It only takes a day or two of messing up your meds to make the demons come back with a vengeance, but it can take days, even weeks, for the meds to work, for the demons to be chased away, for the pain to recede.

So this is what she's been living with, what she's been trying to survive and control and wait out until she came out on the other side. I felt for her before, but now I hurt for her. Because I know the tremendous energy it takes to stay well on a good day, but this fight is too much for anyone to bear.

Tasha sighs then and yawns hugely, and I can feel her exhaustion.

"You're tired," I say, stating the obvious.

"Yeah, very tired," she acknowledges. "But I'm okay," she adds, answering my unasked question. "Really, you can go. I just want to go to bed."

Now's the time for me to make a decision. Do I believe her, take her word for it, and leave her? Or do I try to make her go to the hospital?

I sigh. I love her dearly, but I'm not her mother. Ultimately, it's up to her.

"Okay, Tasha," I finally say. I kiss her on the head. "Get some rest, sweetie. Things will look brighter in the morning."

She manages a wan smile. "Sure, I know. You're right."

We hug, and then I leave, driving myself home, hoping I did the right thing.

The Date I Never Wanted

TONIGHT MY DATE didn't come by way of *Flame* or *Couples* or *Relations*. It didn't come by way of flirtations in a bar, or a chance meeting in the grocery store, or a continuation from another previous encounter.

It came from a 2:00 am phone call from a frightened twelve-year-old girl, the daughter of my friend, who had been awakened by the sound of her mother violently retching in the bathroom.

Melanie's voice was hitching when she called, but she told me enough that I got to the house right after the ambulance left. I picked up Tasha's exhausted, terrified children, and together we rushed to the hospital.

On the way, I tried to learn a little more about what had transpired in the few short, critical hours since I left.

"Tell me exactly what happened, sweetie. Can you do that?" I say to Melanie, who is doubled over herself in the passenger seat.

"I woke up," she says, her voice hoarse. "I don't know why, but I knew something was wrong. And then I heard the crash in the bathroom and the sound of my mom puking."

I reach over and squeeze her hand and she grips mine.

"I went in there, and there was throw-up everywhere. She looked… gray. Like, dead," she says, and her voice catches.

Hunter huffs from the backseat. "It shoulda been me that found her," he mutters. I look at him through the rearview mirror, and he has a pained expression on his face.

"Was she conscious, when you found her?" I ask gently.

"Barely," Melanie says. "She kept saying, 'I'm so sorry', but all slurred, like she was drunk or something."

"And that's when you called 911?"

Melanie nods. "Yeah. And then I got Hunter up, and he helped me hold her until the ambulance came."

"You guys did great. You did the right thing."

By this time, we're pulling into the hospital parking lot, and Melanie clears her throat. "Um, I don't know if it matters, but I found this on the floor." She reaches into her pocket and pulls out a prescription bottle, handing it to me.

I put the car in park and take the bottle, which is empty. 'Klonopin', the label reads. *Shit.*

"This is really important, Mel. I'm glad you brought it."

She nods solemnly, looking much older than her eleven years.

We rush into the ER, and I instruct them to sit while I go to the check-in desk.

A nurse in scrubs looks up from her phone. "Can I help you?"

"You just brought in Tasha Simpson, possible overdose," I say, cringing to hear myself say the word.

"Are you family?" she asks, and I hesitate for a moment.

"Yes. Her sister," I say, hoping I won't have to prove it somehow.

"She's being evaluated now," the nurse tells me. "It might be a while. I'll let them know that you are here."

"Thank you. But there's something they need to know—I think she overdosed on Klonopin," I say, pulling out the empty bottle.

Her eyes widen slightly as she takes the bottle. "Do you know how many she took?"

I try to remember how many were in the bottle when I was there earlier. I don't know the number of pills, but I do tell her that the bottle was almost half full a few hours before.

"Also, the doctors should know that she threw up several times. I hope… I hope that's a good thing."

She gives me a kind smile. "We'll let you know."

Then I go back to the waiting area and take a seat with the kids.

"What did they say?" Melanie asks, and I tell them.

She's sitting in a double seat next to her brother, and she collapses against him. He puts his arm around her and pats her arm, and it warms my heart.

"She'll be okay," I tell them, and I hope to God it's true.

I pull out my phone to text Gretchen: '*Tasha's in the hospital. She OD'd. I'm here with the kids and we're waiting to hear if she's going to be okay.*'

I don't expect a response for several hours, since it's the middle of the night, so I put my phone away and glance at the home improvement show that's playing on the wall-mounted television.

We are all dazed, exhausted, waiting and hoping to hear some good news, and we all three are startled at the swish of the automatic doors. I turn to see and am surprised to see Malcolm striding in.

He rushes to the kids, who immediately stand and pile into his arms. "Are you all right?"

Melanie tears up, but she nods, and Hunter puts his arm around her. "We're okay," he says. "Just worried about Mom."

Malcolm steps back and searches their faces. "Have you heard anything? How is she?" Malcolm asks.

Melanie hiccups. "We don't know yet."

Malcolm hugs her again, kisses her roughly on the top of her head. "I'm sure she'll be fine," he says. Then he turns to me, looks me up and down, taking my measure. "I'm assuming you're Claire. We need to talk."

"Of course," I say. The kids collapse onto the seats again as I follow Malcolm back through the automatic doors into the cool night air.

There's a bench on the sidewalk and we take a seat together.

"So what the hell happened?" he asks, not looking at me. Anger and frustration radiate from his body, and it's scorching and justified. He spins a key nervously on his key chain, as he visibly tries to reigns in his emotions.

Incongruously, I'm struck by what a big beautiful black man he is. He's tall, several inches over six feet, and built for man-candy calendars and bringing down bad guys. But it's his face that is arresting, exquisitely handsome, like he was the mold that God made for perfection. Still, it's the fact that he doesn't seem to know it, or at least doesn't flaunt it, that makes his magnetism so quietly powerful.

No wonder his and Tasha's children are so damn gorgeous.

Anyway, tonight is not the night for admiring beautiful specimens of manhood. So instead I watch the traffic lights on the street in the front of the hospital—they are flashing yellow, as they are programmed to do in the middle of the night, and there is not a car in sight. After a beat, I tell him what I know, and he rubs his face before abruptly rising. He paces the length of the portico, cursing.

"How did you find out?" I ask hesitantly, curious to know, but not wanting to draw his ire.

"The dispatcher didn't know we were divorced. She gave me a heads up."

Malcolm is a cop at the local precinct. Of course it makes sense he would find out.

Now he whirls on me, fixes me with his cop gaze on me, and I squirm. "When's the last time you saw her? Did you know she was this bad?"

I hesitate, thinking how to answer. The truth is, I've always believed Malcolm to be this rather benevolent figure in our collective post-divorce melodrama. He and Tasha have had their issues, many of them caused by her illness and her impulsive, sometimes destructive behavior triggered by her bipolar episodes. But he's been decent to her, even after the divorce, supportive of her spending time with the kids. He's the most decent of our three ex-husbands. He deserves a real answer.

"I saw her earlier tonight," I finally say. "She was bad, but I thought she'd make it through."

"Shit. This is utter bullshit. She has always been irresponsible and selfish, but why in the hell would she surround herself with people just like her? Like you?"

"I'm sorry?" I say, taken aback.

"You met at the psych ward, right? Obviously you are only making each other worse. She needs stability, not more nut jobs."

I suck in a breath. He can't be speaking about me. I'm a businesswoman. I'm responsible. I'm not a "nut job." "Excuse me, Malcolm, but you don't know me." *I'm not like her,* I think, but I don't say it. Because I feel an unexplored shame at the thought.

He collapses on the bench, his anger exhausted. "I can't believe she did this to our kids. They shouldn't have to go through this."

He was right, of course. And I feel like absolute crap that I messed up so royally. Not only did I not insist she go to the hospital when I had the chance, I didn't think about what it would do to the kids if she did something stupid. The truth is, I didn't want to believe that she would do something like this.

"I'm sorry," I say. But it's not enough.

He sighs and stands. "I'm taking the kids home," he says. He asks for my phone, adds his number to my contacts and hands it back. "Let me know when you hear something. The kids will want to know."

"I will," I say, and then I follow him back inside.

I give the kids tight hugs goodbye, and then they are gone.

I MUST HAVE DOZED OFF, because I wake to sunlight streaming in the glass doors and Gretchen hurrying through them, scanning the room for me.

When she finds me, she rushes over to me and grabs me in a hug.

"Oh my God," she whispers.

"I know," I say.

We sit, gripping each other's hands. "Tell me exactly what happened," she says, so I do.

When I'm done, she swipes at the tears that spill over. "I think we should pray," she says.

I nod. That is precisely what we should do. We close our eyes, holding hands, and she says a prayer for Tasha's full recovery.

When we've finished, I tell her about my conversation with Malcolm.

"He was so upset," I say. "He had every right to be." I shake my head. "I screwed up, Gretchen. I didn't make her go to the hospital when I had the chance. I should have known."

"It's not your fault," she says. "You couldn't have known. You believed her—you can't fault yourself for that. Plus, she's an adult. She's responsible for herself."

I hear her, but I don't quite believe it.

"What do you think Malcolm is going to do? Do you think he'll take the kids away?" she asks. That is our worst fear.

"I don't know."

We're both silent as we contemplate the possibilities, and we're startled when the doctor comes out.

"Are you the family of Tasha Simpson?" he asks. There's no one else in the waiting area.

"Yes, that's us," I say, standing. Gretchen is standing so close I can feel the heat coming off of her. She grabs my hand as we wait to hear what the doctor has to say.

"We treated her for an overdose of Klonopin. She's currently sedated, and we don't yet know the extent of any damage. Honestly, it probably saved her life that she vomited some of the medication out, not to mention, from what I understand, her vomiting is what alerted her daughter that she needed help. So let's thank God for that."

We both nod.

"In any case, I believe she's going to recover, but I'm not sure about any long-lasting effects of the overdose at this point. Once she wakes up, we'll do an evaluation. Barring any complications, we'll transfer her to the psychiatric hospital as soon as she's physically stable."

"Thank you, doctor," I say.

"Yes, thank you," says Gretchen.

He shakes our hands, then turns to go back through the swinging double doors.

We sit together on the bench. "Thank God," I whisper.

"Amen," she says.

ELEVEN

Life in Pictures

STILL AUGUST

GRETCHEN PULLS UP into the driveway, and I'm waiting for her on the front porch. I hug her tightly when she walks up, and then follow her inside.

"Have you heard from Tasha?" Gretchen asks as we take a seat on the couch.

"Yes, she actually called me today," I tell her.

"How did she sound?"

"She sounded good—better. Her meds have finally kicked in. They put her on a new one in addition to the ones she was already taking. And she's not having the Bad Thoughts anymore. She said the therapy is going well, and that she feels better than she's felt in a long time."

"Oh, thank you, Jesus!" says Gretchen.

"She said she was going to call you during phone time tomorrow night."

Gretchen smiles. "I can't wait to talk to her." Then her expression turns serious. "Are you ready to do this?"

Today is a momentous day—it is the day I'm choosing to do something that I've not been able to make myself to do before now.

Something that may seem small and insignificant to some, but which holds tremendous meaning for me.

I've decided to look through my photo albums, to survey the history of my life with Noah, in an effort to continue moving towards healing, to continue moving towards *moving on.*

And maybe to understand a little more. The anger was good, healthy even, but I still don't understand the most essential question —*what happened to us?* Before I can move on with Brandt or anyone, even myself, I need to understand.

Gretchen, bless her sweet soul, has volunteered to be here with me as I go through this emotional exercise. She's sentimental, like me, and, despite being in a relationship now with a decent man, still has a longing for the life she once had. Though she's never said as much, I can tell it in the way she reminisces, how she sometimes seems shocked to remember, in conversation, that she's no longer living in the home with her first love and their twins, that her intended life has somehow splintered off and continued without her.

So I appreciate that she is the one that will be here for me— Tasha is great when you need someone to help you feed your fury and indignation, when you need a partner for screaming into the night and breaking stuff. But Gretchen is the one that understands —sometimes you just need to mourn.

"Yes, I think so," I say.

We begin to prepare for this great event in ceremonial fashion, in order both to relax ourselves and simultaneously cleanse any negative energy. So we light some sage candles on the island and pour ourselves two crisp, cold glasses of Chardonnay, and we place the stack of albums between us.

When we're seated, Gretchen raises her glass to me. "Here's to saying goodbye to the past and hello to a brand new future," she says.

"Cheers," I say, with only the slightest of hesitation, and we clink our glasses and then take our first sips. "Let's do it," I say then, setting my glass down. She does the same, and we begin.

I've not stacked the albums in any particular order, and it's been so long since I've looked at them, I don't remember which is which in terms of year or vacation or other occasion. So I'm surprised, and reminiscent, as I open the first album and see pictures of the Grand Tetons in Wyoming. This had been one of our favorite trips, back when he seemed to enjoy my company.

I've always enjoyed photography, particularly of breathtaking scenery like this, so we flip through four or five pages of photos of mountains and lakes, bald eagles in flight, and wildflowers spread across sprawling foothills. And I'm finding that this slow revue of the past is not too terribly painful, though perhaps a little wistful.

It's on the sixth page that I first see it—a missing photo, an empty space where a picture had once been.

"I guess I took that one out and put it in a frame," I say, though I don't recall where it might be, as I mentally catalog the framed pictures that are positioned throughout my home.

We continue our journey, and within a few more pages, I find another empty slot. It is next to one that holds a picture of me, which Noah must have taken.

"That's weird," I say, and begin to flip through more pages at a more rapid pace.

I come across another missing slot, then another, and then I notice a theme, a common thread to the missing photos, and it really is through the process of elimination, of reverse logic—there doesn't seem to be any pictures remaining that contain Noah.

I sit back, take a sip, as Gretchen peers at me curiously. "You okay?" she says.

I don't want to think it, of what it might mean. But it's almost undeniable. "The missing pictures... I think they are the ones of Noah."

"Are you serious?" she says, grabbing the album, flipping through them herself. When she's finished, she sets it back on the counter. "Why would he do that?"

Maybe it's a fluke, I think. I grab another album—it's filled with pictographic memories of Italy, from our tenth anniversary vacation, back when I insisted we take romantic trips as a way to try to mend the crumbling foundation of our marriage. Back when my desires still held some significance to him, albeit waning. I flip through the first few pictures, mostly beautiful architecture and scenery, Basilicas housing the bones of saints and apostles, and then I come to the first empty spot. My stomach twists and I feel ill as I quickly flip through the rest of the book—again, all the photos of Noah are missing.

"I... I don't understand," I say, as I try to wrap my head around the missing pictures, what it might mean. I can't bring myself to look in the other albums in the stack, to confirm that they too contain half the story, half of our life together.

I realize now that, though we'd agreed in the divorce that we would each get copies of all of our pictures, so we'd both have a complete set, he had never requested them. I assumed it was because he made his own copies while he had possession of my house. But now... now it seems as though he didn't *want* copies of our photos, of our life together. *He wanted to erase it.*

A stabbing pain pierces my chest, and I double over.

"Are you okay?" Gretchen asks in alarm.

But I can't speak, can barely breathe. And then I have a horrible thought.

"Sweetie, what is it?" says Gretchen, reaching for my hand, which is shaking. "All the color just drained from your face."

But I don't answer, instead I jump up, pausing to steady myself as the dizziness and nausea threaten to overtake me. Once it subsides enough for me to stand without falling, I rush to the buffet in the dining room, where I keep the album I'd not intended to look at today—the one that represented the best of our marriage, the beginning, happy hope for it.

My wedding album.

I retrieve it clumsily from the cabinet as my hands are shaking violently, and I place it on the table. Gretchen is by my side now, and she sees what I've unearthed, understanding at once the importance, and the depths of my fear.

"I can't do it," I whisper, and slide it towards her. She gives me a grim look, then nods. She slowly opens the front cover, and we both gasp at what's inside—where there used to be facing photos of the blissfully happy, dreadfully young bride and groom, only my photo remains. And then she turns the page, and as she does so, she reaches over to grip my hand—because where once was our wedding portrait, merging the happy bride and groom of the previous pages into one hopeful couple, now there is a ripped photo, leaving only a bride, torn away where once the groom had stood next to her, smiling.

My breath leaves me, squeezed out by the piercing pain in my chest, and I collapse in a heap on the floor.

There have been so many ways that Noah has hurt me—during our marriage, and even more so during the divorce. But this is one of the most hurtful of all, this degradation of our memories, this tangible erasing of our life together. I know it has been a long time since we've been happy. And in fact, there were many years when he deliberately treated me terribly, apparently (in retrospect), wanting to hurt me… I've never figured out why, exactly, other than at some point during our marriage, he grew to hate me. My mother says it's because he hated himself, and he couldn't face that, so he directed his self-loathing onto me.

But there were years, in the beginning especially, when we loved each other. When we wanted to be together, to have a life that was anchored in our commitment to each other. Those college kids that fell in love nearly two decades ago and became grown-ups side-by-side, they had something, something special worth remembering. More than just worth remembrance, I had believed, up to this point, that what we'd once had was even worth treasuring, clinging to, as a reason to believe, besides the obvious and overwhelming gift of our child, that our years together weren't a waste.

But he stripped those reasons away with his defilement of our photo albums, *our wedding album*. He stripped them as bare as the empty photo slots and rendered them, and our entire life together, meaningless, worthless.

Gretchen closes the album—we've seen enough—and she guides me gently to the living room and eases me onto the couch. Sitting beside me, she takes my hand, our legs touching in solidarity.

She sits quietly with me for a while as I try to cry. Because this hurt, like it's twelve steps too far. He's already destroyed me, he didn't need to destroy all of our past as well. That was wholly unnecessary, and frankly cruel.

And I don't understand—how could he want to erase it all? Didn't he ever love me?

My tears won't come because they are dried up in protest of one more ounce of pain. And this is pain.

"Why?" I finally say. "How could he do this? I… I don't understand. How could he?" There are more words, but they won't come either. All of my avenues of expression have abandoned me.

Gretchen takes a deep breath, as though she has something to say. She takes her time though, chooses her words carefully, and then turns my face so that she can look into my eyes.

"Sweetie, that man you thought you knew, that you thought your husband was…" she pauses, looks down at our hands which are intertwined. "He's been gone a long time." She looks at me again, her eyes full of sympathy, making sure that I'm paying close attention. "Maybe… maybe he never existed at all. I think it's time you let the fantasy of him go."

When Gretchen says this to me, something in my memory triggers, pulling at my consciousness and transporting me back to a moment from my time at the psych hospital, as though delivered by some divine providence to a recollection that must hold some importance for me.

It's the last day of Group, and there's a new guy sitting in the empty chair next to mine writing intently in his journal. I don't want to interrupt him, but I'm also curious, and that wins out. So I sit down and introduce myself.

"I'm Lucas," he says, after I tell him my name.

"Nice to meet you, Lucas." He's young, can't be more than twenty, and bright-eyed with coffee skin and a flat-top fade hairstyle. He's wearing a flannel shirt, unbuttoned, over a white wife-beater, and his jeans are sagging below the waistband of his white boxers. But he doesn't look like a punk—there's something sweet about him, and I instantly feel a kind of protectiveness toward him.

At this point, we've all shared our stories about why we're here, and while my new friends, Gretchen and Tasha have already graduated and moved on, my shyness has completely worn off, even with newcomers. Plus, focusing on others is a momentary distraction from my Depression. So I come out and ask him about his story.

"I was doing good in school, for real. Like not really honor roll, but almost. But then I started getting mixed up and I couldn't understand what all they were trying to get me to do. You know, what I needed to understand, or what problems to work out and stuff." He reaches up and twists the stud in his ear, a nervous habit. He sighs. "That's why they said, or my mama said, I had to drop out."

He meets my eyes, just for a moment, and then looks down, as though what he sees there is too much. "They told me I have, uh, schizophrenia," he tells me, stuttering over the word. "But they're wrong. 'Cause I know what that is—it's when you see people that ain't really there." He slaps his hand down on that table, but it's not an aggressive display, rather it's insistent. "I *don't* have that."

He seems distressed, so I pat his hand. "It's okay, Lucas. I believe you."

But he doesn't respond. Instead, he turns to the chair beside him, slightly agitated. "No, I already told you. I ain't hungry. Go on without me," he says, then rolls his eyes to me and smiles a little, like we're sharing a joke, like he's conveying his annoyance with a persistent friend.

Except, the chair is empty.

A chill races across my neck.

Veronica comes in then, today's facilitator, and all eyes are on her. She writes on the board, "Radical Acceptance," and that's when I realize I've cycled through the entire program. I'm an old-timer now, a "repeater" with the tenure of those with either severe mental problems or really good insurance. I must be the latter, since my psychological evaluation came back diagnosing me with "acute major depressive disorder indicated by situational factors," and with no "suicidal or homicidal ideations." This diagnosis, though real and recently debilitating to me, seems pale in comparison to bipolar disorder, type I and type II, both cruel and pervasive and lifelong. It seems especially pale in comparison to suicidal thoughts, psychotic breaks, schizophrenia.

And after hearing some of the terrible stories from some of the other folks, stories of attempted suicides and addictions, horrible histories of violence, rape and molestation, my own tale of woe seems woefully inadequate—psychological and emotional abuse at the hands of my husband. It's hard to even describe what he does to me, because most times its subtle and passive aggressive. But it's still mean and meant to demean and control me, and that's what these dear screwed up people have helped me to understand.

Veronica clears her throat at the front of the room. "Let's get started," she says, and we all take our seats. I look to the seats once occupied by my new friends Tasha and Gretchen, now held by other faces, each carrying their own burdens.

"Radical acceptance… What does that mean to you?" Veronica adjusts her loose-fitting pants and looked around expectantly.

Several people give answers, and they are not dissimilar to the sentiments expressed the first time we had this lesson, three weeks ago.

"Pain is a part of living. Sometimes it is useful, as it can drive us to make change," Veronica says slowly, pushing past her tendency to slur with careful enunciation. "This kind of pain can be really powerful—it can push us to get out of an unhealthy situation, to take steps to make our lives better." She looks at us then, really looks at each one of us, in turn.

It's funny, how I've heard this topic before, but I'm hearing it differently now, There is something in the lesson, something that applies to my current, present pain, a realization born over the course of my time here and cemented in this final reinforcing discussion—I can choose to make my pain productive. I can, finally, let it help me get out.

Veronica seems to focus on me then, like she is delivering me a message, even if it wasn't for that day, even if I didn't know I needed it yet: "Radical acceptance is when you're not fighting reality anymore. It's when you realize you can stop fighting that you can finally move on."

And just like that, I'm back to the present.

Gretchen has been patiently waiting for me to return, to process what's happened, to come to my own conclusions. And as the memory fades, I reflect how I'd thought that the primary gift that Group had given me were the reactions of my fellow Group members, the confirmation of what I'd felt but could never prove under Noah's constant manipulations. It was what I'd needed at the time to come to terms with the sickness in my marriage, and ultimately gave me the strength to leave it. And of course, it gave me the gift of my two best friends. But that wasn't its only gift to me. And I finally get what Gretchen is saying, realizing that the answer had been there from the beginning—from Veronica, yes, but also from Lucas, and all the other people I met in Group and have grown to treasure along the way, especially my two sisters.

Stop seeing what isn't there, and accept the truth. Maybe then I can finally move on.

Armed with this new charge, I take a deep breath and remove the desecrated wedding photo. Because facing the emptiness is better than preserving what was torn in half. And when that's done, I resolutely grab a photo album and begin replacing the empty spaces with photos from the back, and Gretchen quickly joins in. We move photos around to fill in the empty spaces and tell a different story, maybe a truer one. And I realize that maybe I didn't actually know my husband, or at least the man he came to be, and maybe that was part of why he grew to hate me—because I didn't see the real him.

Or, because what I saw in him was more than he could ever be.

Date #1 of Maybe Being in Love - Brandt

I'M FIRMLY MOVING ON. I believe that I've finally come to terms with my marriage and who my ex-husband was in ways I've not done before now. It's been hard, but I'm finally starting to let go of the past and my pain along with it.

Is it coincidental that, at the same time I'm finding the strength to let go, I've also found someone that I feel something with—someone I might be able to find happiness with? Or is it because I'm letting go that I can finally let someone else in?

Maybe God is facilitating all this, reaching out to me to pull me from the pit. Gretchen would say so. And I want to have her faith.

So maybe, just maybe, Brandt is the next chapter in all that. Maybe he is a path, or at least stepping stones along the path, to my new, brighter future.

Which means it's time to speak to Brooklyn about him. Up until now, I've protected Brooklyn from my forays into dating. I only see men when she's at her dad's, and I don't mention them to her, ever.

But now, I think it's time.

I wait until the end of our time together, not sure how to broach the subject. It's Friday, and her dad is scheduled to pick her up at 6:00. Her school had an In Service day, so we spent the day at home together, making pancakes with whipped cream faces for breakfast and skipping lunch in lieu of buttered popcorn and Harry Potter movies. It was a delightfully slovenly, decadent day, and we'd both enjoyed it thoroughly.

Currently, we are watching Hermione slug Malfoy in the face and cheering her on, when I reach down to pause the movie.

"What the heck? I like that part," says Brooklyn, throwing a piece of popcorn at me but grinning.

"I know, I know. Me too," I say, throwing some back at her. "But I want to talk to you about something. Or actually, I need to ask you something."

She turns sideways on the couch to face me, drawing her knees up to her chest. She plays with her long, red side ponytail.

"Sure, Mom," she says, and smiles in encouragement, only her eyes betraying her slight reticence.

I take a deep breath and plunge right in. "What would you think if I started dating somebody?"

She stops playing with her hair and hugs her knees. She puts her head against them, and I sit up, alarmed, worried I've upset her. But then she looks at me, and her expression is contemplative but not upset, as she goes back to playing with her ponytail. She shrugs. "I don't know. I guess it would be kind of weird."

I let out a breath, not realizing I was holding it. "How, honey?"

"Just to see you with somebody else that's not my Dad would be kind of weird."

"Okay," I say, unsure where to go from here. She's studying her hair, stretching out the curls and letting them go to watch them bounce back.

She looks at me then, releasing her hair. She lowers her knees into a cross-legged position, and I'm suddenly transported back to when she was in pre-school, and the teachers taught the kids to sit "criss-cross applesauce."

But she's not that little girl anymore. "Look, Mom. It's not that I think you and Dad are getting back together. I know that's not going to happen." She pauses, maybe to see if I'll correct her. I don't, and she sighs. "But it's still kind of rough, you know? I'm still getting used to everything, I guess."

"Sure you are, baby," I say, reaching over and smoothing a stray strand of hair behind her ear.

She smiles at me then, and it's only a little sad. "Someday I know you will probably be with somebody else. Maybe you'll even get married, because you like being a wife."

Interesting.

"But I hope… I hope it's not for a while. Because I like having you to myself."

I pull her to me and she folds into my lap, all gangly and tween-ish, and I hug her tight, cover her head with kisses. "I like it too," I say, and try to hide the waver in my voice.

"You're smothering me, Mama," she says against my shoulder, and I release her. She scoots back, smooths her hair. Then she flashes me a brilliant Brooklyn smile.

"Who needs men anyway, right Mom?" she asks, and I beam back at her.

"Right, baby girl!"

I HAVE to fight back tears when she leaves. It's always hard when she leaves, my stomach dropping and twisting in on itself at the thought of not seeing her for several days. But when we connect like we just did, especially right before she goes, it's soul-ripping. I hug her tight at the door and she lets me, but then her father taps the horn twice and she breaks away from me.

"See you next week, Mama," she says, as she climbs into the car, and I wave and don't bother to wipe away my tears. Because for one, that will just draw attention to them. But also, I know it won't make them stop.

And when she's gone, I think about our conversation. *Well, shit.*

I mean, I get it. This has been tough on her, and she's handled every single bit of it like a champ. She has the absolute right to say when she's hit her limit. And this is it.

But does that mean I should stop seeing Brandt? Or only that I need to keep it separate from her, for now, for as long as it takes for her to be ready?

Because the truth is, I'm falling for the man, and it feels really incredible. Like with endorphins and serotonin and dopamine and all the good stuff my brain usually screws up. And in bits and spurts, I remember what it is to feel good. Not merely happy, which is elusive and subjective and not really measurable, but actually *not sick*, and that's a whole hell of a lot better.

And damn, that would be a hard thing to give up.

I'm still unsure what to do by the time I've finished getting ready and head to his house for dinner. But then he opens the door and scoops me into a sweeping hug, and I smell his spicy scent and feel his heart beating through his chest against my cheek, and a thought emerges in my head—*I love him.*

I love him.

I love him!

And now that I've thought it, the words feel like they are pounding against the confines of my skull, rolling around on my tongue, wanting to be released.

It's weird, how when you start to love someone, the words want to come out. They want to be given, like a gift, and of course reciprocated, but that's almost a minor point. They want to be declared, as though to formally stake a claim in a small love plot that will hopefully grow into a Big Love Garden.

And I really want to say them. But I don't—not yet. Because what about Brooklyn?

As he lets me go and looks into my eyes with a gaze that says I'm the best thing he's ever seen, I think about what Brooklyn said, and I'm utterly torn.

Damn, I'm not sure I'm strong enough to let him go.

Still, I love my daughter, and I make a decision. I will respect her needs and feelings., so I will keep Brandt a separate part of my life for as long as my not-so-little girl needs. And when she's ready to entertain the idea, I'll introduce Brandt into our life slowly, so she can grow accustomed to it. I can be patient with that part, because I want her to be okay most of all. And as I feel the tenderness of his welcoming kiss, I'm confident that Brandt will understand and be patient, too.

DINNER IS GOING to be a lovely affair—he's recently subscribed to one of those meal-kit services, and he's making us a brown sugar-baked salmon with asparagus. I offer to help, but he insists he wants to do this for me, so instead I sit across the counter of the island as he cooks, and sip on a glass of zinfandel.

I should be feeling great, especially with these new love feelings surging, but something is nagging at me—something about the way he keeps looking at me when he thinks I don't notice, how he's nervously keeping up a running conversation, when normally our conversations our slow and easy.

It makes me wonder if there are things he wants to say to me, too.

But then he joins me at the table, and for a while our conversation returns to its normal, comfortable rhythm. It's not until he brings the dessert he's made—a chocolate, flourless cake made from scratch—that I realize that my earlier instinct was right. There is something on his mind.

I wait patiently for him to get to it, worrying that maybe it's bad news, but then thinking he wouldn't cook for me from scratch just to break up with me. And then he begins.

"Claire, you know I care for you deeply," he says, and looks at me with fathomless eyes, his expression pensive, as though he's waiting for me to say something.

But I sense some danger lurking. "I... yes," I say, uncertainly.

"Well, then, please know I'm asking this from the best place. But I would like to understand more of your illness, and what exactly you are doing to get better."

"Oh," I say, and feel my body relax slightly. I hadn't realized I had been tensing my shoulders so tightly. Of course he would be curious about this. And he deserves to know. So I describe to him my years of therapy, culminating in Group Therapy where I met

Tasha and Gretchen, and then I, reluctantly, tell him about the numerous medications I take.

"And do you take your medications correctly?"

"Of course!" I say, because I'm religious about that. I despise being sick, and I say so. "No one wants me to be well more than I do," I tell him.

"What about therapy?" he asks, reaching out for my fingers, which I am unconsciously drumming on the table. I let him take them, but they are clammy and I hope he doesn't read anything into that.

I give him a squeeze and sit back slightly. "I did therapy," I say.

He sighs, just a little, but I take it as judgment. "But what about now? Shouldn't you be in therapy now?"

"I was in therapy for six years," I say, ignoring the tightness that's growing in my chest. "At some point, you exhaust every possible conversation with your therapist."

He regards me for a moment, chewing on that. "Did you ever think about finding another one?" he asks after a moment.

This time, it's me who sighs. How do I explain this to someone that's never had mental illness? "You know that group therapy is very intensive therapy, right?" I ask.

He nods.

"Well, that was a real break-through for me, to help me see the things I couldn't before. It helped where my therapist could not, because it wasn't only about my specific memories or working through specific therapeutic techniques, it was about listening to other people's stories, people who had been through similar things and horrible things not similar at all, and feeling understood. And it was about them hearing me and seeing their reactions to my experiences." I look down at my jeans, smooth my napkin and fold it into a perfect triangle. When I look back up, he's staring at me intently. "I don't know if the other therapy, the one-on-one simply wasn't as effective for me… Actually, I think we had just, like I said, exhausted it. But this was a culmination for me, and it gave me a more external perspective that was really helpful. So that I wasn't so wrapped up in my own head. So that I could validate that not everything that was happening *was* in my head."

This time, it's Brandt who looks away, swirling his wine in its glass distractedly, while he sorts out his reaction, what he wants to say next.

When he turns back to me, I instantly tense, clenching my stomach and gripping the sides of my chair seat. Because I believe I read condescension in his eyes. Judgment. But surely not. I want to give him a chance, believe that he'll truly try to understand and not jump to conclusions.

"What about Tasha and Gretchen?" he asks then, and this catches me off guard.

"What about them?" I ask, my fingertips going numb as they grip the seat.

"Do you think they are holding you back from, you know, really getting better?"

"No!" I say, instantly defensive. Then I take a deep breath to steady my heart, which has jumped up to near-myocardial speeds. "They are my therapy now. They are the new iteration of it. You have no idea how helpful it is to have friends that truly understand your mental illness in a way no professional ever could, and who never judge you for it. And honestly, they are my sounding board now to help me figure out when my thinking is whacked, and also to help me work through painful memories. So I am getting therapy—with my friends."

I cross my arms and feel my heart thumping in my chest.

I can feel the tension between us like a series of strings that are pulled so tight, you could ping one with your finger and it would make a sound. He takes a slow sip of his wine, stirs a crumbling bite of cake around his plate with his fork.

But I won't speak. I want to hear exactly where this is going, what he is trying to say.

"Claire, I can see I'm upsetting you, and I don't mean to," he says after an interminable pause. "I want to see you get well. Get your life back."

That kind of pisses me off. I feel heat rising up my neck, my face, and into my scalp, which prickles. I take another deep, calming breath. "And you think I don't?"

He doesn't answer. Instead, he says something that seems completely incongruous to me. "It's just, I wonder if Tasha and Gretchen are really good for you. I know you think they are your therapy, but that doesn't seem... healthy. They are pretty ill, too. Plus..."

I can barely breathe now. "Plus what?" I ask.

"They seem like a bad influence. They are not professional women, not really like you at all. They are... ugh, I don't want to have to say this."

"Say it."

"They are, well, kind of low class."

I gasp. "Excuse me?"

But now that he's spit it out, this deplorable thought that he's been leading up to, it all spills out. "I think maybe they are bringing you down. I mean, you've been out of work for over a year. Your divorce was bad, I know. But you should be over it by now. At least, you should be past the worst of it. You should be better. The fact that you're not, that you're still not working, makes me ask myself, why?"

I am so angry, and so shocked, I can't find words. What. The. Hell??? I don't even know where to begin to respond to all the horrible things he said.

This is where my brain, of late, lets me down. It doesn't find the words that normally would be lining up to come out. But no! I won't let him say those things while I sit here stupidly, afraid. So I force myself to take a moment—I close my eyes, and order my thoughts with deliberation, as though I'm plucking them out of a card catalog and putting them in a neat row. And while they won't be as articulate as they normally would, I know I have to say them anyway. Because it's important.

He seems to sense that I want to speak, so he waits patiently, the only sound coming from his fork mashing and scraping and then mashing again the disintegrating cake on his plate. There's a dark, cakey crumb stuck in the corner of his smug, tight lips, and as I fight the urge to rub it off with some force, all I can think is, *You're not so damn perfect.*

I gather myself and take in a long slow breath. And then I speak. "First of all, you have no right to judge whether or not I should be 'better' or not. This is my illness and my journey, and like I said before, no one on this earth wants me to be well more than I do. Second of all, you know nothing about what I've been through or about depression or about treatments—you are not a doctor, or a therapist. You are not qualified to offer anything but support as a… whatever you are to me. Third…" The blood roars in my ears and I can feel my cheeks flush with anger and frustration. "Third, you have no right to judge my friends. They are… they are my sisters. And they have been my lifeline. They have been here for me when no one else was, and they never judge me because they understand everything. Plus, they have taught me how to laugh again. And I don't give one shit how much money they make or whether they have a 'suitable' job or a good enough address. None of that matters one bit."

He watches me closely, and I imagine it's because he's gauging whether I'm becoming hysterical, but then maybe I'm reading too much into it. When he speaks, he doesn't address most of my points. The crumb tumbles off when he says, "There are other friends, or even your family."

I am angry, and I don't owe him any explanations, and I don't have to justify myself. But I have feelings for him, and I want him to understand. So I tamp down my anger and frustration. "There are no other friends," I say back, slowly. "I've never had friends like these, maybe because I've never been a friend like they are to me, like I am to them now. And my family… my dad helps me all the time, but he can't be here. He works full time in Cincinnati. And as for my mom, she came to stay with me in the beginning, when I was a drooling mess. She stayed for a month, and I appreciated it so much. But by the end, I wanted to kill her, and it was hurting her feelings that I was getting annoyed. Because I didn't and don't need to be mothered. I'm a grown woman."

I pause, let my blood pressure lower, sit in the silence. And then

I reach for his hand, because I want him to get this. He hesitates for a fraction of a second before he grasps my fingers, interlacing his with mine.

"I need all of them—my parents, my doctors and therapists, and my friends to get through all this. And I am a lot better. Not totally there, but better than I was. You need to know that. But you also need to know this," I say, and pause again. I want to tell him this, because he needs to have realistic expectations. But I'm also afraid to say it out loud. Because I don't want it to be true.

But I'm a braver woman, now, than I once was. "You need to know that I might always be ill. And I might never again be the person I was."

His fingers, where they had been stroking mine, freeze. But I don't falter. I look straight into his eyes. "This may be who I am now and, if you want... whatever this is between us to work, you have to be okay with that. And so do I."

I release his fingers with a squeeze and lean back. I sit there, eerily calm now, and wait. Wait for his continued judgment, or his disbelief, or his acceptance. But whatever his reaction, I've spoken the truth.

He scoots back in his chair, carefully places his napkin on the table. Then he gets up and comes around the table to me, and pulls me up and into his arms.

"Brandt..." I say into his neck, and I don't realize until this moment how much I wanted this, his acceptance.

"Shhh," he says as he holds me tight. We let our bodies speak after that, and really, no words are needed. And when I'm driving home, I feel a strange sort of peace.

I listen to music on the way home, singing along loudly and with feeling to Rihanna and Alicia Keys. I don't notice the text until I pull into my driveway.

I see that it's from him, and I wonder, hope, that he's said the words he couldn't say when we were together—that he loves me.

But he doesn't say that at all.

'This isn't working for me. I think I need more from a partner than you are willing or able to give. I'm sorry.'

TWELVE

Holiday at the Twinkie House

SEPTEMBER

GRETCHEN and I hold hands as we wait in the reception area of the psych hospital. Tasha has sounded good on the few short phone calls we've had with her, but we can't help but be worried for her. Not so much that she's still suicidal right this second, because she does sound better. But we are worried how she will do once she's out of the hospital and has to face everything that happened.

Gretchen's hand is sweating in mine, and she's nervously drumming her fingers of her other hand against her thigh.

"Wish I had a smoke," she says, and I nod in commiseration.

And then the locked doors open, and our friend walks out holding a reusable grocery bag overstuffed with clothes. She looks skinnier than normal and her hair is an exploding mess, but her face lights up when she sees us and we rush to meet her with a hug.

"I missed you girls," she says into our shoulders as we stand and hug and *absorb* each other.

"We missed you so much," I say, and she feels tiny in my arms.

When we pull apart, she smiles at us and there is a peace in her eyes I haven't seen since I've known her.

"You ready to go?" says Gretchen.

"Just let me get my contraband. The Twinkie House is strict," she says with a good-natured wink. She gives a paper, a discharge form of some sort, to the receptionist, and the receptionist then walks to a back wall of lockers. She unlocks one and drags out Tasha's massive purse, and I think, *Sweet, thoughtful Melanie must have sent it with her to the hospital.*

Tasha thanks the woman with a genuine smile, and then turns to us. "Let's get the hell out of here. I need a decent cup of coffee and a smoke like a mother fucker."

We drive to a nearby coffee shop, and Tasha's introspective but calm as she and Gretchen smoke with the windows down. I know I'll smell like tobacco for the rest of the day, but I don't care. I'm just so thankful to see Tasha feeling better. So when thoughts of Brandt creep in, I tamp them down. The sadness and disappointment can wait.

When we get there, we all order coffees and then Gretchen scopes out a table with comfy chairs in the back.

Once we're settled in, Gretchen jumps in. "So, how are you really doing?"

Tasha closes her eyes for a moment. When she opens them, she fixes them on us. "I'm actually doing well. Better than I've been in a really long time."

"For real?" I say, and I'm so relieved.

She nods, fraying, grown-out locs shaking. "Yes, for real. They put me on a new med, and I feel great. I mean, all things considered. And I finally really realized that this is all up to me—whether I'm bat shit crazy or not. Or at least to some degree. I have to take my fucking meds, like, every day."

"Uh, that's what I've been telling you," I say, and she smirks.

"Yeah, yeah, don't rub it in." She blows on her coffee, takes a careful sip. "It's not that I didn't kind of already know that. I'm not an idiot. But I guess I didn't realize how important it is."

Gretchen's nodding. "Yes, of course. Meds are super important. So what did they put you on?"

Tasha lists four different ones. We know them all.

"Oh yeah. I've been on that first one," Gretchen says, indicating the main one. "It made me hyper and took away a lot of my sex drive."

I slap her arm. "Don't tell her that!" Then I turn to Tasha. "I'm so glad you found a combination that's working for you," I say, as I think about my own cocktail and its minimal effectiveness.

"Me too!" says Tasha and shrugs. "And my sex parts still feel normal," she adds, reaching down to pat them, but I stop her before she can do so. She laughs, then turns serious. "For real, though, I'm going to take them like I'm supposed to. I've decided I have to do that for me and for my kids. Because I don't want to put them through that shit again."

I don't say anything, but I'm so glad to hear her say this.

"Have you talked to them?" asks Gretchen.

Tasha looks away, gazing out of the window at the dense tulip poplars that line the sidewalk. "No," she finally says. "I called them, but Malcolm said they were still really upset about what happened and he thought it was better if they didn't talk to me until I was totally better and out of the hospital." Her voice is melancholy as she says this, but then she turns to us bright-eyed. "But I'm going to call them today, because I need to see them and tell them how sorry I am for what I've put them through. I need them to know how much I've changed. I can't help having this damn bipolar bullshit, but I'm going to take better care of myself and my illness."

"I'm so proud of you," I say, giving her arm a squeeze, not liking the sharp feel of the bone beneath her skin.

"Tell me what's been happening with you guys?" Tasha says then, bouncing in her seat as she draws one leg up under her. She looks at me, gives me a wink. "How's sexy business dude, Brandt?"

Gretchen tosses me a worried glance, and my stomach turns over on itself as a prickle of dismay spreads from my scalp along my neck and cascades down my back and arms.

Tasha's excited expression turns to concern. "Oh, fuck. What happened? I can see it's bad from your face," she says.

But I can't speak. Because I miss him and I'm bitterly disappointed in him and it all really hurts.

"They broke up," Gretchen says, speaking for me.

"Oh no, for real? I thought he was a good guy, from what you said," she says as she pats my knee. "I'm sorry, Claire."

"It's okay," I say, but my voice wavers as I fight the tears that are stinging my eyes.

Tasha gives my knee a squeeze and sits back, clutching her coffee. "What happened? Do you feel like talking about it?"

Gretchen looks at me questioningly. I haven't told her much—certainly not what Brandt said about them—but I know she's been curious.

"He didn't understand my mental illness. He said he didn't understand why I wasn't better yet. He thought I wasn't trying hard enough."

"Asshole! What right does he have to judge?" says Tasha, her brown eyes ablaze with indignation on my behalf.

Gretchen's nodding in agreement. "That's kind of bullshit, if you'll excuse me saying so. He obviously doesn't get it."

"Damn right, he doesn't get it," says Tasha. "What's he think, that you freaking like being sick? Like you aren't doing everything possible to get better? That pisses me off!" She plucks a string off her pants and tosses it on the floor. "He doesn't fucking know you at all!"

"I thought he did," I say. "I thought I was letting him know me. Maybe he did know me, and he didn't like who I am." My voice catches at this, and I take a deep shuddering breath, trying to maintain control.

I've already spent several hours upset over the loss of this relationship, the future I thought we might have had together. I've probably lamented too much, disproportionate to the time we spent together. I get that—but I was so ready to be happy. I really thought my relationship with Brandt was sent from God to help me find happiness.

Instead, I've fallen back into the pit of Depression.

"Well, then fuck him," says Tasha. "You deserve better than that, girl. Don't you think different for one second."

"I agree," says Gretchen. "And if he wasn't the one, you have to have faith that God still has the right person out there for you, and He'll send him your way when the time is right."

I give my girls a teary smile and they reach across from their chairs to hug me. I'm still in the pit, but as usual, they help light the way out, and I will climb toward it.

We sit for a while longer as Tasha tells us about some of the characters she met in the psych hospital and how she and another girl that was in for suicidal thoughts couldn't stop laughing when the music therapist literally sang Kumbaya. She's a good storyteller, and even I'm smiling a little by the time we've finished our second cup of coffee.

"Okay, girls. It's been real, but I need to get home so I can call my kids and hopefully see them this afternoon," Tasha says, standing and stretching her tiny frame.

"Of course," says Gretchen. "I'm sure they're anxious to see you."

"And I gotta make an appointment with my hair girl. They don't know shit about maintaining black hair at the Twinkie House. My locs are a mess."

We all hurry out to my vehicle and pile in, and I drive the short distance to Tasha's place. She's upbeat and optimistic on the drive over, already planning to clean so that she can have the kids over later and talk to them. I'm slightly jealous, once again, that she has an ex that is flexible about such things.

By the time we pull up, Tasha is planning her cleaning playlist, and Gretchen is missing Carson. And while I've enjoyed their company, my socialization energy is spent and I'm ready to go home and take a nap.

It's Gretchen that notices someone walking away from Tasha's front door as we pull up. He's dressed in street clothes, but I don't recognize him. "Who's that guy leaving your front door?" asks Gretchen.

Tasha sees him then, but shrugs. "No idea," she says, as we walk her up the sidewalk. He notices us as we approach and he stops and waits. He's holding a package.

"Can we help you?" asks Gretchen as we get near. We're all hesitant to get too close, and I have my phone in my hand, emergency call button at the ready.

"Latasha Simpson?" he says, his voice low but deliberately calm, as though in an effort to be non-threatening.

"Yeah, that's me," Tasha says.

He hands her the package. When she takes it, he says, "You've been served," and then hurries around us and down the sidewalk to the parking lot.

"What the hell?" says Tasha as she stands there too shocked to move. Gretchen gently takes the envelope from her hands and pulls back the tab closure. She slides out a stack of documents and we all huddle close to read them. The first is labeled "Emergency Custody Order," the second, "Temporary Restraining Order."

Tasha's hands fall away, and we have to lurch to grab the documents before they fall to the ground. Tasha collapses onto her knees. "He wouldn't," she says, as we pull her up and help her inside.

When we get her seated on the couch, Gretchen hurries into the kitchen to fetch a glass of water. Tasha has gone an ashy pale, and we are both worried that she's going to faint. When Gretchen returns, Tasha barely takes a sip, but sits clutching the papers as we huddle close to her to read them together.

They are true to their ominous titles—Malcolm has gotten a judge to sign both orders, giving him full emergency custody of the kids and requiring Tasha to have no contact unless supervised by Malcolm, at his discretion. The reason cited is that Tasha has demonstrated that she is a danger to herself and others. A hearing date to rule on permanent custody is to be determined.

"I can't believe this," Tasha says, as she lays the papers on the coffee table, her hands shaking. "That fucker! Why would he do this?"

I take a deep breath, because she always tells me the truth, and I need to do the same for her. "Because he's scared for his kids," I say, and she looks at me slowly, like she's trying to process my words. "He's always been a decent guy and treated you fairly. But I saw him at the hospital. You scared the shit out of him, and he was very upset about what Hunter and Melanie went through. And honey, it was really awful on them. I was there. It was bad."

She lets out an awful sob. "I know," she says, and buries her face in her hands as she cries.

Gretchen can't speak. This triggers painful flashbacks for me, but at least I can remind myself that losing Brooklyn is in the past. But it must hit so close to home for her—not that she's legally prohibited from seeing her kids, but she still doesn't see them, just the same. She sits white-faced, lips a thin grim line, gripping Tasha and rubbing the top of their clasped hands over and over like a touchstone.

But this doesn't have to be a parental death sentence. I believe, I hope, that Tasha has turned a corner in her willingness to really take responsibility for her illness. And maybe this is what it will take to make it stick—that she must always take her medicine, because the alternative, and its repercussions, are too terrible to contemplate. Bipolar disorder is not curable—at least, not with today's medicine. So this is her life, and it always will be.

"Tasha, look at me," I say, and she does, and her face almost breaks me. The despair there is completely unfamiliar on her, but is all too familiar to me. It's like looking in a mirror. But I take a deep breath and fortify myself, because my friend needs me. "This is not the end. This is the beginning of a new time for you and your kids. Because you are going to prove to Malcolm and the court that you can treat your mental illness and be a safe and responsible parent for Hunter and Melanie. That is now your number one priority. And once you convince them and get joint custody back, you are going to spend the rest of your life proving to them that you love them enough to take care of yourself. That they never have to worry about this again."

I push away the fear that there may be times that her sickness overcomes even her best efforts and complete medication compliance, because that is a discussion for another day. But she's listening to me, so I press on. "Do not let this beat you. This is actually an understandable response from Malcolm. It's up to you to prove yourself, and I know you can do it. You are so strong and bright and wonderful. Your kids need you. You can do this."

She nods at me and squares her shoulders as she wipes away her tears. "You're right," she says, and Gretchen shudders beside her, biting her lip to keep her emotions in check. "I can do this, and I will. Because my kids deserve it, and so do I. I'm going to show them how good a mother I can be."

"You were always a good mother," I say. "Just an ill one. You can't ever forget that again."

"I won't," she says. "I promise. I really get it this time. Maybe this is what I needed. I will show them all."

We hug her and only leave when she assures us she's calm and at peace with the situation and what she needs to do, at least for now. I'm worried, but I have to trust her—because if I can't, then maybe no one can, including her kids.

It's up to Tasha to make it real.

The "Date" I Don't Remember But Will Never Forget

SOMETHING IS BUZZING. Loudly. But I can't quite reach it, can't quite tell what it is.

My eyes won't seem to open, though I will them to, and I feel as though I'm swimming through gelatin towards a surface I can't quite find.

I try to understand what's happening, where I am, and I see a flash in the distance of my mind—the bar. I'd gone by myself, upset about Brandt, but not wanting to be alone. *Afraid* to be alone. Not looking to hook up with someone, only wanting to be around people. And my friends were not available—Gretchen was busy with Chris and Carson, Tasha had been working.

So I went to the bar. That I remember, as I slip and slog through the thick opaque substance, trying to find the light.

I went to the bar, and I sat at the counter and chit-chatted with the bartender who I know a little from our many visits there. He was nice, but distracted by his many patrons, and that's when the guy sat down beside me. He was attractive, I remember, though I can't quite recall his face. He was good-looking, though, and attentive, and he bought me a drink or two, which I said wasn't necessary but didn't really mind.

The buzzing is so loud. I want it to stop, but at the same time, I feel that it's important to find it, to swim toward it like it's a beacon.

And then I hear a voice.

"Hello?" It's a man's voice, slurring the word, sleepy-sounding.

There's a tinny reply I can almost make out.

But it's *his* response that gets my attention, that ultimately helps me emerge from the sludge.

"Who's Claire?" he says, then laughs, a low rumbling sound.

This time, I can hear the voice on the phone clearly.

"The fucking girl that owns this phone! And you better find her quick, you goddamned mother fucker!"

There's a nudge on my shoulder, and finally my eyes open. I'm in a room—a bedroom, and the early morning sunlight is streaming in across us. Across a bed. Where there is a naked man beside me. And as I acknowledge this curious fact, I can now feel sheets against my bare skin, and I realize with sluggish alarm that I'm naked too.

"I think it's for you," he says, and hands me my phone.

"Hello?" I say, and it's hard to get the word out. My voice sounds scratchy and far away.

"Claire, thank God!" Tasha says. "Where are you?"

I look around again, at the Quaker style dresser, at a chair in the corner covered in clothes.

"I... I don't know," I say, slowly.

"Get the fuck out of there now," she says. "Get your shit and get the fuck out. And don't hang up!"

Suddenly, I feel afraid. I wrench myself into a sitting position, swing my legs over the side. It takes so much effort, and I wonder how much I had to drink. I look back at him, worried that I'll see his hands reaching for me, that he'll restrain me. But he appears to have gone back to sleep. This sight fortifies me, filling me with adrenaline that helps me overcome my stupor enough to retrieve my clothes. They are strewn across the floor—except my panties, which I can't find—and I put them on. My purse is on the dresser and appears, at quick glance, to be intact. I grab it and go to the door. It leads into a living room that is sparse, dominated by a giant TV on the wall. And then I'm in the hall of an apparent apartment complex. I don't know which way to go, so I start wandering down the hall, and I eventually come upon the elevators. When they open, I stumble inside, press the 'L' three times, two because my hands are shaking and one extra for good measure.

By the time the elevator dings and the doors open, I spill out of them, barely seeing the lobby, I'm so intent on getting outside. And then I'm through the outer doors, on a street I don't recognize, shielding my eyes from the intensely bright glare of the sun.

I reach into my purse and grab my phone, it still shows an ongoing call with Tasha.

"You there?"

"Of course I'm here! Are you out?" Her voice is raised with alarm, louder than normal, which is saying something.

"Yes," I say.

"Oh my God, Claire. You were supposed to text me when you got home last night. Where are you?"

"I'm not sure," I say, trying to remember where I left my car. And while I can't specifically recall parking last night, I deduce that I probably parked in the garage we always use when we go downtown.

I look around, trying to get my bearings, but it's no use. I don't recognize anything. However, I can see the skyscrapers of downtown in the distance. So I start walking towards the Batman building, which is near my normal parking garage.

There are no cars around. It's too early for traffic, particularly on a Sunday morning. But the streets are clean, well-maintained. The area appears nice, safe. That at least gives me some comfort, as I walk toward the tall buildings in the distance.

Tasha is saying something, but it takes a minute for my brain to catch up.

"I'm sorry, what?" I say.

"I said, do you see any cabs? Are you close to your car?"

"No, and not exactly. But I think I can get there. It just might take a while."

"Do you feel safe?"

Again, I look around. "Yes," I say, and it's true, at least in terms of my surroundings. That's all I can focus on for the moment.

"Call me back when you get to your car," she instructs, and we hang up.

I walk for a while, and as I do, I try to remember details about the apartment building, about the man in the bed. It's useless. It floats away like a waking dream.

My thoughts are muddled and slow, and I quickly grow frustrated as I try to remember the night before, the bar. How many drinks did I have? How did I end up in some stranger's apartment?

After some amount of time, I'm not sure how much, I can feel that the sun has risen higher in the sky. The birds are chirping in the small clusters of trees that are planted in aesthetically designed intervals along the sidewalk. I'm beginning to hear the hum of cars, the screech of bus tires at nearby intersections. The city is waking up.

And the tall buildings still seem far away.

In my purse, my phone buzzes. It's Tasha.

"Hello?" I say, and I can hear the hint of mounting anxiety, the repressed fear, in my voice.

"You there yet?"

"No," I say. "It's a lot farther away than I thought." My feet are hurting. My wedges are cute and relatively comfortable, but not meant for long distance walks on hard city streets.

"I'm coming to get you—you probably shouldn't be driving anyway, from the sound of it," she says. "Find some street signs and tell me where you are."

I see street signs at the intersection up ahead. When I get close enough, I read them to her.

"Hold tight," she tells me. "I'll be there in twenty minutes."

I look around and see a small courtyard leading up to a condo building. There's a planter that faces the street, and I take a seat along the edge and wait for my rescue.

As I wait, I try to remember more about being at the bar. I focus on that part, because I'm not ready to think about the rest. But it's no use. No matter how hard I try, I don't remember much more. The guy is still a blurred face companion that may have been named Jack or Josh or Jacob. I still don't remember having more than a drink or two, and I definitely have no recollection of how I got to the apartment.

After several minutes of futilely scouring my mind, trying to piece together the bits of memory that remain, untethered, in my rattled brain, a cute little Yorkie approaches me on a leash, his owner pulling him back with an apologetic smile.

"Sorry about that," the owner says. "He's friendly."

"It's fine," I say, surprised to find that my voice is working again. I reach my knuckles out to the dog, who promptly licks them. I reward his kiss with a scratch behind the ears, and then the owner is leading him away, holding a pooper scooper in anticipation of a productive walk.

As I watch them until they are out of sight, a quick beep of a horn draws my attention to the street. I almost weep with relief at the site of Tasha's car at the curb.

I rush to get into the passenger seat, and then the tears begin to fall.

"Oh, honey," she says, hugging me awkwardly across the console. "Are you okay?"

"I don't know," I say, as I buckle my seatbelt and take some deep breaths to calm myself.

She pulls away from the curb without another word, and it's several blocks before she speaks again.

"Do you want to tell me what happened?" she finally asks. "Who was that guy?"

I'm looking out the window, trying to sort that out for myself. Without turning around, I reply, repeating my initial response, wishing I had another answer. "I don't know. I don't remember much of anything. I think…"

I pause then, hesitating to put into the words the thought that has been circling my mind for the last thirty minutes as I try to sort out the events of the night.

I face her then, though she's watching the road. "I think I might have been drugged," I say, and it seems like it could be true yet at the same time fantastical.

Her head whips around to look at me. "Shit, really?"

I nod, and she turns back to her driving. "Holy fuck," she says.

"Yeah," I agree. The thing is, nothing like this has ever happened to me before, this lost time, the inability to remember anything. Hell, I normally don't even drink that much, and definitely didn't intend to last night, given that I'd gone out alone.

"Why do you think that?" she asks after a brief moment, a pause to let this disturbing possibility sink in.

"Because I only remember having two drinks, and I was going to be careful not to get drunk. And I've never been blackout drunk before. Ever." But there's more than that, as I try to articulate how foggy, how *off* I've been since I woke up. "Plus, everything is so fuzzy this morning. I can't think straight. Not like hungover, like *confused*."

She glances at me again, and her expression is pained. "Did he…?"

Right at this moment, and very intentionally not a moment before, I begin to take a full physical inventory of myself, now that she's raised the question I haven't wanted to consider. I think about my naked body, how I felt cold, exposed, waking up in a bed next to his naked body. I think about my missing panties, how even now I keenly, physically notice their absence, and how my clothes were scattered around the room.

I think, though every particle of my psyche screams at me not to, how I can feel a stickiness between my legs, how my upper inner thighs are slightly sore, as though I've been ridden hard.

"Yes, I think so," I whisper, and I turn away instinctively to hide my horror, my instant shame.

"Fuck, Claire," she says, her voice shaking with shock, anger. "Fuck, fuck, fuck."

I don't know what to say, so I say nothing, just stare out the window, tears spilling out, streaming silently down my face.

Fuck.

She takes my hand, and I look at her slowly, wretched and wrecked.

"We have to go to the hospital," she says gently. "I'm taking you to the hospital."

For some reason, this idea fills me with panic. "I… I can't," I say, fighting the hysteria that is bubbling up in my throat. *That will make it all real.*

She pulls over to the side of the street, puts the car in park, and faces me. Taking both of my hands, she looks at me with such sadness, such pity. "Honey, you were raped," she says, and that's the tipping point, collapsing my tenuous strength into sobs.

She takes me into her arms as best she can, and I cry. "I know," I whisper, and that single, simple acknowledgement breaks me inside.

She takes me to the hospital anyway, but I stop her before she can get out of the car.

"Tasha, wait," I say. "This is pointless."

She's puzzled. "What do you mean?"

"There's nothing to tell the cops. I don't know the guy's name or what he looks like." I try to recall the apartment number, the building, the street, but it's no use. "I don't even remember where I was."

She sits up straight as something occurs to her. "Did you take a picture of his license?"

"I don't think so. It wasn't a date. And I barely even remember meeting him."

"Check your phone anyway," she says.

So I do. The last photo I took was of Brandt and Elijah sitting in an armchair together reading a storybook. The picture that should be there, the one I always take if I'm truly on a date, is missing.

"Nope," I say, collapsing further into myself.

"Well then they can test you, do DNA or whatever."

"And compare it to what? They probably won't even believe me. I mean, I don't even know what happened. Maybe I went there on my own accord."

"Bullshit. If you were fucking drugged, it's impossible for you to… what's the word?"

"Consent," I say.

"Yeah, fucking consent. No fucking way that's consent! And girl, you were roofied. I've never seen you so jacked up from drinking. I bet they can test for that."

"Maybe they could," I concede. "I'm not sure if it's detectable or not…"

"See, there you fucking go. Let's go get you swabbed or pricked or whatever." She goes to open the door, but I grab her arm.

"But, what's the point? Even if we prove I was drugged, *I don't remember anything.* There's absolutely nothing that can be done. I'd be questioned, put through all that, for nothing. I… I don't think I can do it."

And, though I don't say it out loud, *I'm ashamed.* I know all the rape literature. I know that victims are *never* to blame. But I still feel shame. I went to a freaking bar alone. Some people, lots of people probably, would say that I put myself in a dangerous position. Maybe even that I was asking for it.

Damn! I hate myself for even thinking this. I know it's messed up. But I feel dirty and slutty and to blame. And while I hate that piece of shit, asshole rapist that did this to me, I kind of hate myself right now, too.

"Please, Tasha. I can't. If it would do any good, I… I would. But it won't. It will only make me have to relive, or imagine what happened, in excruciating detail for cops and doctors for no reason. They'll do an exam, take swabs of my… my vagina, for what? Please," I say, gripping her hand. "I just want to go home, go to sleep, try to forget."

She looks at me for a long time, her fierce, protective, warrior nature warring with the truth of what I'm saying, the futility of the situation. Finally, she nods.

"Okay, Claire. I'll take you home. But I'm not leaving you alone."

"Tash…"

"No, don't argue. You don't need to be alone. I'll hang out in the living room and watch something on TV, and you can go to bed. I want to make sure you are going to be okay."

There's no arguing with her, so I nod, and she puts her seatbelt back on and pulls out of the parking lot.

We're quiet on the drive home. I don't have any words right now. And before long, we are pulling into my driveway. My body feels limp, boneless, like a wet noodle. I'm not sure if it's from the lingering effects of whatever drug might be in my system now that the adrenaline has worn off, or if the mental and emotional exhaustion has sapped all of my strength, but Tasha has to help me out of the car. We walk into the house with me leaning on her small frame, and when we get inside, she takes me straight back to my bedroom.

"Shower," I say, and it sounds small, weak.

She starts stripping off my clothes, and pauses but doesn't comment when she sees that I'm missing my panties. And then she's lifting me again, supporting me with her body as she takes me to the bathroom. She opens the shower door, grabbing me a towel and washcloth from the linen closet as I step inside.

She looks at me dubiously. "You got it from here, honey?"

"Yes," I say, and she seems to briefly consider camping out on my bathroom floor before finally deciding that I truly can handle showering on my own.

"I'm right out there if you need me. Just holler."

I nod. "Okay."

And then she's leaving, closing the door softly behind her.

I reach to turn on the water, already knowing that I won't be able to get it hot enough—that while I can wash away his skin cells and sweat and semen, I won't be able to scrub away the violation. I won't be able to cleanse myself of this profound disgust I have for my most precious, private parts, for my defiled body.

I wish I could shed it completely, get a new, fresh one. I don't want this one anymore.

I scrub myself, and at first I'm gentle, careful not to aggravate the soreness in my thighs, in the folds between my legs. But then something changes—a rush of anger and revulsion washes over me, hot and relentless as the steaming water, and now I want to feel the pain, to scour it until it flakes away, till I've sloughed off the damaged parts and am left with the underneath. And I try, but it makes the aching worse, more pronounced—like an exclamation point to the rape. So I give up, or recognize that I'm as clean as I'm going to get, and I sit on the floor under the stream until the water turns cold, reaching up, shivering, to turn it off.

Tasha must hear its cessation, because she comes in before I can even stand up and has the towel open and waiting for me by the time I step out.

She murmurs to me as she helps me towel off—comforting, meaningless phrases like, "It's okay," and "Good girl." But it *is* a comfort, if a small one. When we've finished, she has clean panties for me, a t-shirt and pajama pants, which she tugs onto my useless, limp body like she would a small, sleepy child.

She pushes the covers aside and helps me climb into my bed, and I can't help but flash back to the bed from this morning—the naked man, the twisted, tacky sheets—and I beg God for relief.

It's the first time I've prayed since I woke up.

Tasha tucks me in and kisses my forehead, and I close my eyes and pray, again—this time for a quick descent into a dreamless sleep.

THIRTEEN

Sangria is Great for Drinking Games

STILL SEPTEMBER

TASHA GIVES me three days of solitude. Three days of hermit-like isolation and self-pity, before she and Gretchen show up at my house, unannounced, on a pretty Indian Summer day. It is a day that has become once again indistinguishable from the rest, given the fact that my Depression has returned with a vengeance, and so there's nothing to mark their passage—most notably, still no work to require my presence. Nothing but the slow preparation for my time with Brooklyn, but that's still days away…

So they show up and let themselves in with my spare key, because they know where I hide it. They are attempting to make my proprietary recipe for sangria in the kitchen when I'm awakened, and I emerge from my bedroom to my two girls who, because it's still hot as hell outside, are already in the bathing suits they've donned to bear the heat or, in Gretchen's case, to facilitate a tan, Caesarean scars and stretch marks bared for all to see. They hug me, but not overly so, just the perfunctory kind of embrace we share at every meeting, and they invite me to join them at the island as they chop strawberries and stir the concoction they are so thoroughly botching.

But I don't care. I'm not ready to talk, and they are not forcing me to, and so I'm finding some comfort in their pressure-free presence.

When they've finished mixing the sangria, Gretchen pours each of us a large tumbler full, and they wait for me to change into a swimsuit myself. When I emerge again, Tasha grabs my Bluetooth speaker, and I follow them onto the patio where she helps spray us down with the SPF 15 tanning before taking the reclining lounge chair that's beneath the umbrella. That's her spot, while we take the two that are in the sun. Tasha grabs my phone and turns on my Justin Timberlake streaming station, syncing it to the speaker.

Thankfully, though, the first song actually is JT, and they get their sexy back in horrid harmony, but one that eases the weight on my chest, be it slightly, just the same.

After a while of listening to music, Gretchen reaches over to turn it down.

"Aren't you going to ask me where Carson is?" she asks, and laughs. "You're very observant today."

"Oh, yeah. I'm sorry," I say, as I truly had not noticed his absence before now. "Where is he?" I ask, mostly because I feel an obligation to do so. In all honesty, I can't generate any genuine curiosity on my own.

"He's at Mother's Day Out at the Goodlettsville Church of the Cross," she says. "It's free!" she adds gleefully.

"Oh, good, honey," I manage.

"No, you don't understand," she says. "This is my freedom! Chris is working all the time, and I never get a break during the day. Now I do! And Carson is going to learn so much, being with the other kids. He's already been saying lots of words. He even said 'I wuv you,' after I told him I loved him the other night before bed."

"Aww," says Tasha. "That's adorable! What else is he saying?"

"Well, he's been saying 'mama' and 'dada' forever, but now he can count to four and say 'ready, set, go!'"

"Cute little stinker," Tasha says.

"Good for you," I say, and I try to bring my cheeks up in a smile. I'm not sure it works.

Tasha eyes me sideways from behind her sunglasses. "You're

sucking at being you right now," she says. "You haven't even said anything about my new hair."

It has changed again. They look sort of like braids, but ropier, not like the ones she used to have. And there are some blond streaks in them.

She sees the blank expression on our faces. "They're Senegalese twists, your ignorant white girls. Aren't they gorgeous?"

Gretchen gives an enthusiastic endorsement, and Tasha eyes me. I nod, but I can't bring myself to say any more words, so I turn away.

"Okay, that's it," Tasha said. "We've tiptoed around this bullshit long enough. Let's just get it out there." She turns around then in her chair and sits upright with her feet on the ground. "Gretchen, sit up, we're going to play a game with Claire."

Gretchen does, but I refuse to move from my reclined position. I'm not sure I have the energy to.

"What game are we going to play?" Gretchen asks, taking a sip from her fruity drink.

Tasha taps her chin. "Hmmm," she says, as she contemplates, but seeing Gretchen sip on her pseudo-sangria gives her inspiration. "I've got it!," she says. "Life Sucks, Drink Sangria!"

Gretchen says the words I can't manage to. "What is that?"

Now Tasha's eyes are alight with mischief. "It's where you say what sucks about your life and then you have to take a drink of sangria."

Gretchen claps. "Well, hell! We should be great at this game!" She laughs at this, and my mouth twitches despite my disinclination to feel anything but misery today.

"I'll go first," Tasha says. "Let's see, where to start, where to start… Oh, I know. I let toothless Diego feel up my titties for a handful of hydrocodone, and his fingers felt like someone was trying to sand off my nipples." She takes a hearty drink.

"Eww," says Gretchen, and I can tell she's a little shocked. I never told her about that part of the mess that led up to Tasha's overdose.

But I agree. *Eww.*

"Okay, I guess it's my turn," says Gretchen, scratching her head as she thinks. She nods when it comes to her. "I quit liking sex because of my psych meds and my ex-husband got tired of waiting for me to give him a blowjob again. So he found someone else to do it."

"You know what to do!" Tasha says, gesturing to Gretchen's cup.

Gretchen drinks deeply, and then she's gesturing to me.

But I can't do it. I can't say the words. "I'm... I'm not ready," I manage, and they only look at me for a moment before Tasha speaks up.

"Then you at least have to drink. Forfeiture of a turn does not... what's the word, Claire?"

"*Negate*," I think, but I can't say it.

"Oh, hell. I'll get it. I just need a minute... Um, it doesn't *eliminate* the drinking requirement," she says rather formally, emphasizing her word choice, which she came up with on her own and seems appropriately proud of. I'm proud of her too.

She gestures to me, so I do take a drink, and it tastes better than I expect.

It's Tasha's turn again. She takes a deep breath, then dives right in. "I recently tried to kill myself, and I had to spend two weeks in the Twinkie House."

"Well, that is a good 'life sucks' moment, for sure," Gretchen says. "Drink up!" Tasha does.

Gretchen is fully in the spirit now. "Okay, me next. I accidentally got pregnant, and thank God for sweet little Carson, but I was freaking forty-one years old and waaaaay past wanting any more kids!"

Tasha points to Gretchen's glass. "Oooh, girl. You drink that shit up!"

And then it was my turn again. Tasha looks at me expectantly, but I shake my head and take a drink before she can say it. Still not ready.

"Okay, so I guess it's back to me again," she says. "Hmm, so much to choose from..." She's dumped her chin in her hand and she's tapping her forehead contemplatively. But it's all a show, because we know her worst. "Oh, I know! My ex-husband has taken my kids away, and I don't know when or if I'll ever see them again!" she finally says, and takes a huge swig.

Gretchen clinks her cup with Tasha for that one, and then she speaks her worst. "And I haven't seen my daughters in over a year!" she fairly shouts, and then she is drinking while Tasha chants some fraternal chugging mantra.

And then it's back to me again, and I think about what my girls have said, what they've been through. Their pain is real and terrible too, and yet they have not given in to despair. They continue on, because life does that—it marches on, whether you feel like it or not. And this realization makes me immensely proud of them, because they are admirable of the highest order.

Tasha and Gretchen are looking at me now, waiting for me to speak, waiting to see if I can name my pain and begin to accept it. And Tasha's about to give up, I can see it—not in a judgmental way, but in complete support of me and whatever time I might need.

But then I clear my throat and they both pause. "I…" I start to say, coughing a little into my hand, because my voice has been unused these last three days. "I was drugged and raped by some guy, and I don't even know what he looks like," I finally say, and Gretchen gives me the kindest, sad-eyed smile. "Or even whether he was any good," I add, smiling a little myself. Because it's an inappropriate joke, and I don't mean it at all, that there would be any conceivable possibility I would ever think it was 'good', but just saying it reclaims a little of my power.

They are both shocked at first, and then Tasha barks out one of her giant laughs. "Damn straight," she says. "He better at least have had a big dick!"

And then we're all laughing, because you have to either laugh or cry in such matters, and then it's Tasha's turn again.

"My vagina is slackening," she says. "I keep front-farting during sex!" Gretchen and I both look at each other for a moment, trying to work out that term and what it means.

Then Gretchen's eyes grow huge. "Are you talking about a pussy fart?" she says, and she can barely squeak it out through her laughter.

Tasha is crying and can only nod and maw out some sounds that indicate, 'uh-huh' in the most hilarious fashion.

When Gretchen finally catches her breath, she says, "Girl, you gotta do the Kegels. I've got three damn kids, and I do them every day. Hell, my pussy is so taut, it locks onto Chris during sex and won't let go. It's like a vaginal vice-clamp! Why the hell do you think he stays with me? My cock-eyed nipples?"

At this, I fully lose my composure, and the laughter springs forth like a fount. I laugh and laugh, the way only my girls can inspire, and I love them so fiercely right now, my heart physically swells, as though to wrap them up and hold them close within it.

When we're finally spent from laughter, Tasha looks at me but my words are used up for now, the most important ones being disbursed. She winks at me and says, "Okay, ladies. I have one more."

Gretchen and I smile at each other and at Tasha in anticipation.

Tasha leans in a bit, like she's telling us a secret. "I don't know if this is a 'life sucks' moment or not," she begins. "It's all according to your perspective." She's trying on her big words again, and apparently finding that she likes them.

Gretchen expresses the impatience we both feel. "Freaking tell us already, Tasha!"

"Well," she says, leaning in further, rather conspiratorially. "I had sex three times last night."

Gretchen's eyes widen. "No shit! With who?"

At this, Tasha erupts in laughter again, and when the hiccups she's prone to take over, I'm not sure she'll ever spit it out, but she finally does. "With myself!" she says, and we roar till the physical pain of laughing so hard has thoroughly pushed away the emotional pain of the day.

When we finally come down, we sigh with contentedness, and we enjoy a few moments of silence in each other's company, listening to the birds and the cicadas and the wind whispering through the trees—until I notice the intense look of concentration on Gretchen's face.

"Gretchen, are you okay?" I say, growing concerned that she's about to cry for real or maybe feeling a twinge of discomfort somewhere.

"Oh, sorry," she says. "Was doing a Kegel."

And we're crying again.

Thank God for my girls.

Date #1 With Finn; Also, Screw the Fear

IT'S BEEN a while since I've had dinner with a man. I've avoided men, since the Incident. But now I've confirmed with my second set of blood tests that I don't have a life-threatening STD and I've recently broken my vibrator from over-use, and I thought perhaps those are signs that it's time to get out there again.

So here I am, getting ready for my first date in a long time—almost six months. I'm nervous but trying not to let it stop me. I can't live in fear, because that's not really living. I literally need to get back out there, for my own sanity.

Gretchen has texted me again. She's not been sleeping, and cleaning obsessively. I've never seen her truly sick—she'd already been stabilized with medication by the time I met her at Group—but I know these are her particular precursors to full-on mania.

I'm about to respond when my phone rings. It's Tasha, though, not Gretchen.

"Hey girl," she says when I answer. "Just met with my lawyer. She is pleased with my doctor reports, because I'm killing it with taking my meds like I'm supposed to."

"I'm very proud of you," I tell her, meaning it. I paid for Tasha to get a lawyer months ago, and she advised Tasha to live with supervised visits for a while, during which time she can see her psychiatrist monthly and have documented proof that she's taking her medication properly. She also advised her, after discussions with her psychiatrist regarding Tasha's addiction issues, to come off of all benzodiazepines and also to attend Narcotics Anonymous. Tasha tends to be impatient, but it seemed like a sound strategy to me, and I told her so. Not only that, she legitimately needed to change her way of managing her illness, for her own sake as well as her kids.

"This is going to work, right?" she asks, like she does every month or so.

"Yes, this is going to work. And honey... regardless of what happens, this is the right thing to do."

She sighs. "I know. I just miss them. Two hours a week with my kids, with Malcolm breathing down my neck, is not enough."

"I understand," I say, because I really do. My own memories of supervised visits with Brooklyn are almost too painful to think about.

"So tell me about this guy," says Tasha, changing the subject.

"It'll probably be nothing. But I liked his picture because he looks normal—cute but not too cute to be arrogant about it, with kind eyes. And he seems funny on his profile, and has been very polite in our messages. But seriously, I'm not expecting anything. I just... don't want to feel afraid of men anymore. I feel like I have to bite the bullet, because I know, logically, that not all men are scumbag rapists."

"Well, then, I'm proud of *you*," says Tasha. "And if you do bite that bullet, try not to bite it off. Dudes don't like that."

I laugh. "Oh, okay, thank you for that bit of advice. You're crazy."

"Yes, I know. And that's why you love me."

We say our goodbyes then, and it doesn't register that I forgot to mention Gretchen until after we hang up. But I'm running out of time and I still haven't finished my hair. I'll mention it to her later.

I'M wary as I drive to the restaurant, which is an Irish pub that's supposed to be authentic. I'm not sure I'm entirely ready to do this, but I choose to be optimistic. After all, things have been going a little better for me in the last couple of months. I did a consulting project and, while I wasn't at the top of my game, I didn't choke either. I completed the project, collected my paycheck. I call that a success. My improvement in this area I will attribute to time, working through my issues with my unofficial therapy group (i.e., the girls), and the marginal effect of my medication. I have chosen, at least so far, not to resort to ECT. While the concept of remission is appealing, it also seems unreal, like unicorns and rainbow pathways to alternate worlds. And the possible side effects are scary, the memory loss in particular. I need my memory for work—it is essential. Plus, I couldn't stand to lose any of my memories with Brooklyn, even if some of my other memories I could do without.

When I arrive, I can hear an Irish reel from outside—a fiddle and a mandolin along with a drum of some sort race through a song with no discernible beginning or end. It's festive but loud, so I'm pleased to see Finn sitting at a table near the back, far from the music.

He waves to me when he sees me and flashes a huge, crooked grin. It's endearing. He stands and gives me a quick hug when I reach him, then holds the chair out for me to sit.

"Thanks!" I say. "Wow, this place is cool," I add, looking around. There are Irish lutes hanging from the walls and dark mahogany walls and bar. People all around the dining area are tapping their feet, and an enthusiastic older couple near the band are actually dancing a jig.

"It's the place of my people," he says with a wink. "My name is Finn Murphy, after all. Can't get more Irish than that. Though to be honest, I do have two German grandmothers. Hence why I can't have a Guinness without also craving strudel."

I laugh. "I won't tell," I say.

We talk about what's good on the menu and order an assortment to share. He also orders a Guinness, sans the strudel, and I order a Bailey's. By the time our drinks arrive, we've dispensed with the preliminaries – where we live, how long we've lived in the Nashville area, how awkward on-line dating is.

Then the topic turns to what we do for a living.

"I'm a financial consultant," I say, and am pleased that, due to my recent engagement, it's a true statement. He asks a few follow-on questions, and I explain as best I can. "Not very exciting," I add.

"On the contrary! You're like a number ninja! Or maybe it's your cover, and you're actually an assassin."

"Like *The Accountant?*" I say, referring to the fairly recent movie.

"Oh, no, much cooler than that. Like Alias but with a calculator."

I laugh, because I loved that show. And while the conversation is a bit nerdy, he seems legitimately nice and he's making me laugh. That's a talent.

"How about you" I ask.

"I work as an audio engineer in the music industry. That's my day job. But I'm really a songwriter in my heart of hearts, in my 'way down deep,' so to speak." He says this with a wink and a sparkle in his eye that makes me smile.

"Songwriting seems so hard to me," I say. "And I love songs. Like, to sing them. I'm terrible remembering song titles, but if you sing a couple of bars, I'm off and singing it. In fact, I'm highly susceptible to song suggestion. But don't mess with me on that."

"Oh, I'm going to!" he says, laughing. "That sounds like tremendous fun! But songwriting isn't as hard as you think."

"How do you even think of what to write about? That seems like the hardest part. Well, and all the rhyming. And the melody."

"You have to be open to inspiration from anywhere. Like, we could write a song about something in your day today."

I raise one eyebrow. "I doubt that. Until meeting you, it has been completely boring."

He mimics my eyebrow raise, or tries to. "I've always wanted to do that..." His eyebrows raise in tandem, then he squints one eye, but it doesn't work. I laugh as he shakes his head. "I'm easily distracted," he says. "But let's get back on point. Of course we can! Tell me about your morning."

I think back, recounting a pretty boring day to myself. "I guess the only not-very-interesting thing that happened was that the donut shop gave me a free extra glazed donut, which of course I ate and immediately regretted. I have to limit myself to only one or else I gain three pounds. And then I have to eat 100-calorie soup, which is basically bullion-flavored water, for three days to offset it. So you see how an extra donut might *seem* nice, but it's actually a curse."

"I can work with that!" he says, clapping his hands and rubbing them together. "Hmm, let me think…" He composes in his head for a few moments, and I sit back and wait expectantly.

"Okay, I've got it!" He says, and arranges his hands like he's holding a guitar.

"Is that your air guitar?" I say and laugh.

"Why, yes it is," he says and smiles back. He does an imaginary strum and begins to sing:

DEAR DONUT SHOP, don't give me that extra glazed.
  I shouldn't have come to you anyway.
  I'll be eating soup for days…
  Dear donut shop, don't need those donut holes.
  Those extra pounds you give me
  Make me outgrow all my clothes…

I'M SMILING NOW, but he grins and holds up one finger, signaling me to wait for it—and then he breaks into the chorus.

OH DONUT SHOP, you don't know what this means!
  Such a love/hate feeling…
  You make me stretch my jeans…
  Oh donut shop, you're so good!! And yet so bad…
  Your chocolate cream-filled slice of heaven
  Was the best I've ever had…

· · ·

I'M FULL-OUT LAUGHING NOW, as he breaks into his fade-out, strumming all the while…

OH CALORIES... so many calories…
   It's even better than sex…
   But so many calories…

"WAIT–YOU have to hear my guitar solo," he says, riffing it up in silence on his imaginary guitar.

When he finishes, I break into applause, as do the couple of tables nearest to us, and he bows in his seat, but with a flourish. Then he carefully places his air guitar in the seat next to him, which makes me laugh again.

It feels good to laugh with a man.

Now that the applause has died down, I hear the buzzing on my phone. It's near constant.

"I'm sorry, my phone is blowing up. I'd better check it, in case it's an emergency."

I pull it out of my purse and see that there's a series of missed calls and texts from Gretchen.

*Missed call**
Text: 'Claire, I'm calling you. Please answer.'
*Missed call**
Text: 'I'm getting worried. This is not like you.'
*Missed call**
Text: 'Claire, you didn't answer my call. Are you okay?'
*Missed call**
Text: 'I'm freaking out here, Claire. Please tell me you're okay!!'

All of these occurred within about three and a half minutes.

I text her back: *'Yes, I'm fine. On a date. Are YOU okay?'*

She quickly fires back: *'Yes! I'm good! Perfectly wonderful, as a matter of fact! Didn't mean to interrupt your "date"!! Call me back when you're done!! Doesn't matter what time!'*

That is a lot of exclamation points for one text stream. It sets off alarm bells in my head.

"Is everything okay?" says Finn, and he sounds genuinely concerned. His brown eyes really are warm, kind-looking.

"I'm not sure," I say honestly.

"You're not trying to ditch me, are you?" he says with a half-smile, but there's insecurity in his voice.

"No, not at all," I assure him. "I'm actually having a good time," I say, and now I'm the insecure one, wondering if he's feeling the same way.

But he lets me off the hook. "Me too," he says.

The rest of the dinner is pleasant, filled with lots of talking, some of which I come to discover is contrived for a specific purpose. It's after he's sprinkled the conversation with odd phrases like, "Don't stop believing," "I want to know what love is," and "Naughty girls need love too," that I recognize he's baiting me with song suggestion. Granted, the last one, which was quite the non sequitur despite his valiant attempts to bring it naturally into our conversation, was the giveaway. Or maybe it was when I started singing Samantha Fox under my breath and his triumphant response that was the actual tip-off.

"You've been messing with me!" I say, giving him a playful shove.

"Who, moi?" he says blinking wide with mock innocence, at odds with his devilish grin. "It's just so fun!" he adds, when I shove him again.

By this time, many of the patrons have left. Now it's mostly drinkers that remain. "Oh, wow. What time is it?" I ask, pulling out my phone.

"Late," he says, but I barely notice. I see that Gretchen has tried to call four more times, followed by more texts:

'Everything's all good here! Checking in to see if your date was over! Don't worry about me!'

And then, *'I'm freaking exhausted, so off to bed for me! Don't worry, I'm good to go! Talk to you tomorrow so I can hear all about your date!!'*

"Something wrong?" he asks, and I look up at him. All the

joking is gone, and he's concerned, his brown eyes radiating that kindness that originally drew me.

"I hope not," I say. "But I guess I should go. It's later than I thought."

"Oh, sure, of course," he says, suddenly nervous.

I don't want him to feel nervous. I place my hand on his. "This was fun, Finn."

His face lights up with the sweetest, cutest smile. "I think so, too, Claire. I hope we can do it again."

"I think that's a distinct possibility," I say with my own wink.

He walks me out, and I'm wondering if he's going to make a move, though I'm kind of hoping he won't. Not that I'm not attracted to him, because I am. But I'm still a bit raw, and distrustful, and so far, he has been so good.

He leans in and I freeze, but he doesn't kiss me. He gives me a sweet hug, two arms but not full-bodied, and precisely the right duration.

"Goodnight, Claire," he says as he opens my car door for me.

And that's it—I'm driving home, thinking through the highlights of the date, smiling at the memories, and trying not to worry too much about Gretchen.

FOURTEEN

Hotel California

MARCH

IT'S a couple of days after my date when Gretchen sends Tasha and me a group text. A couple of days of not being able to get in touch with her, other than via a few sporadic text exchanges. In them, she insists she's fine! That she's handling things better than ever!

Tasha and I have discussed it, discussed our growing concern at the odd tone of her communications. But Gretchen's not answering her phone, and so we take her at her written word, even if she sounds a little off.

But the group text is troubling: '*Girls, this may be the last time you hear from me from this number. Things are not what they seem. Please don't worry—just pray!*'

This time, we don't wait for her to answer her phone. I swing by and pick up Tasha, and we make a bee-line for Gretchen's place.

Tasha texts her to let her know we are coming.

"Did she reply? What did she say?" I ask, as I make my way down streets I don't normally travel, past pawn shops and liquor stores and empty storefronts with boarded-up windows.

Tasha reads from her phone: "She says, '*Not necessary! But will be good to see you. Better to talk in a safe place.*'" She sighs, leans her head back on the seat. "What. The. Fuck?"

"I don't know, but I'm worried."

"Me too."

I almost pass the apartment complex—the sign is small and insignificant compared to the neon tire store sign and the Quick Mart next to the entrance, and the complex itself is tucked away down a long drive so that you can't see it from the road. I've been here before, but it's like my brain doesn't want to remember the way. Maybe it's because I rarely come here unless something is wrong.

Gretchen is standing outside when we get to her apartment. She's clutching a ragged purse with one hand and smoking a cigarette with the other, and I can see it shaking before we even get out of the car.

Her white-blond hair is wild and curly, and it trails out behind her as she hurries to greet us. She negotiates a grasshopper green Datsun with a trailer hitch and a motorcycle with orange flames and a basket on the front.

"You are just in time," she says to me and Tasha as she opens the rear door, and then she's climbing in the back seat and rolling down the window so she can continue to smoke.

Chris is holding Carson in the window, helping him wave goodbye to us. Carson sports a wide-open toddler grin, and Chris kisses him on the top of his fuzzy head as he lets the curtain drop.

I wave back, but Gretchen doesn't. "Are you okay?" I ask, as we back up, and slowly then make our way out of the sad apartment complex. She's clearly not.

"There's stuff going on here that you have no idea about," she says.

Tasha reaches back to squeeze her hand. "Like what, honey?"

"You don't want to know. Trust me—it's better that way."

Neither of us responds, but we share a quick look, careful not to let Gretchen see.

I drive the two miles to the city park and we pull up alongside a silver mini-van with a dent in the rear fender. There's a family walking down by the pond—two parents and a little girl. The girl has a bag of bread in her hand and she's feeding the small flock of ducks that have surrounded them.

Gretchen eyes them suspiciously, so we guide her away from them toward an old picnic table covered in bird crap, like nature's mocking version of a Jackson Pollock painting—decidedly unintentional and consisting, literally, of shit. I select a spot with the least amount of defilement and she plops down across from me, Tasha beside her.

Now that we're here, I'm not sure how to start. I'm relieved when Tasha does it for me.

"So what's wrong? Talk to us."

Gretchen shakes her head. "So many things. So many things," she says, taking a long drag from her cigarette. It distorts her face, aging her. "There's so much that you two don't know about. You wouldn't even believe it if I told you."

"Like what?" I say, but she doesn't hear me because she's become distracted eyeing the family. I glance over as the dad scoops his daughter up and out of reach of the now frenzied ducks.

There is a crushed Dr. Pepper can on the ground and a rolled up napkin stuffed between two boards in the table. Gretchen jumps up and retrieves them, muttering under her breath as she throws them into the nearby barrel trashcan with unexpected force.

"Cleaning up here, there and everywhere. Because who the hell else is going to, that's what I'd like to know."

But we're patient, and she eventually sits back down and takes a drag, patting her hair with her free hand. I repeat the question, and this time she answers. "Well, for starters, Chris got physical with me. I was running a bath, and he literally threw me up against the wall. Said it was an 'accident,' the door 'stuck' and whatnot." Her air quotes are angry. "But stumbling is not an excuse. And a door doesn't grab wrists. I had to kick him to get away. I suppose that's a 'good excuse...,'" again, the angry air quotes, "... for why the neighbors called the police."

Tasha's eyes grow wide. "No shit? Did they come?"

But I'm shocked. "Why would he do that?"

"Yes, they came, but they were watching anyway." She waves her hand in the air. "They know what to look for."

I attempt to keep the conversation on course. "What happened when the police came?"

"That old 'he said, she said.' That was it. No charges pressed, blah-blah screw the order of protection, everything is hunky dory." She leans in. "But I know better."

Tasha pats her own cigarette out of the pack she's been carrying and sticks one in between her lips, flicking a lighter against the tip. "What the fuck are you talking about?" she says out of the side of her mouth as she lights it, squinty and barking, like a wise guy in an old gangster movie.

"Jonathan," Gretchen says, leaning back and slapping her hands on the table, careful to preserve her cigarette. As if invoking her ex-husband's name explains everything.

Uh-oh. It is always a bad sign when she brings him up. "What's Jonathan got to do with anything?" I ask, though I'm almost afraid to.

"He's got people everywhere. I see them, even though they try to hide. That's why I'm trying to talk quietly," she adds, gesturing toward the family who is obviously completely disinterested in us. "You should keep your voice down. I've seen that van before. It parks across the street from my apartment. Pretty convenient, wouldn't you say?"

I hesitate about whether to argue with her as she takes a deep drag, and blows smoke that swirls around us in a cloud. I can tell she's getting agitated, so I try to be gentle. "Honey, Jonathan's not having people watch you."

"Don't you dare underestimate him," she hisses, grabbing my hand. Her fingers dig into my palm. "You can't afford to be a fool about any of this, Claire. Neither can I, for that matter." She lets go and I rub my palm under the table.

She shakes her head then. "We're all in the same boat, if you really think about it. Asshole ex-husbands. Police. What-the-fuck apartment managers. Okay, maybe not you, Claire—mortgages and whatnot. Hotel California."

"I'm sorry, what?" says Tasha, tossing me a look.

"Hotel California. The Eagles. You know, the *code*." She sighs. "It hasn't changed since Group."

Tasha's eyes widen and I am sure my expression equally conveys my confusion. Gretchen looks pointedly at us. "You know the line! I can't say it out loud, but it's how you think you've escaped, but you're really trapped? Remember?" Her eyes are wild, insistent. "Just the tip of the iceberg. But I can't write it down anymore. That's why they took my journal at the hospital. For the *Code*."

Tasha looks at me then and we silently communicate—do we try to convince her that her thinking is completely distorted and, for lack of a better term, jacked up? Will it even do any good? I feel so impotent, and I know, without a doubt, that she needs help beyond what we can give her. I try to think of the words to say to convince her that it's time to go back to the hospital. But Tasha doesn't wait for me to be tactful or delicate.

Instead, she crushes her cigarette in a knothole on the table surface and grabs Gretchen's arm. "Gretchen, look at me," she says, and Gretchen does, expectantly. "I love you, girl, but you know me —I don't sugarcoat for fuck. And honey, you're talking bat shit crazy right now."

I wince—I can't help it—and I wait for Gretchen's reaction. But to my surprise, she merely pats Tasha's hand and smiles a sad, sympathetic smile. "And that's exactly what they want you to think," she says.

The words, the look on her face, are a sharp stab to my heart.

By unspoken accord, Tasha and I decide to take Gretchen on a walk around the pond. Gretchen sets a brisk, manic pace, and we adopt our best power-walker forms to keep up. We start toward the end opposite of the family, hoping she'll forget about them, but she looks for them every few steps anyway, to be sure they're not following.

She keeps up a steady stream of chatter as we walk, and it's disjointed and yet follows her own kind of logic, threads that lead to other threads that lead to simultaneously obvious and yet ridiculous conclusions.

By the time we've circled twice, the family is gone, and Gretchen finally starts to slow. I can't imagine the energy it takes to be hyper-vigilant, paranoid, and power-walking at the same time.

She hugs us tight at the car when we suggest we take her home. She suddenly looks exhausted.

"I don't know what I would do without you girls," she says. "I have to have people in this life that I can trust. It is beyond essential to my sanity and to the safety of all involved."

We hug her back and herd her into the car.

As we pull out into traffic and head back to her place, I have no doubt that Tasha and I are sharing the same, quiet thoughts, as we take turns glancing back at our friend, now sleeping, in the back seat.

How do we help our dear friend when she doesn't know she's sick?

Date #... Suspiciously Still Really Good
With Finn

I'M NOT sure what to think about Finn. It's not that he hasn't been wonderful, because he has. He sends me sweet texts throughout the day to let me know he's thinking about me, and he sends or brings me fresh flowers just because. And our dates have been awesome—not sexual so far, but companionable and fun. We went roller skating, which I haven't done in years, but which I still rock at, btw. Though I will admit I was sore in muscles I forgot I had for a couple of days after. We went to see an indie movie about a love story intermingled with incredible food in the French countryside and then had wine and cheese after so we could discuss. And we've been to several music venues, supporting other struggling artists in solidarity, and slow dancing to the music both when and when not appropriate. But mostly we talk. About philosophy and spiritualism and humanitarian crises on the other side of the world and at our own borders. We are bonding at a soul level, because we *hear* each other. He helps me understand what I believe in, when I've never before had the time or the energy to ferret out my deepest foundations for myself. I am a deeper person for knowing him, and it connects us.

And he still hasn't tried to get me into bed, which I both appreciate and am suspicious of at the same time.

The truth is, he seems really great, and I think that's what scares me. Because Brandt had seemed great, too. What if I can't trust Finn? What if he's not what he seems?

What if he lets me down? I'm not sure I can handle that again.

Tonight, he's coming over to cook for me. Apparently, he's quite the accomplished amateur chef, so he's going to make me mushroom risotto for dinner. I'm preparing a cheese and charcuterie board, with wine of course, as an appetizer, and feeling nervous, because it's the first time he'll be coming to my house, and I'm not sure what that means. I don't know where this is going. I want a relationship, and not only will I not tolerate abuse of any sort, I also don't want games or other bullshit. And that also means I need someone that is not going to judge me because of my Depression. I need someone that's going to understand it and be supportive of me. And I need someone who is exactly who he seems.

Bottom line, I don't want to waste my time, or his either, for that matter. So I think tonight is a good time to have some hard discussions.

He arrives on time bearing fresh daisies and an armful of groceries, which I help with as soon as I open the door. He kisses me after we've unloaded everything on the counter, and it's lingering and sweet and also sensual. I feel something stir in me that draws my body to his, and he tugs at my waist for a moment but then lets go.

My vagina protests, but my head and heart appreciate his respect.

We chat as he gets dinner going, me propped on one of the island stools while he stirs and sautées in front of me. Then it's time for it to simmer, so he joins me for wine, cheese, grapes, tapenade and a selection of Italian meats.

"Oh, yummy," he says, as he takes a bite of aged Irish white cheddar and tapenade on a cracker.

"Why are you not married? Is something wrong with you?" I say, jumping right into this conversation that has been weighing on my mind. But I say this with a laugh to lighten the tone.

He sits back, a little surprised, but he doesn't protest. "I was married for five years. Until my early thirties."

My eyes widen. "Oh, really? What happened, if you don't mind me asking?" I have already told him some about my marriage and divorce on previous dates. Not *ad nauseam*, but an appropriate amount for him to understand what I've been through and some parts about where I've been—though I have not yet told him about my Depression.

But this is the first I'm hearing about this.

"I used to work for a world relief organization, and that's where I met her." I raise my eyebrows at this, but say nothing. I'm learning all kinds of information tonight. "We lived all over the world for a while, working in different countries that had various crises that needed our help—hunger, medical care, disaster relief. And we loved it. Or at least, I did. It was an existence that suited my free-spirited side. But then she got promoted, and they wanted her to work at the headquarters in DC. I struggled with that huge change in lifestyle. I mean, we were used to living in huts or tents or dilapidated tenements and having very few belongings, and doing really meaningful work in a way that we saw the direct impact. And all of a sudden she wanted the corporate life and a mortgage. She thought I should want that to."

"So you left her?"

"No, not exactly. At first, we tried the long distance thing, because I didn't want to give up the work in the field. But then that was not working, so I decided to live in DC with her and go back to school. But I struggled with it, and she got frustrated being the primary breadwinner. Plus, she hit thirty-five and suddenly she felt like her biological clock was about to come to a hard stop. She wanted a baby, and I thought that would add to the stress in our marriage. Eventually, we decided we didn't want the same things anymore."

I chew on that for a few minutes. What does that say about his ability to commit long-term? I mean, no one ever said marriage was easy.

He speaks to my concerns before I can even voice them. "I know what you're thinking, that we didn't try hard enough. And maybe we didn't. But it is what it is, and I was a different person back then."

Hmm. "In what way, and what changed you?"

"Well, after we divorced, I went straight back into the field, and I lived kind of wild and free, you could say. There were a lot of women in a lot of different places, women who weren't looking for anything long-term either. And, full disclosure, there were some questionable smoking sessions in Southeast Asia and a few existential mushroom experiences in South America as well. I guess I thought I was fitting into the culture, so to speak. That's all behind me now, of course," he says with a smile. Then he sighs, runs a hand through his dark curls, making them stand up. "My life drove my family crazy because they never saw me, and my mom in particular was convinced I would never settle down and have a family."

"Didn't you want that?" I ask.

"I did… someday. But then I got cancer. Testicular. I came here to Nashville to be close to my parents and get my treatments, and when they were over, my whole future looked different. My dreams of one day having a child of my own were gone, and my 'someday' became 'never.'"

"I'm sorry," I say, and reach over to squeeze his hand. He squeezes back before letting go. We both take a sip of our wine and we sit in silence, each thinking about what he's said. It's heavy, his story, and he's in the past for a few moments before he returns and continues.

"After all my treatments were over, I realized my wandering days were over too. I was too old to live like a vagabond any longer, and the things that weren't important to me before became more important—things like being near my family, and maybe finding someone to live this life with. It's cliché, but facing your mortality in a way you have so little control over changes your perspective. I mean, they always say that, but it's true. I'd been in dangerous spots many times—in my work in Africa and the Middle East, especially—but that was also exciting. This wasn't."

He reaches for the board and I hand him the toast so he can add some gorgonzola and prosciutto. I don't know if he's really hungry after telling that story, or if he's occupying himself so he doesn't break.

He takes a bite, gazes out the window into the night. "Everything changed, I had to figure out where to go from there. I got a marketing degree when I went to college originally, but I never used it because I went straight into charity work, basically working my way up. So marketing was out. Plus, I'm not sure I ever really liked it—I'd only picked it because my dad wanted me to do something in business, and marketing at least has some creativity involved." He smooths down his hair. I guess he can feel that it was standing on end.

"Anyway, I started to think about what I'd like to do for a living, besides travel the world helping people, and I thought of music, because I'd always loved it, always played guitar and sang and messed around with arrangements and lyrics. But this time, my head wasn't so in the clouds. I had to pay real bills—I couldn't rely on the meager living expenses being funded by my job in some third world country, or on the virtually non-existent income of a struggling singer/songwriter. And I actually decided I wanted a car and a mortgage, because you need all those things if a good woman is going to take you seriously someday as a potential mate." At this, his mouth turns up on one side, and he gives me a wink. But it's tempered with the seriousness of the discussion.

"So I went back to school to be a sound engineer, got a job off Music Row, and I pursue my passion in my spare time. All very sensible and grown-up, if I do say so myself." He smiles and raises his glass to me, and I clink it against mine.

"Yes, quite so," I agree with an answering smile. That was not such a bad past. It does give me slight pause that he can't father children, but maybe my time has passed for more biological children, as sad as that is. And honestly, maybe I couldn't handle another child, anyway.

And that sucks, but there it is.

He must see something in my expression. These days I'm not great at hiding my emotions.

"What are you thinking? Did I scare you away with any of that?" He looks worried, and that warms my heart. Not in pleasure at his discomfiture, but because he doesn't want to lose me.

But he doesn't know my shit yet.

"No, Finn. I'm just thinking that there are some things you need to know about me, too," I say, straightening my spine and inhaling deeply in preparation.

He sits back, but he doesn't look afraid. "I'm ready for whatever you have to tell me," he says, and I believe that he means it. "But first let me stir the risotto." He kisses my cheek and goes around the island to the simmering skillet on the stove. I like watching him— now that he's unburdened himself on me, he's visibly lighter, even knowing that I'm about to tell him something that he might not expect. He hums Blackbird, one of my favorite Beatles songs, to himself as he works, and I'm filled with warmth when he joins me again in his seat.

"Okay, lay it on me. And don't be gentle," he says. I push him playfully, but quickly sit back, bracing myself for his reaction.

I tell him all of it—about my Depression, and how it may have originally been situational, but now it's become a part of my life. About how I've not worked much in the last two years, and why that is, but also how hard it's been on me and who I've always believed myself to be. How I'm getting a little better, but that I'm still not great and may never be again. And about Tasha and Gretchen and how sick they can be, but also how loving and brave and integral to my life.

I even mention how worried I am for Gretchen right now, how crazy she's been sounding, talking about codes and constantly on the look-out for people that are "watching" her. I don't leave anything out. Because I'm not messing around, and I'm not going to waste one more minute on someone who doesn't get it.

"So that's pretty much it. A big pot of fucked-up soup, that's what my life has turned into. My friends and I have accepted it, and it works for us. But I'm not going to apologize for it. You either accept that I'm a mess, or we need to agree to just move on."

And then I wait for it—the judgment, the rejection. I don't even

ANGELA HOKE

relax when he stands, without words, and pulls me into a big, full-body hug.

"You are an incredible woman," he says into my hair.

I shudder. "Why?" I say, because I don't understand. I'm damaged, battered, but not incredible.

"Because your strength is boundless. I've seen you struggle to heal, and you never ask for pity. You fight your way down a path and when it ends at a cliff, you backtrack and look for another. And I've seen the way you love your friends, and the way you love your daughter. Even though I've never met them. I see it because of how you talk about them, how you hurt when they hurt, and you revel when they feel joy. You get knocked down but you claw your way back up, and you bring your friends and daughter along with you." He pulls back, looks into my eyes.

"What you've told me reinforces what I already knew—that you are amazingly strong, stronger than I've ever had to be."

I widen my eyes. "You had cancer," I say.

"Yes, but I knew what my enemy was. I could see it, and I had a clear path to fight it. It wasn't confounding, just shitty luck. And, everyone got how sucky it was and jumped in to help me without question. That's the only good thing about cancer—people get it, and there's no judgment."

He leads me to the stools at the island and he takes my hands as we sit. "Getting cancer was the first time I ever had to be a grown-up. You've had to be a grown-up your whole life, always responsible. That's a heavy weight to bear. And to have a manipulative spouse and a depression that defies logic and treatment, those are the kinds of burdens that people don't understand. And that makes it even harder. And I gotta admit, the way you love your people is intoxicating. Not like a good glass of whiskey that burns hot and then slowly fades, but like an addiction that forms new neuro-pathways in your brain. It is self-sustaining."

He smiles at me. "You have a heart a big as Old Hickory Lake. Bigger even, and a lot more pure because that lake is gross."

I laugh, but it turns into a little sob. Because I want this so much

198

—to be accepted, especially now that I'm this different, broken person.

And not because I need a man, because I don't. I've learned, these past months especially, how to be alone.

But if he, by all appearances a good, honest man, can accept me, as screwed up as I am, maybe I can accept me too. And that's the hardest part.

He pulls me back into his arms and holds me tight until finally I release my fears and tension in waves, starting in my temples, moving down to my neck and shoulders, and finally in my chest and stomach. I literally melt into his embrace, and he holds me up.

It feels amazing. When I tilt my head back to look up at him, he's gazing at me so tenderly, I melt again, metaphorically speaking, and I press my lips to his. He kisses me deeply, and my head spins, and suddenly I'm filled with desire. I press myself to him more fully, and he feels it and responds, running his hands under my shirt and along my waist and lower back. I clutch him to me, shivering at his touch, and push my hips against his. He moans into my mouth.

And then the stove timer goes off. I feel the change in his body instantly. What was fire and desire calms into affection, and after a moment, he pulls away and puts his forehead down to meet mine.

"I hate that thing," I say.

"I know, but I'm glad it went off. I don't want our first time to come out of our vulnerability. I want it to come from love," he says softly to the backdrop of the beeping stove.

"I hope we don't have to wait too long," I say, our lips still raw and engorged and only inches apart.

"Don't worry," he says back. "It won't be long."

FIFTEEN

A Rocket Trip Down the Rabbit Hole

APRIL, FOR THE THIRD TIME

IT STARTS with a frantic phone call from Chris: "Gretchen is at the Snappy's gas station. You have to help me!"

He's awakened me from a nap, so I'm trying to clear my head, focusing on the twilight that's streaming through my blinds. *Damn, I didn't mean to sleep so long.* I am firmly a day-napper. I like to lie down when the sun is bright, and wake up when it's still bright. Somehow, these self-imposed constraints on my nap behavior make me feel like my napping is controllable, not interfering with my overall daily existence.

"Carson, don't eat that! Give it here," he's saying, which brings me back into our conversation, and reminds me that I don't know what he's talking about or what is happening.

There is commotion in the background, and then heavy breathing as he comes back to the call. "So can you help?"

"Chris, what are you talking about? Tell me what's going on."

He blows out a big breath, and it is amplified in the phone. "Gretchen took off from the apartment. On foot. Me and Carson have been driving around looking for her for two hours. I just found her at the Snappy's on the corner of Dickerson Pike, and she won't get in the car."

Oh, hell, I think. She's gotten worse.

"I'm afraid she's going to run off, that I'll lose her again. And I've got Carson with me…"

"Okay, okay. Let me get dressed and I'll come. Try to keep her as calm as you can."

"I'll try," he says, and we hang up.

I throw on a t-shirt, no bra, and yoga pants and search briefly for my flip-flops. Then I'm out the door. On the way, I try to call Tasha, but she doesn't answer.

It takes me almost thirty minutes to get to the gas station, and it's fully night by the time I get there. I'm beyond relieved to see Chris's gray Taurus parked along the edge of the parking lot, and Gretchen pacing just beyond it under a bright streetlight. She's burning a track in the six-foot patch of pavement, as she stalks first one way then the other, smoking a cigarette that has an inch of ash clinging precariously to its base.

I pull up next to Chris's car and get out. He's sitting on the hood, trying to wrangle a squirming Carson and keep him from escaping.

"Daddy, I want down!" he says. "I want Mommy!"

Chris visibly sighs in relief when he sees me. But I give him no more than a cursory nod, as all my attention is focused on my friend. I approach her slowly.

"Gretchen?" I say, and she whips her head around at the sound of her name.

I hear Chris in the background. "Let's go inside and get a snack," he says to Carson, and then they're walking toward the store.

But I can only look at Gretchen, who I'm watching closely to look for signs that she's ready to bolt. But to my surprise, she tosses her cigarette and runs at me.

"Oh, Claire!" she says, slamming into me and hugging me fiercely. "You don't know what I've been through!"

I hug her tightly back, and she is shaking, trembling through every extremity as though wired with electricity.

"It's okay," I say into her hair, which is oily and stringy and smells like stale tobacco.

Finally she pulls back, and I suggest we get in my car to talk, thinking that confining her will make it harder for her to take off. But she refuses, backing up.

"I can't do it, Claire. I can't get inside something so small." So instead I persuade her to go sit on a nearby bus stop bench.

It's once I'm seated next to her that I can smell the body odor—the unwashed, sweaty smell of someone who has forgotten, or is unable, to bathe. But the scent is whipped away by the low wind as she promptly fishes another cigarette from the purse that's slung on her shoulder, her hand shaking as she tries to light it. I reach out to steady it and she mutters a thank you.

When she takes the first long drag, she seems to settle back into the seat a little, calming a bit. But I know it will be short-lived, so I seize the opportunity to try to have a conversation with her.

"So what happened, sweetie?" I say gently.

"It's all a mind fuck," she says, and is instantly agitated again. "Chris said this and that, psych meds and caseworkers and restraining orders, and it's all bullshit. He can't take my child away!"

I'm taken aback, but only a little. The state she's in right now, I wouldn't necessarily blame him for wanting to get Carson away from her.

"Is he threatening to take Carson away?" I ask.

"Words and phrases, they all mean the same thing!" she says, and her eyes are so wide the white shows. They are slightly yellow, I notice. "He knows what he's doing. He knows exactly what he's fucking doing. Just like Jonathan. They are all the same, and I don't have to fucking live like this."

"Okay," I say, not sure what to say. She's ranting and making absolutely no sense. She needs to go to the hospital right now. Thankfully we're not far from one—ironically, the one where we met. I try to think of a way to say this that won't cause her to run off into the night.

She grabs my arm. "There he is." Sure enough, Chris is coming back out of the store with Carson. They're holding packages of powdered donuts. "That mother fucker. I don't want this shit. He's not who he 'claims' to be." She makes air quotes with her fingers around the word.

"What do you mean?"

"He's not the great electrician with a good job that everybody thinks. He's just a man. A small, pathetic little man. I deserve a real man. A man that loves and respects everything I stand for."

"He seems like a good man…"

"You're fooled! Like all the rest! That is his freaking superpower, besides wining and dining at the local bar."

He actually does seem like a decent man, though. Not perfect, I'm sure, as no one is. But he stands by her even when she's sick, and that's saying something. That actually says a lot.

Chris convinces Carson to climb into the car so they can sit and enjoy their spoils, but he looks at me questioningly. I shake my head —what that means, I'm not sure. I guess it means that I've not yet made much progress.

It's a delicate process.

Gretchen stops talking to take another long drag, and settles back again, momentarily marginally calmer. So I decide to try once more to find out what happened, if nothing else, to try to lead into why she needs to go to the hospital.

I don't look at her, rather I stare straight ahead at the passing cars and the dark trees on the other side of the street, and I speak softly. "Gretchen, can you tell me why you ran from the apartment?"

But that instantly re-ignites her fury. "Who says I ran? Did that asshole say I ran? That's fucking typical. Spinning stories. It's what he does best."

"But… you did leave. You walked a good three or four miles to this gas station."

"Fuck! Why can't a person get away once in a while? Why does it have to be a big fucking production? I need a break sometimes, you know. Carson is a lot of work, and ass-wipe over there is not that much help. But of course he's fucking dad of the year."

Wow. She feels fully justified. I choose my words carefully. "I'm sure you need a break. But walking down these busy streets when it's getting dark is dangerous, Gretchen. And no one knew where you were."

She stomps her foot. "I'm not a goddamned child! I don't have to account for my whereabouts like a prisoner release program. I have rights!"

Then she whips her head around and glares at me. And in a disturbingly quiet voice she says, "Holy shit, you're fucking in on this, aren't you?" She physically leans back from me, scooting away on the bench.

Oh shit.

"I'm not in on anything," I say, but she's shaking her head at me, slowly, as though in disbelief. Or, in her demented mind, disturbing realization. "Gretchen, do you hear me?"

"Then why the fuck are you here? How in the world did you know to show up here, in this exact spot, on this exact night?" She's getting up now, and I reach out for her arm, but she snatches it away.

"Chris called me," I answer honestly. "He's very worried about you. You're…" I pause, gather my courage. Because I know it's the truth, and I know she needs to hear it. But I also know that it will set her off like nothing else. The scariest thing about Gretchen's illness, when it reaches its foulest, most vile point, is worse than anything that Tasha and I must endure. Because Gretchen, bless her sweet soul, *doesn't realize she's sick.*

But I say it anyway. "You're sick, honey."

"Oh, fuck you, you fucking bitch!" she spits, jumping away. I'm stunned at her words, by the look on her face.

"Gretchen, I…"

"Don't even try to come up with some excuse! You are fucking in on the whole damn thing!" She turns away and starts walking, and my momentary paralysis releases me. I jump up to go after her, as I hear Chris opening his car door, calling for her.

But she's walking fast and ranting words that are being carried away with the wind. I jog to catch up and grab her arm tight, and it's a good thing because she tries her best to pull away.

"Assault!" she screams then, and I do let go. But to my surprise, she doesn't immediately run off again. Instead, she puts some distance between us, ten feet or so, and glares at me with absolute hate in her eyes.

"Gretchen, please listen…" I begin, but she cuts me off.

Her voice has turned calm, cold, and somehow that is worse. "I'm not going to listen to a goddamned word you say, you fucking cunt. You and your judgmental life and your so-so house, and your fancy fucking college-type job. You have fucking Ev-Ery-Thing." She draws out that one word, as though to do so makes it true. "You judge from your fucking high horse and we're all little piss-ants under your feet. But you want to know the truth?"

As I stand there, once again stunned into silence, a glob of slobber drips from her lip. She's drooling from the intensity of her anger.

"Your husband was fucking smart to ditch your ass. You are just a slut-whore bitch who can't even fucking get out of bed to take care of her own child."

I feel like I've been sucker-punched in the gut, and I grab one rasping breath before my airways spasm and leave me gasping.

"Gretchen," I sputter, and it comes out like a cough, weak. But then she does the worst thing. She *smiles* at me—an ugly, bitter, demented grimace that transforms her usually sweet, pretty face and leaves her old and rotting and ugly.

I stand there for a moment, frozen by the intensity of my confusion, of my hurt. And then my breath comes back and an unnerving calm settles over me. And *I walk away*.

"That's right, bitch!" she screams after me, but I don't care. I know full well how sick she is, but I think she might have permanently broken something between us. And I'm not sure it can be repaired… certainly not tonight.

So I walk, while she screams repugnant words at me that swirl around in the breeze, and I don't try to capture them. And when I get to Chris, he is standing outside the car, his mouth open in surprise and dismay, and he can't even form a coherent sentence when he attempts to speak. "What… what?"

"Call an ambulance," I say. "Or the police."

"I already did," I hear him say as I go to get in my car. But then the ambulance pulls up, followed by two squad cars, lights flashing but no sirens. They block my exit, so I collapse into my car seat and leave the door open, as uniformed persons spill out of their vehicles.

Chris comes to me first, holding Carson's hand, on his way to meet the officers and paramedics. "Can you please watch Carson?" he asks, and his eyes are pleading. They are a very bright, appealing pale green color, I notice for the first time—normally, all I see when I look at him is the mess of woolly beard and mustache that cover his face. But now I see his eyes and they are kind-looking.

I'm drained, hurt, shutting down, but I say yes. Because, what else can I say? That's my sister's little boy.

So I climb back out of my car and take Carson's hand and try to lead him away, but then Gretchen's running at me, screeching, her white-blonde hair flying out behind her like a tailwind. "Get away from my son, you fucking whore!"

But she doesn't make it far. The cops were calm and orderly, slow-moving, when they arrived, but now they spring into action, catching her and bringing her down to the ground in one deft motion.

Chris runs up to them, and the two other policemen reach for their stun guns and he halts. "She's sick," he says. "She's mentally ill, and she's very, very sick. Please don't hurt her," he begs with his hands raised in the air.

The officers facing him relax their postures and approach, presumably to take his statement, while the other two officers lift Gretchen off the ground and move her toward the nearest squad car.

But she barely seems to notice, because she's screaming at me the whole time. One of the officers talking to Chris breaks off and approaches Carson and me.

"Ma'am, are you involved in this?"

"I'm her... friend," I say. "And this is her little boy."

"You fucking, snobby cunt-whore! That is my fucking son!" Gretchen screams as they push her into the backseat.

The officer turns to me. "Ma'am, it might be better if you left."

I'm devastated. And indelibly wounded. And utterly defeated. Tears are streaming down my face, and I swipe them away. I look down at Carson, who is straining to release his hand from my grip.

"Mommy, mommy!" he cries, but I don't let go. Not until Chris walks up and gently removes his son's hand from my grip and scoops his little boy up into his arms.

But then the door to the squad car is shut, and while I can barely hear Gretchen screaming, now it is punctuated by sobs. I don't want to look, but I can't help it, and I see the most pitiful sight —my dear friend's face is contorted in a silent scream of agony on the other side of glass.

"We'll take her to the hospital," one of the other officers says to Chris. "Will you follow?"

"Yes," he says, and then walks away without another word to me. Not that he owes me anything—we are both, I suspect, equally wrecked by the events of the night. And he is absorbed with holding a small child that is now sobbing into his shoulder, and the thought of the tasks to come—admitting Gretchen, against her will, into the hospital.

The remaining policeman gives me a polite nod and turns to follow his partner to their car, and then the caravan of vehicles is leaving, and I'm left standing, alone.

I get in my car then, close the door, buckle my seatbelt. But I cannot drive, cannot formulate how to crank the ignition, how to find my way home.

So, instead, I simply sit and weep.

Date #... There Must be Something
Wrong With Him

I'M in a foul mood when Finn gets to my house for our date. I could say it's PMS or a shitty day at my consulting gig. But the truth is, I can't stop thinking about what Gretchen said to me.

Tasha has told me five times if she's told me once not to take it to heart, that Gretchen was out of her head. But if she was out of her head, how did she know exactly what to say to speak to all my secret fears?

Because what if my divorce was all my fault? What if I was a shitty wife, and a shitty mom, and I deserve everything I've gotten?

How can I ever hope to have a real relationship with a good man, when I don't actually deserve it?

And that makes me suspicious of Finn because clearly something must be wrong with him, that he wants me.

When he walks in, he greets me with a slow kiss and a long hug, both of which I normally love. Tonight I'm tense and stiff in his arms, and I'm sure he can sense it. He pulls away and looks at me questioningly, but I'm not ready to talk about it, might never be ready to voice the ugly thoughts that are circling my brain. So I keep my face neutral as he offers me a smile and a final kiss on the forehead.

"What's on the menu for tonight?" I ask, gesturing to the grocery bag he set by the door when he walked in.

He picks it up now, and leads me to the kitchen. "Arctic char with a basil pesto sauce and broccolini."

"Sounds really good," I say, because it does, damn it.

He removes the cork on a bottle of Shiraz that he's brought and pours us both a glass.

He raises his glass to mine. "To another beautiful night with delicious food prepared for a gorgeous lady by an incredibly sexy chef, all of which we get to enjoy together," he says, and we cheers each other.

He gets to work preparing dinner, having me chop some herbs with some wicked sharp chef knives he brought with him in some cloth compartmented wrap thing, specifically for this purpose. He has been working on a new song for a while now, and he sings his latest version for me, and I find myself unconsciously harmonizing with him.

He stops mid-chorus when he hears me do this. "What are you doing?"

"Oh, I'm sorry. I do that—I harmonize with songs that I like. I didn't mean to mess you up."

He sets down his towel and spoon and comes around the island to where I'm seated and gives me a spontaneous kiss and a squeezing hug.

"No, don't stop! I love that you are doing that! It sounds so awesome with your harmonies, and it makes me feel like we're creating music together!"

He's alight with happiness as he looks at me, and I can't help but smile back, even though I'm thinking that this is all too good to be true. That this wonderful, sweet, romantic man is either secretly an awful person, or else he is not getting who I really am.

This can't be real.

Once dinner is ready, he lights candles on the island and refills our wine glasses and we take a seat next to each other. I've been trying to keep up conversation because he has really done nothing wrong, and I know this, but to be perfectly honest, he's done most of the talking.

This is not all that unusual—he's a talkative man, and I like that about him. I feel like I never have to worry that silence will overtake our relationship.

So I think I'm fooling him pretty well, and that's a good thing. No sense voicing my doubts when I know they are probably not rational.

But even knowing this, I'm still thinking them.

But to my surprise, he does notice. I guess I was not paying attention when he asks me a question, and he calls me out on it.

"Is everything okay?" he asks. "You've been awfully quiet tonight. Are you... are you feeling okay?"

Aww, shit. He means, am I depressed. I don't know whether to be pissed off at the question or appreciate that he's concerned about me.

I think I'll settle on being pissed off, because what if his apparent concern is actually a lead-in to tell me how to fix myself, or worse, the beginning of him realizing the extent of my issues and him hitting the road.

"Yes, I'm fine, Finn. Just because I'm not especially talkative does not mean I'm falling apart."

He sits back in his chair, surprised at the vehemence in my words. "I didn't think that," he says carefully. "You haven't said much about Gretchen lately, since she was taken to the hospital. You worried about her?"

I sigh, suddenly deflated.

"I honestly don't know what I am. It was really awful, and she said some things that were... hurtful," I say, but what I think is '*true*.'

"It must have been terrible. For her and for you," he says. "I can't imagine somewhat I love being that mentally ill."

"Yeah, well, she can't exactly help it," I snap, and I jump up, walk around the island and then curse when I slosh my wine on the floor. "Damn it."

"Let me help," he says, and that annoys me even more. Who fucking said I needed help?

But he's already kneeling on the floor with a towel, wiping up the spill, and then he's taking the glass out of my shaking hand.

He wants to say something, I can see it in the way he's looking at me, but he's hesitating. Probably afraid I'll snap at him again.

"Say it already," I say, bracing for whatever it is.

"Can we sit, please?" he says. "There is something, but I'd like for us to sit."

Oh here it fucking comes. The judgment, the pity, the break-up that is inevitable. "I'd rather stand for this," I say sharply.

"Please, Claire," he says, taking my hand to lead me back to our seats. Reluctantly, I let him, because I want to trust him. So much.

Once we sit, I brace again. But I don't say anything. I'm not going to make this easier on him.

He looks at me with aching tenderness for several seconds before he takes a deep breath. "I'm not quite sure how to say this…" he says, and I hold my breath.

I don't comprehend him at first when he finally continues. Instead, I expel a deep whoosh of air and ask him to repeat it.

"I know that you struggle with your depression, and that you fight it like a demon. Or an avenging angel. Whatever metaphor you prefer. I also know…" He pauses again here and studies my face. I'm not sure what he finds in it, but he seems resigned as he continues. "I know that it still is always right at your back, hanging on to your shirttail even on your good days."

I can't help it, I think, swallowing the hurt and disappointment and willing myself not to get upset. But the words won't form. Because everything I feared is happening. It's too much for him, exactly like I knew it would be.

"I absolutely hate seeing you struggle so hard. You deserve more of a life than that," he continues, and all I can think is *Please, get it over with. Say it and leave so I can cry without you watching.*

But he doesn't say that. "I've been doing some research," he says, pulling a folded sheet of paper from his pocket. "I've looked into alternative treatments for treatment-resistant depression, and I've found something I wanted to show you." He hands me the paper, and my hand shakes as I unfold it.

I'm looking at it, trying to understand what I'm looking at, but I don't have to actually read it because he explains. "It's called Transcranial Magnetic Stimulation, or TMS," he says, and his voice is timid. "It's supposed to have the same beneficial effects of ECT in that it wakes up your brain, the part that's not working so well, but it doesn't have the side effects. No cognitive issues or memory loss. And you don't have to be put to sleep or miss work or anything. It works like an MRI, with magnets."

I look up at him, unsure what to say. What does all this mean?

"Are you trying to fix me?" I say at last. "Do you think I'm damaged goods?" I ask him. *Because I do. Say you think so too, because that I can believe.*

"No!" he says, taking my face in his hands. "I think you are the most beautiful woman. Sweet love, I just think you deserve to enjoy how wonderful you are more fully. You deserve to live a better life."

It's the first time he's ever called me that endearment, and something warms in my chest at the sound of it. But I'm still wounded and afraid.

The tears I've pushed back come anyway. "Are you saying that you don't want me the way I am?"

"You listen to me right now, Claire Colson. I am NOT saying that. I am saying that I want everything for you, not for me. I will be here no matter what."

He wipes my tears away with his thumbs, as I fight to keep them from flowing freely.

"Why?" I whisper. "Why do you want to be with me?" He hasn't said 'love' yet, I notice. But I'm starting to feel it all the same, and I don't understand it.

"Because you are smart and funny and lovely, and it is as if God made you for me and me for you. I wouldn't leave you now if you turned into a vampire and tried to suck my blood." It's a joke, and he smiles a little.

But I don't smile. "What if I can't be what you want? What if I can't be a good girlfriend, or maybe wife, or anything more than this broken person? I might never be more than this," I say, and it reminds of a very similar conversation I had with Brandt, one that didn't turn out so well.

"What I want is for you to be you, whatever that means. Because being you, exactly as you are, is perfect and right. And, Claire, listen to me." He takes my hands. "I do not believe for one second that you are irretrievably broken, because like I've said before, I see the strength in you. You have been very badly bruised, but you are healing, little by little, step by step. And one day, you won't be standing on the edge of the hole anymore, and another day, not long after that, you won't even be able to see it. You might not forget it's there, but it'll just be a dot on the horizon, indistinguishable from the trees and the fence posts and the fishing ponds."

"I can't picture it," I say.

He brushes his fingers down my cheek. "What's that, love?"

I sigh. "I can't picture a life where I'm not on the edge of the hole. I can't picture what feeling *whole* again might look like."

His eyes soften. "I can picture it. I can picture it all, your happiness and also mine. Your strength is a monolithic, granite mountain that endures. It towers over my own strength, which is nothing more than a twig and stick shanty I threw together to weather a passing storm. But your mountain and my shanty are stronger together. You can shelter with me, and your granite will keep the wind away. And we'll make pictures together—pictures of a life that is different and brighter than it was before."

What is he saying? "How can you know that?"

"I know all this because I'm in love with you. And I'm in love with you because I know all this. And nothing about what you've been through or what you go through scares me. On the contrary, it makes me so completely in awe of you."

I look into his dark eyes and they are depthless and loving and true. "Is this for real?"

"So, so real," he says, and kisses me. And because I'm still emotional, not crying, but raw, he draws me, wordless, into the bedroom and after laying me down, he lays down beside me. And then he holds me until I fall asleep and for the rest of the night. And his presence, with no expectation other than to be there for me, makes me feel truly safe with a partner for the first time, maybe ever.

It may be the most precious gift I've ever received from a man.

When I wake the next morning in his safe, protective arms, I feel lighter and something else… hopeful.

And I whisper what I knew last night but was too overcome to say—that I love him too.

And that, for my own sake and not his, I want to give TMS a try.

SIXTEEN

Maybe It's Better Not To Remember

MAY

THE SKY IS A BRILLIANT, cloudless blue on this otherwise ordinary day. Except, it's not ordinary, because today's the day we are supposed to pick Gretchen up from the psychiatric hospital where she's been for these past weeks. I should be happy—excited to see her, pleased that she's doing so much better. But I can't quite wrap my head around seeing her again. We haven't spoken since that awful night at Snappy's gas station, and I'm not sure I'm ready now. She changed everything between us with her words. And I'm not sure where that leaves us.

Tasha knows all this, knows what went down. I told her the basics about what happened and some of the wretched details that I could remember, but it's not the same as her witnessing it. And there were some things that were too terrible to repeat.

Even so, she appears to have other ideas.

"Suck it up buttercup and put on a bra. You have to come with me. You have no choice in the matter—she's expecting the both of us," says Tasha, standing in my kitchen drumming her fingers on my counter and jingling her keys in the other hand. I'm still seated at the island, sipping coffee and not at all sure that she's right.

"You weren't there, Tash. You don't know all the horrible things she said to me," I say. I shiver in remembrance of the hatred in her eyes, of the awful words that came out of her mouth.

Her tortured, silent scream in the police car window.

"I know it was bad." She drops her purse from her shoulder and onto the floor and takes a seat beside me. "But honestly, I'm not sure she remembers. She asks about you every time I talk to her, about why you haven't called or visited."

Again, I flash to Gretchen's enraged face. Gone in my mind is the Gretchen I once knew. Or at least, she's harder to conjure than the demented version. "I just couldn't do it," I say.

"I know that, but my point is, she doesn't. And you have to remember, she had ECT while she was there and from what I understand, that can really fuck up your memory."

I sigh. "I know. I hate that for her. I can't imagine being so sick that the doctors decide ECT is the only course of action."

Tasha steals a sip of my coffee. "Well, after her meltdown went nuclear, she went all catatonic and shit. That's what her doctor said."

This gives me pause. I've avoided asking too many questions about how she was doing, other than generalities. I wasn't sure what I would do with the information, as I was not ready to see her. Or forgive her. But now maybe it's time I know.

"What else did they say about her? Did they explain why she got so sick?" I ask. Gretchen had given Tasha, well both of us actually, the approval to talk to her doctor and clinical team in her presence. Tasha went. I didn't.

"It was really kind of sad. They said that her illness had most likely gotten worse and her medication wasn't keeping up. They prescribed new shit and upped what she already took. You know, it kind of makes sense now that her mom killed herself when Gretchen's kids were little. I mean, this crap is hereditary as hell. I think about that with my kids all the time."

"I didn't know she killed herself," I say. Gretchen had only told me that her mom died suddenly, and then a few years later her dad died of cancer. I had assumed stroke or heart attack.

"Oh yeah. She told me lots of random stuff when I went to see her, stuff that came up in her therapy and whatnot. But you're missing my point. They said her illness had gotten worse, and she was just kind of like smiling in the corner, all chill. It was almost creepy. Her brain is freaking fried, is what I think. So she doesn't remember shit. And bat shit crazy Gretchen has gone back into her hole."

That makes me really sad for my friend. First that she got so sick and didn't realize it, and now that she's weirdly serene and doesn't remember any of it. How horrible.

"So you gotta come. She will be heartbroken if you don't, and she won't understand why. In fact, you might want to think up some excuse to explain why you haven't called or visited too. Because I'm sure she'll ask."

I finally acquiesce and try to put my own feelings aside for the sake of my friend. But I'm nervous on the drive over.

As we pull up, we have to sign in with a guard stationed at a huge, ancient iron gate. We're on the list, so he ambles out of his guard shack and manually pulls the gate back to let us through, and we pull up to the rectangular white structure. It is stark with small square windows that look thick and reinforced, though not barred. There's no decoration, no winding pathways or flowering trees, no portico-ed entrance to welcome us. This is definitely not the same facility that Tasha went to and does not have the same pseudo-hospitable feel. Instead, this one is state-run, cold and institutional.

It is certainly no Twinkie House, and I say so to Tasha.

"Yeah, this is more like a HoHo House," she says, making me laugh the way only she can.

Gretchen is waiting for us on a sofa in the lobby when we walk in. There's a woman seated next to her holding a tablet. She looks official, and is wearing a badge, so I assume she's Gretchen's discharge social worker.

I pause at the sight of my friend, who is gaunt and pale, her usually gorgeous hair stringy and limp. Probably no access to good conditioners in the Ho-Ho House. She's clutching a large clear plastic bag with a draw-string top, full of clothes and a book or two, maybe a journal. She stands when she sees us, and she gives us a sweet smile.

Tasha immediately walks up to her and pulls her into a gigantic hug, and Gretchen's eyes leak tears.

"I missed you so much," she says, then gestures for me over Tasha's shoulder, and I join in the hug, because what choice do I have? None unless I want to act like a bitch.

"How come Chris didn't come get you?" Tasha says when we pull apart.

"He had to work and Carson's at his sister's. Plus, I didn't want Carson in this place. I don't want him to see me in here," she says, as she signs an electronic form on the woman's tablet.

"Can one of you please sign as well?" the woman asks. "We need documentation that Gretchen has a safe ride and a safe place to go from here."

"I will," I say, and my hand shakes as I use a stylus to sign the electronic document.

And then we're leaving, all of us too emotional to say much in the presence of the social worker and the receptionist.

Tasha hands Gretchen a cigarette as soon as we get in the car. "I bet you're jones-ing," she says.

"No, actually I quit while I was in there," Gretchen says, lifting her arm to show us the nicotine patch there. "Figured it was a good time to, since I didn't have much choice. But I could use a latte! I've missed good coffee."

"You got it, sister," says Tasha, and we head to the coffee shop. We don't stay there, though. We get our coffee to go and head to a nearby park so we can enjoy the pretty weather.

Once we're all seated at the picnic table, I have a sudden flashback to the last time we did this, when Gretchen was talking about Hotel California and "the code." I'm pleased to see her so much calmer this time.

"So how are you?" I say, not sure what else to ask.

"A little fuzzy, but better," she says. "I missed you." She leaves the burning question unasked, which is why didn't I visit her.

Tasha saves me from answering. "You look kind of like shit, but at least you're skinny."

"Well, thanks, I think," says Gretchen.

"I'm just saying, you were wanting to lose a few pounds. Who knew the Ho-Ho House was the answer."

Gretchen shrugs. "I guess... Not sure it's worth it for that, though."

"Clearly," I say, but then I stop. I don't want to open up any discussions that will be awkward. I'm still getting used to the idea of sitting across from her after what happened when last we were together.

"But in answer to your question, I feel decent. Kind of groggy, but they had me on some sedatives in there. Plus, the ECT made me kind of fruity. My memory is spotty. But we can talk about that later. I actually have good news to tell you." Her eyes light up at this.

"What?" says Tasha.

"Chris asked me to marry him!" she says, and she bounces in her seat, clapping her hands together.

I'm stunned. After the psychosis and police incident, I would have thought that Chris might want some distance. Wow.

"Are you fucking with us?" says Tasha, voicing my confusion but in much more direct terms.

"Not at all," says Gretchen, cocking her head. "Why would you think that?"

Tasha looks at me and gives me a WTF look. I shrug, almost imperceptibly.

Gretchen continues telling us the story. "Well, he doesn't have the ring yet. But he said that after going through all this with me, he definitely wants to make sure he's always here to take care of me. I thought it was sweet, even if it wasn't exactly the most romantic of proposals. But he did get down on one knee in the common room. Everybody clapped."

"Well, I'll be an angry witch's nipple clamp," says Tasha.

"Yeah, that," I say and laugh. "But congratulations!" We both give her hugs then, and she's beaming.

But then apparently I shake my head unconsciously, in

continued disbelief, and Gretchen picks up on it, despite her "fuzzy" mental state.

"What? What is it?" she asks. "Do you not think I should marry him?"

"No, no. It's not that. It's only… the last time I saw you," I pause, try to think of the words to say. I settle on: "You were not very nice to him."

"I wasn't?" She furrows her brow, obviously trying to remember.

"Do you remember when the police came?" I ask, not sure I should go there, but unable to stop.

"Barely," she says. "I remember being upset that he was keeping me under his thumb, and I wanted to get out for a while. And I remember the back of the police car. That's about it."

I sigh. I know Tasha had warned me, but how could she not remember any of it?

Tasha gives me a look then, and I'm not sure if it's a warning, or a "*See, I told you her brain is fried!*" look.

But Gretchen sees it, too. "What! You guys aren't telling me something. Did Chris do something while I was in the hospital?"

I make a decision in that moment to tell her what happened. At least, some of it. And I don't know if it's the right thing, but I think she should know. So I tell her most of what happened, what she said about Chris to me, the state she was in when I found her, and most of the awful things she said to me.

She looks at me like I've grown a third head. "That didn't happen. I would never say any of that," she says. She physically leans away from me on the bench.

Tasha reaches over and pats her hand. "You did, though. You can ask Chris. I'm sure he'll tell you."

She shakes her head, still incredulous. "But I wouldn't do that," she insists.

My heart hurts for her. "You're right—you wouldn't normally," I say, reaching out for her hand. She doesn't reach back though, and so my hand falters and I withdraw it. "But you were very, very sick."

She looks out at the trees, toward a jungle gym across the way. There are a couple of parents chasing small children around it.

She's quiet for some time, and I want to say something, but I don't know what.

"I'm not saying you're lying," she says finally. "I don't think you would do that. And why on earth would you? But you have to understand, I don't remember any of that. It seems impossible to me."

Tasha reaches for her this time, and I feel a twinge when Gretchen reaches back and they clasp hands for a moment. "I know, girl. Trust me when I say, you were bat shit crazy."

Gretchen smiles a little, but it doesn't reach her eyes. She's struggling with all this—it's easy enough to see.

Then something passes over her face, the blood draining away. "Oh God," she says.

I lean forward, reaching out again, and this time she takes my hand. "What? What is it?"

"Do you think that means… I mean, do you think I said those awful things to Macy, too?"

Oh my, I hadn't thought of that. But now, having seen her in full-blown psychosis, it makes sense. Because, like me, why would her daughters lie?

"Yes, honey," I say softly. "I think you probably did."

Her face registers this slowly and then crumples. "Oh, my poor girls," she says, as she weeps into her hands.

There's nothing really to say to that, so we gather close to her and put our hands on her in support, just so she can feel us near.

When she's through the initial shock of it, she calms a bit and I fish a clean tissue from my purse. She wipes her nose and eyes and sighs hugely.

"How do I fix this?" she says.

"Well," I say, looking at my friends, both of whom are staring back at me, hoping I have an answer. I don't, exactly. But I do have hope. "I'm not sure," I say honestly. "But at least now you acknowledge it's probably the truth. And I believe that's the start of healing your relationship with the girls."

"Yeah," says Tasha. "Admitting you have a problem is the first step. I learned that shit in NA."

Gretchen looks at us both intently, takes a big shuddering breath. "Then I will have faith that this is the first step towards seeing my girls again. Maybe all of this had a purpose after all."

Not sure I see any good purpose for someone to have to be that sick, but I don't disagree with her. Because hope is a good thing.

"I'm going to text them," she says then.

I'm surprised, and not sure that's the best idea without further consideration. But then, I tend to overthink things sometimes. "You are?"

But she's resolute. "Yes. No time like the present." She digs out her phone and puts in their names on the text so it will go to both of their phones. Then she thumbs a message. When she's finished, she turns the phone around so we can read what she's typed:

"My sweet loves—I just got over being really sick and had a great realization. I sometimes, apparently, say awful things when I'm sick. Things I don't remember and would never normally say, and things I definitely do not mean. So I want to tell you, I am so very sorry for hurting you with things I've said. You and your little brother are my greatest joy in this life. You are precious gifts from God, and I thank Him for you every day, that I get the amazing privilege to be your mom. Even if I don't get to see you. Please know that. And no matter what happens, I want you to know without question that I love you more than my life."

I read this and hitch my breath at the beauty of it. "Wow," I say. "Just, wow. Gretchen, I don't think you could have said it any better."

Tasha is nodding. "Girl, you about made me cry. That is eloquent as fuck, right there."

Gretchen smiles, genuinely this time. "Thank you." Without another word, she hits send.

Date with Gretchen, the Bride

THE BRIDAL STORE is not crowded for our dress-shopping date—I guess there aren't a lot of brides shopping for dresses in June on a Tuesday morning. I suppose that's the benefit of none of us working regular nine-to-five hours. Plus, most summer brides, except maybe the shotgun kind, shopped for their dresses months ago.

Gretchen has been giddy all morning, talkative and bouncy and more animated than I've ever seen her. Since I've known her, before I saw her really sick, she was always sweet but usually pretty even-keeled. I don't know if this is the new meds buoying her or the fact that we are shopping for her wedding dress.

She's been so excited and chatty, I don't think she's noticed that I haven't been. Or maybe it's that she's used to me being sullen and depressed. I hope that's not it. Because that's a sad freaking statement about how my friends perceive me.

I don't think I'm always the depressed person anymore, or at least not as much recently. I have been doing a lot better, in longer and longer intervals. Then again, Gretchen's missed much of my improvement—first in her psychosis, and then in her hospitalization.

But Tasha notices the difference. I've barely said a word, and she apparently is not going to let it slide.

"What the fuck is up with you?" she asks, when Gretchen goes back with the attendant to try on the third dress.

"What are you talking about?" I say, but I don't look at her. I walk over to the wall of bridesmaid dresses and run my fingers along them, stopping when I find a pretty turquoise one that I pull out a little to inspect.

"I'm talking about you acting like a Sad Sally on Gretchen's happy day. You depressed?"

I sigh. "No, not bad," I say, because while it's never gone, it's not in the front seat right now. "I just… I'm still struggling with Gretchen. It's hard for me to act like none of that stuff ever happened."

"It didn't happen," she says, tugging on my hand and pulling me over to the rose-colored sofa where we sit. "That was not Gretchen."

"But it was. I get it—I know she was so sick, and that she wasn't herself. But I told her, after, what all she said to me, and the thing is, she never apologized. It's like, she put me through hell, she put all of the people that love her through all kinds of hell and worry and stress, and there's no acknowledgement of it whatsoever."

Tasha looks at me for so long I start to squirm. She takes a breath, bites her lip, like she's trying to show restraint in whatever she's about to say.

Uh-oh.

"Okay, here's the thing, Claire. This is the thing about us. We're all seriously fucked up in the head. You think we liked seeing you when you could barely say two words and your hair was this nasty stinky mop on your head? When you sat like a lump of unwashed clothes on the couch while we talked about my trucker dudes and Gretchen told us about her cock-eyed nipples and we tried to make you laugh? Do you think it made us feel good when you didn't answer our questions, or ask about our lives, or remember that we see our kids a lot less than you see yours?"

My eyes fill and I shake my head silently, *No.*

"'No' is right," she says. "It was hard on us—not just that you weren't that much fun," she smiles a bit at this, and I know she's trying to make me smile too, lighten it a little, but it doesn't stop the sting in the words and the burning in my eyes. "No, it was hard because we hated seeing you so sick. We hated that for you and it was hard and stressful and a lot of fucking work to drag you out of that bedroom when you didn't want to do anything but sleep."

"I'm sorry," I whisper.

"You don't have to be fucking sorry," she says. She shakes my arm. "Listen to me, you don't have to be sorry for being sick. You couldn't help it, and we love you. That's it. We love you, and so we love you through your bullshit Depression. And we love, love, love to see you doing better. To see you smile, and even laugh, to get up without us having to physically drag you out from under the covers, to take a shower before you start to reek and even *fucking go to work*. We are so happy about that and for you that none of the rest of it even matters. Because we love you, and that includes the shitty stuff. We. Love. You."

Tears are streaming down my cheeks and I'm having a hard time containing my emotions. Because I love these girls so much, and she is right. I was a Depressed, depressive shit show, and they loved me anyway.

"Damn, I'm a bitch."

She laughs then, swipes at her own eyes. "You're our sister, and you've been there for our shit too. That's our club, and so long as we're not crazy at the same time, it fucking works."

I nod, trying not to sob.

"But here's the deal, Gretchen's sick is what it is. It's harsh and awful, but that's hers, and yours is yours. It doesn't matter. We love each other and we don't hold it against each other. We love each other through it. Got it?"

"I got it," I say, and I swallow, wiping my eyes one last time as Gretchen emerges.

She's a vision of satin and chiffon, and she floats in like a beautiful princess. I'm speechless, but Tasha gasps beside me.

We both jump up and rush to her.

"Gretchen," I say, through my tears that are threatening to come back. "This is the one. You are absolutely stunning in this dress."

Tasha's nodding. "Yeah, girl. This dress makes you look like a bad-ass, goddess-queen."

"Really?" says Gretchen, but then she turns to face the full-length mirror and she lets out a little '*Oh*.' "You're right," she says. "This is the one."

We put the dress on payment plan, and I'm still weepy and emotional — but not in a depressed way, in a profoundly grateful way. Like when something bad happens to someone that you know you love, but you forgot how much until life reminds you.

"You okay?" she asks me as we're leaving, because the friend I love is back from her dark place and she's concerned about *me*.

"Yeah," I say. "Just glad to see you so happy."

"I'm glad to see you have some happiness, too," she says back.

And I didn't realize till she said those words that this is what this is—this absence of Depression, even if it's not constant, is because it's being pushed out by something much better. The good stuff is better than the bad, and maybe that is happiness.

"Me too," I say, and I mean it.

WE GO to lunch at an Asian bistro after to celebrate, and I order a salad with mandarin oranges and sweet ginger dressing. The girls both order fried rice.

I'm still struggling with my overwhelming emotions, and maybe Tasha senses it—she has a way of doing that, they both do.

"So what's up with you and Finn?" she says.

"Oh, it's good," I say, startled at the sudden change in topic, but it's an honest answer.

"Is it like eyes-roll-back good? Or just white guy good?" she asks, wagging her eyebrows.

"What? White guys can be good," says Gretchen. "That's racist."

"I'm one-third white," Tasha says.

"Is that possible?" I ask.

"Plus, I've screwed my share of white guys, and I'm not complaining," continues Tasha without acknowledging my question.

"Trucker dude was talented. He had long arms. He could do me from behind and flutter my butterfly at the same time."

I bark out a laugh and soda comes snorting out of my nose. "Thanks for the mental picture," I say.

"Wasn't he the guy that bit you?" says Gretchen.

"Worth it," says Tasha. "But fess up—what's Finn like in the sack?"

"I don't know," I say, but she's got me smiling.

Tasha slaps her hands on the table. "Wait, what? Are you fucking kidding me?"

"No, for real. He says he wants to wait until we can make love. You know, until we love each other." I don't tell her that we've already said it, professed our love to each other. Because really, there's no time limit on this. And I've been okay with waiting—he's made it okay.

Gretchen takes a dainty sip of her tea. "Don't take this wrong, but I didn't know you could wait."

Tasha laughs at this. "Yeah, what happened to the slut puppy we know and love?"

"I guess I lost her last year when I lost a night of my life," I say, and they instantly sober. I didn't have to specifically call it out, but they both remember all too clearly.

We eat for a few minutes in silence. Then Tasha speaks. "But hold up. What if he's not good? Or worse—what if he has a little penis?"

I laugh.

"No, that's a legit concern," she says, and I'm surprised to see that Gretchen's nodding.

"Tasha's right. You can teach a man some new tricks, but you can't do much with a small penis."

"That shouldn't matter," I say. "If you love someone, you work with what they have."

"Spoken like a woman in menopause who sleeps in a twin bed," Tasha says. "You sure your parts still work good? You're barely forty." She pokes a chopstick in the direction of my vagina and I wave it away.

"Yes, they still work," I say, thinking of the surge of desire I've had several times when I've been with Finn. And also my private sessions with my defunct vibrator.

"That bullshit about 'it doesn't matter' is crap women say that are dating their gay best friend. It's because they ain't ever had none, and ain't ever getting any."

"What if you can't feel it?" says Gretchen.

"What do you mean? How big do you think I am?" I say, mildly affronted.

"Well, you do pee a lot," she says, and Tasha nods.

"We've said it before and we'll say it again. Vaginal rejuvenation."

"Yes, and stop saying that! The pee hole is not the same thing as the v-hole!" I insist.

Gretchen takes a giant bite. "You doing your Kegels?"

"Yes! Why did this conversation become about me?"

Tasha pushes her plate away and lays a hand on her slightly swollen belly. That girl can eat. "Because let's be honest—he's probably waiting because he's afraid you're going to bail when you see his tiny junk."

I burst out laughing. "That is NOT what's happening! He's being a gentleman!"

Gretchen's laughing, too. "She could be right, though. Does he ever draw comparisons in conversation, like that he's trying to convince you that smaller is better? You know, like, 'That skinny hotdog is way better than this giant sausage—look at all the toppings you have room for when there's not so much meat in the way.'"

Tasha jumps in. "Yeah, or like, 'Wouldn't you rather write with this nice sleek pencil instead of that big fat marker? So much more, you know, precise!"

"Y'all are ridiculous," I say, but my laughter is bubbling over and washing away my earlier tear-tracks with tears of hilarity.

We are all laughing, and as we settle down, we settle back into our meal, enjoying the post-laughter high.

Then I smile to myself. "Now that I think about it, there was one thing," I say seriously, and they both shed their amusement and assume concerned looks. "When we made pasta, he did tell me he preferred limp noodles to al dente. Should I be worried?"

They look at each other and then at me and explode in laughter. "Oh girl, you are too funny when you're trying to be funny!" says Tasha.

"I love how we make each other laugh," says Gretchen. "You've made my day perfect."

I beam at her, all my anger and indignation forgotten, because she's right.

SEVENTEEN

What More Can A Crazy Girl Do?

JULY

ON THE DAY of Tasha's hearing, the lawyer preps us in her office first. We go over several scenarios, as well as what points we should emphasize, what Malcolm's lawyer might ask, and what we should say and not say. She tells us we'll only present Tasha's attendance at Narcotics Anonymous in defense if Malcolm's attorney brings up Tasha's past issues with prescription pain medications, otherwise we'll keep that in our pocket.

My part in it all is to be a character witness, someone with a socially acceptable, professional background that is around Tasha a lot and can attest to her dedication to her mental health from a layperson's perspective.

I want to do this, because I believe in Tasha and feel strongly about what I'm going to say. But I'm shaken. Brooklyn texted me an odd message yesterday that I'm not sure how to take. She asked if I was okay, out of the blue. If I was feeling "sick." When I said I was fine and pressed her about her concern, she said her dad was worried about me.

That raised all my alarm bells, because he obviously doesn't care about me at all. So I deduced that he was questioning whether my depression was better. I'm assuming he's put a time limit on it, like people tend to do—even me—assuming that it's been long enough after the divorce that I should be better. But why does he want to know? What is he going to do with that?

I push these thoughts aside because today I have to be strong for Tasha, who is tapping her fingers on the conference table but holding herself together. She has so much riding on this going well.

I helped her pick out her clothes—she's wearing black pants and a white button-down shirt, and I lent her the smallest blazer I had, a gray one I bought in my twenties. It's got shoulder pads, but it's otherwise classic. Tasha looks surprisingly conservative, responsible, and I grasp her flailing fingers and give them a squeeze.

"I will warn you again," says Ms. James, the attorney. "Family court is different from what you see on television. The judge has a lot of latitude on what he wants to ask and see, and certainly over what he decides. But we have a really good case, and I'm optimistic, so you should be, too.

Tasha nods.

"Okay, so are we ready?" asks Ms. James.

Tasha looks over at me, her eyes wide, but she nods. "Yeah, let's get this shit… I mean, let's make this happen," she says, and we get up to head across the street to the courthouse.

The courtroom is wood-paneled circa 1975 with heavy wooden bench-seats that look like church pews, and an enormous elevated podium/desk that serves as the judge's bench. There are two tables in the front, and Malcolm and his lawyer are already seated at one. Malcolm glances up as we walk in, and he gives Tasha a complex look—it crosses from frustration to regret, maybe even affection. What I don't see is anger or hate.

I hope that's a good sign.

I sit in the pew behind the other table, and Tasha and her lawyer sit in front of me. And then we wait.

After a few minutes, a clerk comes in, reads the docket number, and announces the judge—the Honorable William Lansing, and we all stand until he tells us to be seated.

And then it begins. Malcolm's attorney presents his complaint, and the judge reads through the orders. This all is expected. But what I don't expect is what they petition for next, though Ms. James doesn't look surprised, so I'm sure she knew about it.

"We request that the supervised visitation be continued until further ordered, or until the minor children reach the age of eighteen," says the lawyer.

I see Tasha stiffen, and Ms. James lays a hand on her arm.

The judge turns to Tasha's side next. "And what say you, on behalf of your client, Ms. James?"

"We request that the supervised visitation be immediately discontinued and that regular, unsupervised visitation be re-established for the well-being of the children and to preserve the important relationship with their mother, your Honor."

"On what basis, Ms. James?" he asks, as he slides reading glasses onto his long nose. His whole countenance is long—long torso and arms that extend well beyond the sleeves of his robe, a long face with a high forehead.

"On the basis that Ms. Simpson has exhibited over the course of the last several months her diligence in maintaining her mental health, treating her illness with due care and demonstrated responsibility, to the point that she is not only not a threat to her children, but is providing an important example of how to responsibly deal with a hereditary illness."

Smart, I think. In one statement, she has established that mental illness is not Tasha's fault, has pointed out that it's hereditary and therefore might be important for her children to see that it can be handled responsibly, and has referred to mental illness as an "illness" implying that it should be treated no differently than any other.

"I presume you have sufficient evidence to support your position?" says the Judge.

"Yes, your honor. We have documents from her psychiatric hospitalization of last year stating that Tasha's form of mental illness is very treatable with medication and sworn affidavits from Tasha's psychiatrist attesting to Tasha's diligent compliance with her medication in the intervening months, as well as his opinion that she is not a threat to herself or anyone else. We've also brought a character witness, a person with an established professional presence within the community that is very close to Ms. Simpson and who also suffers from mental illness but manages it successfully with treatment."

The judge raises his eyebrows. "I hope you are not attempting to establish your character witness as some sort of informal expert?"

"No, your Honor. Merely explaining her unique position to comment on her observations regarding Ms. Simpsons intense desire to manage her own mental health for the benefit of her children and herself."

"Bring up your statements, then, Counsel," he says, and Ms. James walks around the table and delivers copies of the documents/statements to the judge and also to Malcolm's attorney. Everyone takes several minutes to read through them, and then the judge turns back to us.

When he's finished, the judge turns to Tasha. I expect him to call her to the stand, but he doesn't. "Ms. Simpson, it says here that you have bipolar disorder, and that when not successfully treated with medication, it can lead to suicidal ideations. Is that accurate?"

Tasha looks at Ms. James, who nods at her to answer.

"Yes, your honor. But it's not like I *want* to kill myself, like I plan to or anything. I want to be here for my kids and I want to live. It's more like these bad thoughts come, and I know they're bad, so I try to ride it out as best I can until my meds kick in again."

He leans forward, touches his fingertips together in a steeple. "What do you mean 'again?' Why do you think your meds stopped working?"

"Because I messed them up—basically forgot about them for a couple of days, or sometimes in the past it's because I accidentally let them run out."

"So are you saying that it's accidental?"

"Yes, your Honor."

"Well, that's a concern, Ms. Simpson. If it's accidental, how will you keep from letting it happen again?"

"Oh! Well, because I just won't," she says. "I mean, I finally really get that it's my medicine that keeps me from being sick, and I am very determined to do it right. Because I never want to put my kids through that kind of bull…," she pauses. "I never want to put them through that kind of trauma again. It wasn't fair to them. Plus, I really hate being sick, like despise it. I don't want to be sick, ever again."

He considers her words for a few minutes, not as though he's trying to decide whether to believe her, I think he does. It's more like he's trying to decide if that's enough.

Then he turns his attention to me. "Ms. Colson, is it?" he refers to his paperwork, but doesn't wait for an answer. He looks back up at me. "What is your relationship to Ms. Simpson?"

"She is one of my best friends."

"How did you meet? I see that you were an executive at Originate Global Technologies and are now doing financial consulting. How did you come to be friends with Ms. Simpson?"

"I met her in Group Therapy at the psychiatric hospital when I went there to deal with my very painful divorce and the resulting depression."

"Do you still suffer from depression, Ms. Colson?"

I instantly get nervous at this question. It makes me worried suddenly that he's going to challenge my fitness to have partial custody of Brooklyn. But I push my fears aside, because this isn't about me. "Yes," I say. "I may always suffer from it as it is a chemical imbalance. But I treat it with medication and, like Tasha, I am determined to do everything in my power not to be sick."

"In your observation, has Ms. Simpson been compliant with her medication?"

"Yes, without a doubt. She has a pill dispenser where she parses out the medication by day, with slots for morning and night, and she has an alarm set on her phone so she never forgets to take it. And she sees her doctor every month. In my opinion, she is as diligent as a person can be about managing her illness. She can't help that she has this physical infirmity—no one can. But she's doing everything she can to make sure it doesn't take control. I'm not sure what more she could be expected to do, what more anyone could do."

He regards me for a moment, tapping his Mont Blanc pen on

his desk. I begin to wonder if he's done talking to me, whether I've done enough, whether I've hurt or helped Tasha's case. But he's not done with me after all.

"Do you think Ms. Simpson should be granted unsupervised visitation?"

"Yes, I do, your Honor."

"Why?"

"Because children need their mother. They need her, just as much as they need their father. Tasha's not abusive or negligent—she's caring and loving, and she has this amazing relationship with her kids that makes them feel loved and extraordinary and hopeful about their future. I've seen them together—it is special. They shouldn't have to be deprived of their relationship with their mother because of an illness she cannot help, an illness that they could very well inherit," I say, building on the foundation that Ms. James laid out. All of this I say without equivocation, because I believe it so much.

Here's the part that I'm less sure about—not in its truth, but rather whether it's assuming too much that people without mental illness will understand it and accept it. But I feel like I need to say it anyway, and I just pray I'm not messing it up for my friend.

"But here's the thing. Tasha might get sick again." Ms. James stiffens this time, and I know I'm out on a limb here. "She might get sick, but Tasha will know when she's getting sick. She'll be able to feel if her medication isn't working right. She felt it last time."

At this, Ms. James turns around to glare at me, though Tasha stays facing the front, as though she has complete faith in whatever I am going to say. But I'm committed now, and I have to bring it together to make my point.

"The key to managing her illness successfully depends on Malcolm, too." His side is already staring at me, but now Malcolm's jaw drops slightly in surprise. But I forge ahead. "She has to be able to feel safe enough to tell Malcolm when she's feeling sick and to trust that he will be flexible about taking the kids during that time without fear of repercussions in custody court. That's how this can really work. That way, they are working together to protect the kids, and helping her show them, the kids, how responsible adults manage mental illness."

And in these moments, and with these words, I realize I'm not just addressing the judge. I'm talking to Noah, and everyone else who ever judges someone who is mentally ill but is working her ass off to stay well. Who still gives everything to her kids, even when she feels like shit. Who can still be a good mom, even if she's not quite the mom she dreamed she'd be. And I know that even though, during the divorce, I had no fight in me and I lost, now I'm stronger. I can stand up to him, and I won't let him win. If he comes after me, I'll be ready.

Everybody is staring at me like I have two heads and I shoot up a prayer that I haven't royally screwed this up.

"Mental illness is no different from any other illness, except that it brings with it the belief that you have to keep it secret. That's what gives it power to hurt people. Without that fear, everything changes. No mentally ill person wants to be sick. Without the fear, they'll get help, they'll ask for help. What better lesson can we teach our kids than that?"

I stop speaking then, hoping that what I've said is enough and that he gets it. I'm also hoping that neither he nor Malcolm's lawyer asks whether I realized Tasha was sick before her suicide attempt, and if I did, why I didn't do anything about it. Because the truth is, I was a victim of that fear as well. Fear for her, which was a direct reflection of the fear I had for myself.

He looks at me for a beat, and then he turns to Malcolm's attorney.

"Did you bring any additional evidence in support of your petition?"

The lawyer looks at Malcolm, who shakes his head a little.

"No, your honor, other than the evidence previously provided when the Emergency Custody Order and Temporary Restraining Order were granted—the original police report."

"Anything else from you, Ms. James?" She tells him no. "Okay, then. I'll take a short recess and let you know my decision."

We all rise as he opens a door to his chambers and disappears, then Ms. James and Tasha both turn around to face me.

"That was a big risk you took," she says to me. "I wish you had talked to me about it beforehand. I'm not sure whether it was a good idea or not, but we'll keep our fingers crossed."

"I didn't know I was going to say it," I say, but I'm looking at Tasha. I took a gigantic risk, and if I screwed it up, it's Tasha and her kids that are going to pay the price. I search her face to see if she's upset with me.

But she smiles. "You always know the right thing to say, Claire," she says. "You say the truth, like me. But with less f-words."

I smile and reach across to hug her.

Malcolm is looking at us, and his expression is pained. Maybe I'm reading too much into it, but he seems regretful that it's come to this.

But then the judge is returning and we're all standing again, waiting to hear the decision.

"Please be seated," he says, and puts on his glasses to look at his notes. "I have listened to all testimony and reviewed the evidence presented. I do see cases, fairly often actually, involving mental illness. It often impairs a parent's ability to provide a loving and stable environment for his or her children, and I have to take such factors into account."

I suck in a breath, and I see Tasha do the same. *Please, please, please.*

"So, perhaps I will admit my own bias in that I entered the proceedings today fully expecting evidence indicating that Ms. Simpson neglects or mishandles her mental illness to the callous disregard of her children."

Tasha reaches her hand over her shoulder without looking back, and I grip it tightly.

But he's not done speaking. "I saw none of that. Instead, I see a woman who is working hard to manage her mental illness so she can continue to be a good mother to her children, a fact that does not appear to be in dispute, notwithstanding when she is not in compliance with her medication. Furthermore, I find that there is sufficient evidence to support that she is dedicated to complying with her medication requirements. I also commend Ms. Simpson's wise choice to delay the original hearing in order to give herself time to fully regain control over her mental illness, and to be able to demonstrate that control, before coming into my courtroom."

We are squeezing each other so tightly my fingers are tingling.

"So, I hereby order that the Emergency Custody Order and Temporary Restraining Order be lifted, and that a new custody arrangement order be entered as follows: Father will continue to have primary custody, as such primary custody has not come under dispute before the court, with Mother having unsupervised visitation of two nights during each week and every other weekend, subject to the following conditions: (1) Mother will provide to Father at least once every three months a signed statement from her treating psychiatrist stating that, to his knowledge, Mother is in compliance with her psychiatric treatment plan, and (2) Mother will have the unequivocal right to request, at any time, temporary relief from the regular visitation schedule in the event Mother feels that it would be in the best interest of her children to do so, at which time Father will agree to maintain custody of the minor children during the Mother's regularly scheduled visitation in exchange for equivalent days visitation to be granted to Mother at a future date when Mother believes that such interruption is no longer warranted."

He takes a breath then and removes his glasses. "Ms. Simpson," he says. "You can thank your friend for that last bit, but the rest of what I hope is an acceptable outcome is purely due to you and your hard work. Keep it up. I don't want to see you in my courtroom again. We are adjourned." At that, we all rise one last time as he exits the courtroom, and Tasha and Ms. James turn to me, all of us sharing shocked expressions.

"We did it," Ms. James finally says, breaking into a broad smile. "Great job, ladies. We'll finalize the orders and you should see your kids by this weekend!"

Tasha's eyes fill and she hugs first her lawyer and then me. "Thank you," she whispers into my hair.

"Don't you thank me, I just said the truth. Like you taught me," I say back, and she gurgles a teary laugh.

Then she suddenly straightens, and she's looking over my shoulder. I turn to find Malcolm there. "I'm really proud of you," he says to her. "And I'm glad the kids are getting their mom back. They've missed you."

For once, Tasha is speechless, and then Malcolm is gone, and we are heading out to find Gretchen and celebrate.

Date #... Who the Hell Cares Because It's Bigger Than A Pencil

TODAY IS a momentous day for so many reasons, one of which is that my initial course of TMS treatments has just ended and I actually feel the best I've felt in years, and the other being, I got a job! A real one, not a consulting project, but real, legitimate full-time employment. Yes, it's a lower position and less money than what I had before, but I think I can do the work. And thanks to the success of the TMS treatments, I feel like I can handle it.

TMS has been a Godsend, when all other remedies I've tried have been so woefully inadequate. With TMS, my treatment-resistant depression has miraculously receded from a gaping hole into a remote hazard—not disappeared, but well off in the distance where I can look upon it, observe it even, and then purposefully turn away from it, with the aid of well-timed maintenance treatments. It's far enough in the distance that I don't feel the constant pull of its gravity.

It's liberating. It's freeing. It's hope in its most basic, beautiful form.

It was this new feeling, maybe "remission", if that's what this is, that gave me the courage to try for the job, to think that I could actually do it. And it's all because a very good man who loves me cared enough to take on my obligation, my determination, to manage my illness as his own.

That this person and this gift are both remarkable is not lost on me.

I'm feeling so good, I call my dad on my way home from shopping where I bought some new work clothes for the first time in a very long time. I want to tell him all the good stuff. He and Mom deserve to know the good stuff—they've heard enough of the bad.

I update him on everything and he's so excited for me, and I love that I can bring him happy news for once.

"You're going to do great at this job, Claire," he says, and it's reassuring and exactly what I need—until he says the rest.

"You're not letting things get you down, like you were. Like when the car broke down the other week. You were blue about it at first, but you bounced back. That's night and day different from before."

I don't know what to say to this, because I know he means well, is trying to be sweet. And my dad *is* sweet. He's highly intelligent in a geeky, technical way, quick witted and sharp about things he loves—Star Trek, detective shows, scuba diving. But sometimes he's guileless, and also clueless, which makes certain of his comments hurtful and innocent at the same time.

And I know he didn't mean to hurt me with his words—*You're not letting things get you down. "Letting."* As if this has all been in my control. As if it was simply a matter of me not trying hard enough before, and now I am.

I have to let him go before I betray that I'm injured by these seemingly innocent words. Because I don't want to hurt my dad when I know he was not trying to hurt me.

But by the time I get home, the frustration has built itself into this immense tower, containing all the bricks of misunderstanding and ignorance about my illness that I've stacked aside over these years. Finn somehow senses it and immediately folds me into his arms when I walk in, and he doesn't even know what's wrong.

That's one of the things I love—will always love—about him. No matter what day we've each had, or whether we've just argued, large or small, he doesn't want me to hurt. I don't have to point out the contrast from my ex, even to myself. It's ingrained.

After a few minutes of me breathing hard into his shirt while he holds me tightly, he asks what's wrong.

I pull back from him and take a seat at the island, and he pours me a glass of wine before I begin. The wine is deep and dark and woody, or oaky, or some such adjective that escapes me, and it warms a path into my belly.

"My dad," I say. "He still thinks my depression is a weakness. A character flaw of some sort." I notice how I don't think of it as Depression, with a capital 'D' anymore. It's not its own entity anymore. Now it's this minor part of me, like my sense of humor or my susceptibility to song suggestion.

Finn joins me at the counter, pouring himself a glass. "Why do you say that?" he asks, as he takes a sip. He sniffs it afterward and gives it a quick nod of approval.

So I tell him what Dad said, and while he listens sympathetically, I can already tell he thinks I'm overreacting.

"He was just letting you know he was proud of you," he tells me, confirming my supposition.

"Yes, I know. But the thing is, it's not the car breaking down that made me 'blue.'" I was depressed, therefore the car breaking down felt overwhelming to me. If I had been well, it wouldn't have bothered me. Yes, I wouldn't have liked it, but it wouldn't have made me down. I'm not that damn delicate."

Finn takes my hand, stroking its back with his thumb. "It's not always easy for people who don't struggle with it to understand the distinction," he says carefully. "Even for me. It's been hard for me to understand."

I know he's being kind, but I'm getting frustrated again. Not at him, per se, but that I still have to explain—even to the people I love.

"It's a freaking illness," I say, and my voice wavers with the frustration. "It's the freaking chemicals in my brain. I quote 'bounced back,'" I say, making air quotes with my fingers before continuing, "because I had my TMS treatments. For my illness. Not because of willpower, which I've always had in great supply by the way, or any other stupid reason. Because I treated my freaking illness. If I could overcome my depression, my *illness*, with willpower, I would never, ever be sick!"

Now my chest is heaving and I'm trying to maintain my composure. And then he's taking both our glasses, placing them safely out of reach on the counter, and holding me again.

"It's okay, baby," he says into my hair, and I let him wrap me up and protect me. It's still novel, this feeling of being not a target, but protected. I'm growing to like it.

"I'm not weak," I say.

He leans back, lifts my chin and looks directly into my eyes. "You're the strongest person I know."

"You think so?" I say.

"I know it, and so do you," he says, kissing my nose.

"You're right, I am strong," I say, and it's because I believe it again. Like I did back before all the shit. I thought I was tough then. I'm so much tougher now.

I smile then, because he's calmed me and helped bring me back to this moment. "Thank you for reminding me, and seeing the awesomeness that is me for its unavoidable truth."

"Damn straight!"

"And a strong woman knows what she wants," I tell him, giving him a look I'm hoping conveys my deeper meaning.

His eyes glint with mischief. "And what would that be?"

I don't say another word. Instead, I pull him by the shirt up against me and kiss him deeply.

"You taste like peppermint," he whispers into my lips when we break our kiss. We don't break apart though. We're still nose-to-nose.

"I sucked on one on the way home. Do you like it?"

"Yes, it's sticky," he says, and kisses me again.

"What else?" I ask when I get a breath.

"Your skin is soft," he says against my lips, as he runs his fingertips up my arms. "It's like Charmin."

I laugh into his mouth. "Did you just compare me to toilet paper?"

"Yes," he says quite seriously, kissing me across my bottom lip in small pecks before moving to the top. "It's a good comparison because you're both soft and squeezable," he says, as he reaches around to squeeze my behind.

I squeal and he laughs against my cheek, then trails his lips along to my neck.

"And you smell divine. Like cherry blossoms floating lazily from a pink tree... But mixed with something woodsier, like a creek in the summertime."

His breath on my neck tickles, makes the hairs raise up.

"How do I taste, just there?" I say, and my voice is breathy, like a marathon runner or a porn actress.

He flicks his tongue out, and apparently liking the flavor, he applies his tongue and mouth more rigorously. "Mmm, you taste like a yogurt pretzel."

I laugh. "What?"

"You're sweet, but underneath, there's a hint of salty goodness."

"Hmm," I say, because words are escaping me as he kisses my neck in a slow, wet path up the side of my throat, to the back of my ear, his breath tickling my ear canal.

All on their own, my hands grip his arms, then slip underneath them and around to his back. I pull him tightly against me, as he brings his lips to mine again.

His back is muscled under my fingertips, rippling as he moves his hands down my back and to my waist. He holds me there, his fingers brushing the bare skin under my shirt, making me shiver.

We are so close together, I feel the firmness of him grow against my middle, and I press into it harder.

He runs his fingers rapidly up my back and into my hair. He grips my scalp for a moment, massaging it slowly as we kiss, then runs his fingers back through the length of the strands before wrapping his arms around me tightly, his fingers splayed against my back. He lifts me, just a little, and I gasp.

He pulls back to look into my eyes. "I love you," he says.

"Is it time?" I ask.

"Oh, yes. It's definitely time," he says, and goosebumps of anticipation erupt on my shoulders and race down my body.

He leads me to the bedroom, and I stop him at the edge of the bed and kiss him with all the passion that has pent up over these past months, and then we're falling onto the bed and pulling on each other's clothes. I want him so much I'm pulsing for him in my girl parts, but he pauses our progression to look at me, naked in the moonlight.

"You are exquisite," he says, as his eyes travel over me, from head to ankle and back up again. I shiver under his gaze and the cool night air, and he runs his hand over me, slowly, to warm me.

It warms me all right. I arch my back a little, and he takes the hint, leaning down into me until our lips meet again, his body fully pressed, also naked, against mine.

I reach down and he gasps when I take the swell of him in my hand.

"You fit," I say.

"I'm hoping so," he says and chuckles. "I've imagined it often enough."

"Me too," I say, and the porn star voice is back. "I don't know if I've ever wanted anyone so much."

"I never, ever have, Claire," he says, and his eyes are glassy, full of emotion.

And I can't take it one more second. "Make love to me, Finn. I love you. Make love to me."

He doesn't wait for further instruction, but rather merges with me effortlessly, and then moves his body in a rhythm with mine that makes it seem like we were made to fit together. We make music, moving both in tandem and perfect opposition, until I explode with love as much as pleasure.

My cheeks are wet when we've finished, and he's collapsed on top of me, humming his song, our song, into my hair.

"That was perfect," he says.

It really, truly was.

And I'm quite pleased that I'll be able to tell Tasha and Gretchen what I've very happily discovered—Finn is quite comfortable with giant sausages, big fat markers, and his junk, and with very, very good reason.

EIGHTEEN

Karma's A Real Bitch, and She's on Prozac

AUGUST

IT'S the day before the wedding, which I've graciously offered to host in my backyard, and we are having a rehearsal of sorts and a cook-out tonight before the festivities truly begin tomorrow. The yard has already been transformed. No rain is expected, so we went ahead and set up all the tables, minus the tablecloths, and the chairs, as well as an arch draped with fabric and lots and lots of lighting—little warm Christmas lights and then larger strings of warm outdoor lighting. It's all lit up right now, since the sun is starting to set and it's becoming twilight, and it really is gorgeous.

I'm excited about tonight, of course because I'm happy for Gretchen, but also because my friends are going to meet Finn for the first time. I really want them to like each other. Besides he and Brooklyn meeting and liking each other, which is going to happen tomorrow in the guise of my daughter casually meeting my "friend" who happens to be a guy, this is one of the last boxes on my list to making sure Finn and I really could have a future. Because how could I be with a man that doesn't get along with my girls?

Besides me, Gretchen, Tasha, and Finn, Chris will be here, of course, along with his two groomsmen, one of which is married (though the wife's not coming—has another commitment of some sort) and one of which is single. Tasha has been rather celibate of late, not at her own choice, though I'm proud of her for being selective in her rather heightened state. But nevertheless, she's let us know in no uncertain terms that she's ready for the drought to be over. As she puts it, Victor the Vibrator does the job, but he doesn't suck nipples or retrieve after-sex snacks, and those are important distinctions.

The rehearsal pretense is somewhat misleading, in that the officiant, who they hired off the internet, won't actually be here until right before the ceremony. So basically, this will be a short matter of practicing our timing to the processional music, and then eating and drinking wine or beer, according to your preference, while enjoying the cool night air surrounded by 2,000 twinkling outdoor lights on this gorgeous evening.

The girls arrive first and help me prepare the fruit salad and the chip dip and make a huge batch of sangria, because why not? And it's a good thing, too, because Gretchen has news that is not necessarily meant for Chris to hear.

We all grab a glass of the good stuff and follow her out onto the patio for the big reveal. Once we've taken a seat on my outdoor furniture, all newly cleaned in honor of the occasion, Tasha's patience is exhausted.

"Okay, tell us what the hell is going on before I explode, and I haven't had a good man-orgasm in a while. So that won't be pretty."

"Well," says Gretchen, laying her phone on the table between us. "Jonathan texted me."

"What the fuck for?" says Tasha.

"I don't know. He just said it was important that we talk as soon as possible. At first..." she pauses, titters an awkward laugh. "At first, I actually wondered if he somehow found out about the wedding and was going to try to stop it. Pretty crazy, huh?"

Tasha snorts. "Uh, yeah. Are you out of your mind? You wouldn't want that, would you?"

"No, no," she's quick to say, but I can sense the burning in her face even in the muted colors of the setting sun.

"It's okay to think that," I say kindly. "You guys spent a huge part of your life together."

"Yeah," she says, but looks off, her gaze following some geese that are trying to make their destination before full dark sets in.

"Anyway…" says Tasha, prompting her to continue.

She turns back to face us. "Yes, anyway, I thought I would try to call him now, with you guys here with me. Just in case it's something bad. Because that's the alternative, isn't it?" She gives us a chagrined look.

We both say, "Of course." So, with a deep breath, she lifts the phone up and holds it out so we all can hear, and she pushes the button to make the call on speaker.

He answers within two rings. "Thanks for calling me back," he says without preamble. "There's something going on with the girls, and… I need to talk to you about it."

Her eyes widen, and I see the fear there. "Are they okay?"

"Physically, yes," he says. He pauses then, and I begin to wonder if we've lost the connection. But then he finally speaks. "Raina hasn't been herself lately."

"What do you mean?"

"She's quit volleyball. And she will barely come out of her room. At first, I told myself it was normal teenage stuff. But then Macy came to talk to me—she said she heard Raina crying. *Raina.* That child has not cried more than three times her entire life, and two times were at your parents' funerals."

Gretchen opens her mouth to speak, but no words come out. I think she doesn't know what she's supposed to say.

He sighs heavily into the phone. "I'm worried that she's… depressed. I tried to talk to her about seeing a therapist, but she became irate. That was three days ago, and except to go to school, she's been locked up in her room ever since."

"Fuck," mouths Tasha.

Gretchen looks at us, eyes wide and hands up, like she's asking us what to say. We both shrug. What do you say to a call like this, when you've been completely cut off from your children for over two years?

But Jonathan saves her the trouble of finding the impossible right words to say. "I was wondering... I mean, I know you understand this kind of thing better than anybody. So I was hoping maybe you could talk to her, make sure she's okay, see if we can get her some kind of help."

Holy shit.

Gretchen takes a long drink from her sangria before answering. But her voice is surprisingly calm and clear. "Of course I'll talk to her. I would do anything to help her. But... I don't think she'll talk to me. They have been pretty angry with me, and I don't think she wants to hear anything I have to say."

He's the one who's quiet now, and I again I wonder if we've lost him as the bullfrogs start their evening song.

But then he speaks, and it may be the most surprising part of all. "I'll talk to them. Some of that is my fault, because I blamed you for being sick. But I guess that wasn't really fair. I'll start with Macy because she's the key to her sister, and we may have to take it slow. I mean, don't launch into the depression stuff as soon as you make contact. But I think you could at least reach out. If that sounds okay to you."

Gretchen's face has gone white in the waning light. "Yes," she says, and it's little more than a whisper.

"Okay, good. At least we have some kind of plan. Honestly, I'm at my wit's end. Just... worried. I never wanted this for her. For either of them."

Gretchen swallows. "Neither did I." We reach out and take her hands. She's shaking.

"Okay, bye then," he says and hangs up before Gretchen can say it back.

"Ho-ly shit," says Tasha.

"Yeah," I say. Wow. That was some deep stuff right there.

"I need a smoke," says Gretchen.

"But you quit," I say, as Tasha hands her one and tosses me a look to silence me. I guess now's not the time.

As they both smoke and the light fades, I say, "This is a good thing, Gretchen."

She looks at me in shock.

"Not that Raina's depressed, I didn't mean that. But that you have this chance to reconnect with your daughters, and it's in a way that Jonathan will never be able to. Because you get it. They need you, honey. And you get to be their mother again."

She begins to cry then, and we both rush to hug her.

"I'm sorry," I say instantly. "I'm stupid with what comes out of my mouth sometimes."

"No, it's okay," she says, pulling back from us as we re-take our seats. "It's just that I'm happy and sad at the same time. Is that even possible?"

"Yes, of course it is," I say. "It's a perfectly natural response."

"Hell yeah. Can I just say, we keep things interesting on a boring suburban Friday night!" Tasha says.

Gretchen laughs through her tears. "That we do!"

We are saved from further conversation by the arrival of the men, en masse. It's like they took the 7:00 arrival time quite literally.

Finn has a platter of formed hamburger patties and two bags of buns, and Chris is carrying a bin full of condiments and chips. Two other men I don't know are carrying coolers full of ice and beer.

"Where do you want these?" Finn asks, and I gesture to the table by the grill. He sets them down, then comes over to give me a kiss. Then he smiles at the girls. "How about some introductions? I presume these gorgeous ladies are your friends?"

They smile at him, because he sounds goofy and genuine and not douche-y, and the conversation takes off from there.

WITHIN A FEW HOURS, we have eaten, consumed a varied assortment of libations and played Porno Password and one of those R-rated card games that is only funny when you're drunk. It's gone exceedingly well, and Gretchen and Tasha have both given me big thumbs up on Finn. He even played our song for the group, with me singing harmony, and everyone loved it. It was awesome—this is awesome. This is what our life might look like, and it's awesome.

But Gretchen has been kind of quiet, and Tasha notices it too.

So as the guys head around the side of the patio to the basketball goal to play drunk Horse, we circle the wagons around her to make sure she's okay.

"You doing all right?" I ask her, as we stand there and watch the guys show off their serious lack of skills.

"I don't know. I'm just still kind of in shock, I guess. I don't know what to think or do."

"I can take your mind off it," says Tasha with confidence. "I've been checking out the best man, and I have some serious questions." She ticks them off on her fingers. "First, is he really a plumber? And second, have you seen his 'tool'?"

She bursts out laughing. "Yes, Sam's a plumber that works with Chris, and NO! I have not seen his 'tool'!"

"A real plumber, huh? Mmm. I like a man that knows how to lay a pipe."

"Oh, yeah?" I say laughing. "I bet you do."

"I like a man that can snake my drain," she adds then, and Gretchen rolls her eyes and shakes her head.

But Tasha's on a roll. "I like a man that can roto my rooter," she says.

"Wha??" I say.

"Excuse me??" says Gretchen.

And then we all three burst into laughter, and it seems to break Gretchen from her spell. She's more talkative for the rest of the evening, and when we tell the guys goodbye, she gives Chris a ginormous, take-it-to-the-room kiss in front of all of us.

There are catcalls and whoops and only Tasha says anything inappropriate, which is, "Stop it — you're making me tingle. In my va-jay-jay." She adds that last bit to clarify, in case it wasn't clear.

And then the guys are gone, and it's just us again.

We clean up, and then I ask them if they're ready for bed, but Gretchen shakes her head no.

"Not yet," she says. "I want to message the girls, tell them I'm getting married tomorrow, and that I wish they could be here with me. Do you think that's too much? Jonathan said to be subtle and slow getting into the depression stuff. Do you think that would be okay?"

"I think that would be perfect," I say.

"Me, too," says Tasha. "Exactly right."

So Gretchen types out the text that is addressed to both of her daughters, but she doesn't wait or hope for a response. At least not tonight. And it's late anyway. So with that hopeful end to an overall really good, promising night, we turn in, together.

Because tomorrow is a new beginning.

No More First Dates, And Soul Mates
Come in Threes

GRETCHEN AND TASHA are occupying my bathroom, sufficiently using the facilities in a way that has me heading to the hall bathroom in a coffee-induced hurry. Everything is almost ready, all the preparations have been completed, and I really think it's going to be a perfect day for our friend. Before I rush out, I tell her so, and I think she mostly believes me, even without her daughters. And I worry about that, but only a little. Because right now, I really have to pee, and so I barrel into the hall bathroom, startled to find it also occupied, as the guests have been directed to the downstairs bath. Chris is inside, straightening Carson's shirt and tie, as I so rudely barge in.

"Oh, sorry," he and I both say simultaneously.

He smiles. "I had to take Carson potty, which for some reason involves removing all his clothes. He's very stubborn about that. I thought it might be better if we came upstairs, as his anti-clothing ritual takes a reeeeally long time."

I laugh. "It's fine," I say, thinking about Brooklyn and how she used to sing Vacation Bible School songs on the toilet. Kids are funny.

We stand there awkwardly for a moment, as Carson hangs on

his arm like a monkey, and I eye the toilet longingly. Before we can work out who's going to squeeze past whom as they depart, he asks, "Is Gretchen okay? She's not too nervous, is she?"

I read into that, "She's not manic, is she?" But perhaps I'm over-thinking it.

"She's doing really well," I tell him, and then I pause. "I have to give you credit, Chris. She kind of put you through hell, and you're still here. And I'm glad! Not trying to convince you otherwise, because Gretchen has a heart of gold. But, not many men would stay with someone that can get as sick as she can."

He's distracted for a moment as he pulls Carson away from the tub where he's playing with toys that Brooklyn has long outgrown, but which I can't bear to part with. Then he turns to me. "I love her," he says simply.

Then he hesitates, as though unsure whether to say more. But he ultimately continues. "Plus, she needs Carson and Carson needs her. I want to make sure they have each other, and the only way that can happen is if we're together."

Carson changes his focus then, because he hears some kids laughing outside. "Let's go, Daddy," he says, pulling on his father's hand.

"I guess we better get back outside," Chris says to me. "Don't want to risk accidentally seeing the bride before the ceremony! I hear that's bad luck."

I nod and move out of their way, and then they're gone, and as I quite forcefully relieve my bladder, I ponder what Chris said. Or rather, what he didn't say—which, I think, was that if he and Gretchen weren't together, he wouldn't trust her to have custody of Carson alone.

Wow.

He understands her sickness enough to protect Carson if he needs to, but also loves her, and his son, enough to want to make sure they have each other. That's a rare man, right there.

After completing my business, I hurry back to my master bath, where I find that my friends have completed their transformations.

Gretchen is beautiful when she emerges in her dress.

"Oh, girl. You're going to go and make me cry!" says Tasha, saying what I'm thinking.

"Do I look okay?" she asks.

"Stunning," I say, as I walk over to adjust her hair, which doesn't really need adjusting. I just want to be close to her. Tasha must feel it too, this need to surround our friend—she bends down to straighten the hem of the beautiful wedding gown, fluffing it until it forms a perfect halo on the floor.

"You guys look awesome, too," Gretchen says. "Let me see you, turn around." We obligingly pose for her in our pale yellow summer dresses that are serving as our bridesmaid gowns.

"Gorgeous," she says, clapping her hands. "But talk to me about something, because I'm nervous and I keep wanting to check my phone," she says as we make our way downstairs to the kitchen.

The girls still haven't returned her text, and it's weighing on her. Add that to normal wedding-day jitters, and I can see why she would want a distraction.

"Tell us how it went introducing Finn to Brooklyn," says Tasha, taking a seat at my kitchen bar. I pull a backless stool over for Gretchen so she can sit on it and not wrinkle her dress.

I take a seat myself and peer out into the back where Brooklyn is standing with Hunter and Melanie, and they are laughing. She's so tall standing there, my girl—almost as tall as Melanie. She's growing up, and looks grown up in her blue sundress and Converse tennis shoes.

"It actually went fine. Pretty uneventful. I had warned her ahead of time that I was bringing a new friend to the wedding, which she barely acknowledged. She was busy texting those weird selfies with her friends, the ones where you do something to it that makes your eyes huge or puts cartoon cat ears on your head."

"Are they like filters or something?" says Gretchen.

"I have no idea. The point is, she didn't really pay that much attention. And I talked to Finn ahead of time and told him that we were going to first introduce him as a friend, and then over time we'd help her get used to the idea that we are dating."

Tasha takes a swig from an open Lime-a-rita bottle sitting on the counter. I don't think it's hers, and I make a face. She's nonplussed. "Did that bother him?"

"No, not at all. He was totally cool with it. So anyway, I introduced him as my friend, and she said hello, and then she saw Hunter and Melanie and took off to hang with them."

Tasha's peering inside the bottle now, like there's something suspicious in there. I grab it from her and put it out of her reach, and she pouts.

"Are you disappointed that it was uneventful?" says Gretchen.

I think about it for a moment. "No, I don't think so. That's probably for the best."

"Sure, honey," Gretchen says.

Tasha jumps up. "Oh fuck—is that the music?"

We both listen, look at the clock. It is time! We line up to go out, but just as we do, Gretchen's phone chirps, halting her in her tracks.

It's out of reach, back next to the couch.

"Honey, the music is playing," I say, worried that it might not be from the girls, and also that it might.

"I have to check," she says.

Tasha nods once and runs to retrieve the phone. She brings it to Gretchen, and we all crowd around.

She takes a deep breath and unlocks the screen, opens the texts. It's from Macy.

'*We are both happy for you,*' it says, but there's a "…," below it, like when someone is typing another message.

It chirps again: '*Hope to talk to you soon.*'

"Oh, Gretchen," I say.

Her hand is shaking as she brings the phone to her chest. "Thank you, Jesus," she says, and her eyes are watering dangerously.

"Don't you cry!" says Tasha. "That was awesome, but you are about to get hitched! Save the tears for later!"

She straightens up, sets down the phone on the counter. "Yes, ma'am!" she says, and her smile stretches across her face, and circles the whole world.

"Then let's get the show on the road!" says Tasha, and we walk out to marry off our friend.

. . .

"WHAT ARE THEY DOING?" says Tasha, gesturing over to the far side of the yard. We're both filling up the champagne flutes for the toasts, and as I follow her gaze, I find Finn crouched and my daughter hitching her dress up to her knees. They both assume a runner's stance.

"I think they are about to race," I say rather stunned as we set down the champagne and make our way over. Before we reach them, they take off. For the first several yards, they are neck and neck. Then Brooklyn breaks away, her long stride lengthening and finding its rhythm as Finn stalls and peters out. He makes it to the end, barely, to find Brooklyn standing there grinning at him, but he is heaving, his hands on his knees.

We arrive as Finn catches his breath.

"Did I really beat you?" says Brooklyn.

"For real, you did," he says, gasping as he works to collect himself. "I promise I ran as fast as I could. You are legit an insane fast runner."

Brooklyn's grin nearly splits her face.

Finn stands up fully then and smiles at me. "I guess I'm not as fast as I remember," he says.

Brooklyn pats him on the arm. "It's okay, Finn. You are maybe not as young... I mean, I'm a lot younger..."

He feigns a look of horror and she stalls, mortified. Then he grins, letting her off the hook. "Not bad for an old guy—I get it." He does a half bow to her. "I bow down to the running queen of the kingdom of Nashville."

She straightens her back and places her fists on her hips in a regal stance. "Take my picture," she says to me. "With Finn bowing down."

I blink.

"Mom, come on. Do you have your phone?"

I do. I'm carrying it in the pocket of this dress Gretchen picked out, which is pretty *and* functional.

I pull it out and my two loves ham it up for me, as I snap away.

In the last one, Finn lies on the ground as though thoroughly defeated and she places her foot on his chest.

"Brooklyn…" I admonish, but he winks at me.

Snap.

"That'll be a good one," Brooklyn says, and I can't disagree with her.

She steps back and gives Finn a helpful hand up as the other kids call for her. She starts off, but she pauses as she goes to move past me, lays her hand on my arm. "I like your friend, Mama," she says. I grab her in a hug.

"You're suffocating me," she says into my chest, and I release her.

I hold her at arm's length, gazing at her exceptional beauty, the inside kind that she radiates like an aura. "Mom," she says.

I drop my arms, thinking I'm annoying her, but she has something else to say.

"Dad said your job isn't that great, and that you aren't who you used to be," she tells me, and I suck in a breath.

"But I think you're better. Do you feel better, Mom?"

Tears cloud my eyes, but I nod. "Yes, honey. I really do."

She smiles at me and then she's gone to join Hunter and Melanie and the other kids at the gathering.

"Tasha!" someone yells, and we look back toward the table with the champagne. Sam is standing there holding a flute up questioningly.

"I guess that means we need to get back to it," I say, feeling Finn at my back and liking him there.

"Damn, that man is a tall drink of water. I'd like to toast him," says Tasha as we head back over to finish the preparations for the toast.

"Is that even dirty?" I ask.

She shrugs with a grin.

WE POUR all the glasses as the sun sets, and hand them all out on trays. Sam goes first as best man, and it's a good toast—I know this from the reaction of the guests, as I don't really listen. Instead, I continue Brooklyn's suggestion and I snap photos on my phone. Ones of Tasha eying Sam like he's a side of pork at the Memphis in May barbeque festival; ones of Gretchen, bright-eyed and tipsy, leaning into Chris while he strokes her arm. Ones of Brooklyn and Melanie and Hunter tossing cashews into each other's yawning mouths and then laughing when one lands on the end of Hunter's long nose.

I'm cataloguing it all, this new day, to replace the missing pictures of my battered past. But I now know that I was wrong about them—they weren't holes in my life, those missing slots. They were placeholders for what was to come.

Tasha captures my attention when she taps on the microphone, ready to deliver her toast. She stands on the patio, which is surrounded by the twinkling lights and the tables of guests.

"You know I'm not good at this kind of shit," she says, and Melanie yells, "*Mom!*"

Snap.

"I'm sorry, *stuff*," she says, correcting herself with a grin. "But I do know that I love you, Gretchen. You are my sister, and my friend, and I'm so happy that you've found this happiness. Your new life is starting now, and it's going to be fucking awesome! Sorry Melanie," she says, though she doesn't seem very sorry. Melanie dunks her head into her hand in defeat as Tasha raises her glass. "To Gretchen and Chris!"

Everyone repeats the toast with raised glasses.

Snap.

Tasha hands me the microphone and whispers, "Your turn, bitch," with a smile. "Do that wordy thing you do so well."

I drop my phone in my pocket, content now to be in this moment, even if, up until now, I've been unsure what I want to say. But, all at once, with these people I love—Gretchen, Tasha, Finn and my sweet Brooklyn—standing witness, it's all okay. Because I trust my heart and I believe, somehow, that the words will come. So I begin.

"When I met these two girls right here, I was at the lowest point in my life. I'd lost my husband, my house, my job, and for a little, awful while, my baby girl." I throw Brooklyn a glance, and she gives me the frowny-face that she does when something hurts her heart. "I was this broken shell of a woman, mired in deep dark Depression that was a black, soul-sucking pit surrounding my heart. And then I met Gretchen and Tasha—at Group Therapy, if you don't mind me saying." Gretchen, smiling, shakes her head. Tasha does the hand motion of a guy jacking off, her way of saying "big fucking deal," which almost makes me lose it. But I don't, because these words need to be said.

I pause before continuing, knowing what I want to communicate, but hesitant to do so in front of Brooklyn. But maybe now is the time for her to hear it, or at least this abbreviated version of it. Because I survived it. And that is a beautiful story.

"I was like this puddle of nothing on the floor, and these girls pulled me up, grabbed me out of the pit and the bed and helped me to see the sunshine and put on deodorant and find my laughter again. They taught me what it means to be truly loved by someone who is not my kin, and they loved me so completely, they didn't care that I failed, Every. Single. Day. Failed at being able to work, or think coherently, or even read a stupid vampire book to completion. Failed at being good company, or a good listener, or a good mother. They loved me because they just got it, without judgment, without expectation, and they gave me The Most Precious Gift—the gift of unconditional acceptance."

I look at Gretchen, who is wiping tears from her eyes, and Tasha, who looks mad, because that's what she does when she's trying not to cry.

"These two women, who I never would have met in this lifetime were it not for our common 'issues,' who are beautiful and complicated and fierce in their own right, showed me what it means to be a true friend, and in doing so, made me ready again to be a mother, a girlfriend and maybe, someday, a wife." I glance at Finn who is beaming with pride and love, and my heart swells.

"But most importantly, it made me ready to be *me*. Maybe for the very first time."

"To say these two women are my sisters is understating it, because sisters are usually the girls you're born next to, the ones you don't choose and that you take for granted because they're always there. So trust me when I tell you that if *those* sisters are great, they are that much more special when they find their way to you in adulthood, not through bloodlines but through divine providence, and become the sisters that you always needed, but you never knew you did. Because they are the ones..." My breath catches, but I'm almost there.

"They are the ones that God specially made for me to find, at exactly the moment that I needed to find them." My voice breaks then, and the whole crowd is sniffling and blurry.

I take a deep breath as I near the end. "So today, on this glorious occasion when we celebrate this new beginning for Gretchen and Chris, know also this: this is a new beginning for all of us, for every single one of you here tonight, and for Gretchen and Chris, for Tasha, and for me. It is the day that we say, 'This exact moment, as lovely or terrible, as surprising or ordinary, as uplifting or even as painful as it may be, is so that I *can get to where I'm meant to go.*'"

I pat my chest. "And I know this because all the pain, every last bit of it, and there has been a hell of a lot..." I look at my girls meaningfully, and their eyes are locked with mine, their heads nodding in total, soul-linked agreement. "All of the shit, as Tasha would say, has brought the three of us to right here and now, into this perfect moment, into this beautiful, crazy friendship. And what an indisputable masterpiece it is."

For a moment, there's silence, like a collective intake of breath, as everyone processes the emotions brought on by my words. And then my sweet man sees that as happy as I am, I'm about to break from the truth of it all, and he lifts his glass so high it sloshes out and yells, "Cheers!" as he wipes at his own eyes.

An uproarious refrain fills the night, echoing the sentiment and all that it means with joyful shouts and clinking glasses, and it's loud and beautiful, as though a host of angels are singing on our behalf.

My girls rush to me, and we mash into a chiffon and satin ball of tears and hugs and sisters. And the only words we hear are the ones from within our tightly knit sphere, from the voices we know so well, and are the only ones that matter: "I love you," "I love you," "I love you!"

Flashes blink like fireflies all around us, as guests take ten, twenty, a hundred pictures, enough to spill out and over our albums and frames and paper the floor. And it is exactly as it's meant to be.

Thank You, Reader

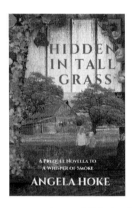

Thank you so much for reading *Missing Pictures*! First and foremost, as a special thank you, I'd love to share a free novella, HIDDEN IN TALL GRASS, with you! It is a prequel to my 4-time award-winning coming-of-age novel, *A Whisper of Smoke*. See the link below:

http://bit.ly/HIDDENINTALLGRASSBonusNovella

And Now My Special Message for You: I am not a mental health expert, a divorce expert, a dating expert, and am not claiming to be. I am not trying to give you instruction in this book, in any form. And, therefore, you should not use it as an instructional book in any way, and I accept no responsibility for this book or its contents as anything other than a form of entertainment.

Rather, I hoped to tell a good story, inspired by an amazing friendship I made out of my own mental illness and attendance at intensive outpatient group therapy, and how my very real friends (code names Emma and Jennifer) helped me heal during the hardest time of my life. This story is fiction, but the feelings and perspectives come from a very real place, my own voice.

So I hope you found love, support, empathy and truth in this story. If you've been through a major life-changing event like a divorce, custody issues with your kids, loss of job, and you thought your life would never recover, I hope you found inspiration. If you suffer from mental illness, I sincerely hope you find the best treatment for you (and never give up on that), but also that you come to embrace a little the crazy or sadness or shutdown mode or anxiety or withdrawal or mania, when it does come (from time to time) as part of what makes you, you (I say that with love, and because I embrace my own crazy, which is specific to me). If you don't have mental illness, I hope you found some empathy from this story, because IT IS NOT A CHARACTER FLAW. And if you do, I hope it helped you feel a little more heard and loved. And most of all, I hope you got from this book that amazing, divine friendships can come from anywhere, and to be open to what God or the universe sends to you. Because they can be the greatest gifts!

I believe fiction is one of the most powerful tools we have as human beings to build empathy and understanding for and with people that may on the surface seem different from us. It is my calling to write and share works that do this. If you think I accomplished this even a little, or if you just enjoyed reading MISSING PICTURES, I would sure appreciate it if you could write a review on Amazon, Apple or Barnes & Noble (wherever you buy books), and Goodreads too, if you are a member. Reviews are how we, as writers, become better and they help us to reach new readers. And also, tell someone about it, as well as all the other great books that you read. So we can literally share the love and support and acceptance. Thank you in advance!

The Story Doesn't End Here: FILLING IN OUR MISSING PICTURES

I have assembled some amazing contacts and sources of comfort, forged from connecting with an incredible group of people:

First—I created a Facebook page to share our mental illness, divorce, or other experiences however you want (subject to group rules), and to provide support for each other. It is called ***Filling in Our Missing Pictures***.

FILLING IN OUR MISSING PICTURES Facebook Page:

www.facebook.com/FilingInMissingPictures

Also, I have created a *Filling In Our Missing Pictures* page on my website, www.angelahokeauthor.com.

FILLING IN OUR MISSING PICTURES Web Page:

www.angelahokeauthor.com/filling-in-our-missing-pictures

On that page, you will find the following:

- A List and Links to amazing **Mental Health Advocates, Blogs and Influencers**
- A List and Links to amazing **post-divorce or toxic/abusive relationship recovery support blogs and websites**
- A List and Links to some **Amazing Fiction and Nonfiction** on mental health, or dating after divorce, amazing female friendships or anything else I find and love and think you would too, as well as to some of those amazing authors

Acknowledgments

As I already mentioned, this book was inspired by some of my own experiences surviving a high conflict divorce and learning to live with mental illness. So there are many people that helped me in *life*, not just with this story, in my journey of writing and publishing this book. I am going to attempt to acknowledge them here.

First, I want to thank my husband James who is a creative talent in his own right and has been my biggest fan and supporter as I worked through a lot of my own trauma writing this book (even though most of it is fictional), and who has shown me what it means to feel truly loved by a spouse. I also want to thank my amazing son for being resilient and patient and forgiving and grateful and empathetic and kind, and for agreeing never to read this book (for obvious reasons)! I also want to thank my parents (Nancy and Dave) for their unending support when I was going through the worst of my depression and for continuing to love and support me in a way I never wanted to need but desperately did, for my brothers and sisters-in-law (Michael, Kelly, Paul, Lisa, Bill and Courtney) for supporting me without question during the divorce (and after), and my Aunt Debbie and Uncle Larry for giving me a place to live that was close to enough to see my son during my divorce when things were at their worst. I also want to express my gratitude for having wonderful insurance and disability coverage from my job at the Big 4 accounting firm where I previously worked, and for those who supported me in taking a very real and much-needed medical leave to address my mental illness and start on the path towards healing.

I want to thank my original beta readers, including Monique who is a talented writer herself and who I know is going far, David (sorry for shocking you!), and Erica, who has become one of my sisters in the years that I've known her – truly one of the people who came into my life post-divorce and reminded me what friendship could be.

I would like to thank Tory Hunter, editor and writer and provider of awesome services like manuscript critiques (which I've used a couple of times), who loved my book and my characters, gave constructive feedback, and helped me believe it might really be as special as I thought it was.

I would like to thank my in-laws (Janet and Howard, Dawn, Bobby, Ethan and Ruth) who took me in when I remarried (to James), and made me feel loved and not crazy. Also, they love my son like he's always been their grandson/nephew/cousin, and sat in the freezing cold at more than one football game.

I want to thank the folks at Crosslin who took me in when I still wasn't totally healed, including Dell who gave me holy water blessed by the Pope to help me when I needed a difficult treatment, but mostly David, Dan and Erica who continue to be my beautiful friends to this day. I also want to thank my new work family at Delek, who gave me a chance despite my odd break in work history, which I explained (thanks, Danny, for not judging me for it and seeing what I could be again – btw, you should not read this!), who challenged me beyond my wildest expectations (sometimes more than I would like!), who supported me as I continued to work on fully getting well (thanks, Nilah) and who showed me love and friendship and reminded me what a work family looks like (Shantel, Viera, Lan, Melinda, Starr, Godswill and Melissa) and helped me fully emerge from the brokenness to be fierce as hell once again.

(And I am truly a bad ass in the board room and with a technical accounting memo, if I do say so myself).

And finally, I want to shout out to my early readers, endorsers, and reviewers who helped confirm to me that this story is special and needed to be told and reconnected me with old friends who have always held a piece of my heart and new friends that can see inside me. And I want to thank my launch team: Monique, Erica, Toke, Valerie, Samantha, Janelle, Leah (my awesome, creative cousin), Amy (a dear old friend), Dorothy (an old/new soul friend), Miyoshi, Cheri, Melanie (another dear old friend), Tara, Tonya, Barbara, Lina, Ashisha and Shantel (you know who you are to me, chile ;)).

But most of all, I want to thank Emma* and Jennifer* (*code names they selected) who are the real-life best friends that found me at my lowest and helped me find a way to accept myself, in all my screwed-up glory, partially by sharing with me theirs, and who have loved me in a way that forever changed me. Because beautiful friendships really can come from the most unexpected places, and even when you have missing pictures, you can find joy in the new ones you make together.

I am truly grateful to God (and all my spirit guides and guardian angels) for putting all these wonderful people in my life, just when I needed them.

Other Books by Angela Hoke

4-TIME AWARD WINNER, A WHISPER OF SMOKE

Amazon Link to A Whisper of Smoke

Also available on Barnes & Noble and Apple iBooks

Check out this FREE PREQUEL!

HIDDEN IN TALL GRASS: PREQUEL NOVELLA TO

A WHISPER OF SMOKE

http://bit.ly/HIDDENINTALLGRASSBonusNovella

AWARD FINALIST,
A PAINTED LILY

Amazon Link to A Painted Lily

Also available on Barnes & Noble and Apple iBooks

Praise for A Whisper of Smoke

WINNER of the 2015 National Indie Excellence Book Award for women's fiction.

WINNER of the 2015 Readers' Favorite Gold Medal for women's fiction.

WINNER of the 2014 Georgia Romance Writers' Maggie Award for Excellence for a novel with strong romantic elements.

WINNER of the 2014 Heart of Denver Aspen Gold Award for contemporary fiction.

FINALIST in the 2015 International Book Awards in women's literature.

"A beautifully written and most compelling coming of age story that's got friendship and history and, not to be forgotten, magic, on almost every page. A marvelous achievement and an unforgettable story."

-- Readers' Favorite

"There is so much to like about *A Whisper of Smoke*. The author does a beautiful job of bringing the reader into the experience of all sorts of things--a girl's first kiss, the first feelings of love as well as the time surrounding the war and all of the unsettling emotions that I suspect went along with the 1960s. This book reminds us of how exciting, beautiful and painful growing up really is."

-- Judge, Writers' Digest

"A poignant and well-crafted story of the tug of love and disappointment... Every family has struggles and dysfunction, and this story treats age old family problems with sensitivity and delightful quirkiness. The love story is a beguiling tale of innocence and passion of lovers caught up in the Vietnam War era."

"Told from a brilliantly vivid first-person perspective, this story … isn't simply a narrative of a love-struck teenage girl. Nor is it simply a tale about familial dysfunction, with closets so full of skeletons that the deadbolts are starting to crack. It is also not just about loss, strained friendships or even regret for paths not followed. It is all of those and more; superbly crafted into an enthralling read that never feels drawn out or emotionally manipulative."

"The relationship between Susanna and Calvin was one of the most heartfelt, beautiful, heartbreaking ones I have read in a long time.... I put this book on the same shelf as some by my favorite authors (Wally Lamb, Jodi Picoult and John Steinbeck). Bravo Angela Hoke on this amazing book. Calling it a great book actually doesn't do it justice. This is a complete work of art!!"

-- *Other Readers*

Praise for A Painted Lily

Honorable Mention in the 2017 Writer's Digest Self-Published Book Awards

"Five Stars… This is a gripping story of love and friendship, of family and a man's search for his roots, and the role played by a woman whose friendship could make a huge difference… I knew there was no way I was going to stop reading because of the power of the prose and the compelling characters. I also enjoyed the historical references and the way the themes are seamlessly woven into the plot. A Painted Lily is a story with a gripping plot and characters that feel as real as they are entertaining."

-- Ruffina Oserio, Readers' Favorite

"Five Stars… Every so often you come across an epic story that remains with the reader for some considerable time, and this is such a story. In a story told with incredible elegance and emotion, author Angela Hoke has spun a web of family secrets, unrequited love, harsh reality, and all gently blended with a touch of romance. The descriptive writing is a credit to the author, who has the ability to make the simplest task or setting a visual experience for the reader. The characters are well developed and endearing and this ensures that the reader understands and empathizes with each one… This is truly an engaging read and one to be highly recommended. Stunning! Such a pleasure to read."

-- Jane Finch, Readers' Favorite

Discussion Questions

1. What do you think it says about Claire that she begins the story, before meeting Tasha and Gretchen, without having any real friends? What do you think about the concept of "work friends" that don't survive the workplace? Does that ring true with you in your own life? Do you have a distinction with your friends?
2. Do you think that Claire's Depression is situational (that is, brought on by her crumbling, dysfunctional marriage), or due to a larger, chemical issue? Is that distinction important? Why or why not?
3. Do you think it's legitimate that Claire considers herself to be temporarily disabled and unable to do her job? Do you think disability should include mental illness, or physical disabilities only? What obstacles does Claire face in her journey to return to her career?
4. How do you think it would feel to be a successful career-oriented woman and suddenly have that stripped away? How do you think that would impact a person's identity? How did it impact Claire's identity?

5. How did Claire's marital issues impact her relationships with men, and her need for physical touch and affection?

6. Do you think Claire's relationships with men over the course of the novel were healthy? Why or why not? Do you think she was expecting too much from her relationships with men? How did this help or hamper her healing?

7. What are the key points in the novel where Claire really moved toward acceptance about her marriage, both what it actually was and how to deal with the painful parts of it? How did Tasha and Gretchen help or hinder this journey?

8. How do you feel about Tasha as a mother? Would you consider her a good mother? Why or why not? What do you think about her suicide attempt in terms of what it says about her as a mother?

9. What do you think about Malcolm's decision to take away Tasha's children by court order? Do you think he was right or wrong? How do you feel like that decision positively or negatively impacted Tasha's mental health and life in general?

10. What are the most significant distinguishing characteristics between the three women's mental illness? Why is Gretchen's particular brand of mental illness so much more frightening to Claire?

11. Do you believe that Claire should have held Gretchen more accountable for the things she said when she was in psychosis? How much accountability should the mentally ill have when they are very sick?

12. Do you blame any of the women for their mental illnesses? Why or why not?

13. Do you think Gretchen was a good mother? Do you think she should have access to her son, Carson? What about to her older daughters? What kind of relationship is appropriate between Gretchen and her children?

14. Do you think the friendship with Gretchen and Tasha was good for Claire? Why or why not?

15. Do you believe that Claire is capable of having a healthy relationship with Finn? Why or why not?

16. Do you believe that Claire appropriately handled delicate matters regarding her divorce, her dating life and her mental illness with her daughter, Brooklyn? Why or why not?

17. How do you think the metaphor of pictures, specifically missing ones, was used throughout the book? Do you think it was an effective way to document Claire's journey? What do you think she learned from the pictures, including the preventive ones, the missing ones and the new ones at the end?

About the Author

Angela has worked for many years in accounting, writing in her spare time. She began writing at the age of eight, when she produced a neighborhood newspaper, until an expose written based on sketchy facts shut her down for good. *A WHISPER OF SMOKE* was her debut novel, and winner of the 2015 National Indie Excellence Book Award, the 2015 Readers' Favorite Gold Medal, the 2014 GRW Maggie Award for Excellence and the 2014 Heart of Denver Aspen Gold Award. It was also a finalist in the 2015 International Book Awards. Her second novel, *A PAINTED LILY*, which was rated five stars by Readers' Favorite, was awarded an Honorable Mention in the 2017 Writer's Digest Self-Published Book Awards. Her short story, *THE CEREMONY* , was a finalist in the New Millennium Writing Contest. She lives outside Nashville, TN with her filmmaker husband and, on breaks, her college-age son, a giant black lab baby girl who has the scariest bark, the wettest kisses, and is a total bed hog, and last (but not least) a slightly neurotic Yorkie that loves his snuggles and can scream like a pre-teen girl.

www.angelahokeauthor.com

Made in the USA
Middletown, DE
20 June 2021